SHADY DEPTHS

A WITCHES OF C.R.O.W. NOVEL

B.L. BROWN

GOOD INTENT PRESS

Book Cover by FantasySpriteStudios

Illustrations by FantasySpriteStudios

1st edition 2023

ISBN 979-8-9879716-1-1 (pbk)

ISBN 979-8-9879716-0-4 (ebook)

Be kind to our merfolk friends. Don't call them human.

To Molly – you know what you did.

If you're related to me, go ahead and skip chapters eight through thirteen. If you aren't related to me, please enjoy chapters eight through
thirteen.

Shady Depths is book one in *The Witches of C.R.O.W.*, a series of stand-alone adventures within the broader Witchy World of C.R.O.W. featuring characters from its sister series, *Witch of the Demesne.*

While it is not necessary to read *Ritual Income* before enjoying this book, *Shady Depths* acts as a prequel, delving into the back story of one of the main characters and the events leading up to his involvement in *Ritual Income.* It is light on the world-building and heavy on the heat.

That being said, dear reader, I'm sorry in advance.

"What we call the beginning is often the end. And to make an end is to make a beginning. The end is where we start from."
T. S. Eliot, Ink Witch

Ways
Fine and Faire

Aragon

Audiomantic *sound*

Augurist *crystal witch*

Chiromantic *Fortune tellers*

Chronomantic *timey-wimey*

Hippocromantic *doctors/nurses*

Meteomantic *weather witch (Donny)*

Obfuscari* *mind witches*

Obnubilari*

Technomantic

Vinefica* *poisons & potions (Rai)*

Corpomantic*

Český-Krumlov

Green Witch *good herb*

Kitchen Witch

Light Witch *soul, truth*

Pastýř *animal handling (shepherds)*

Vestic *diviners*

Spalování *flame witch (Toby)*

Stitch Witch

Svítilna* *wee sparks*

Ways
Forbidden and Foule

To be reported immediately to C.R.O.W.

~~Corpomantic~~

Dark Witch *Master of shades*

Death Witch

* numerous historical incidences identify the marked Ways as At-Risk. Witches of the noted Ways are observed closely by their demesne's Aural Insurance Adjusters and assessed for Fine and Faire aura every five years.

ONE

Inky black water lapped against the seawall, curling over ribbons of ice clinging to the jagged rocks. Keir set his foot down lightly, testing the set of the stone. His boot sole slid easily over the rock face, the algae that long ago clogged the pores of the non-erosive stone now frozen over.

He tugged at the collar of his wooly-pully and huffed, willing his nerves to be as calm as the warm puff of breath clouding in front of his face. Though iced over, the stone was firmly set in place. Lowering himself and spreading his arms wide, Keir brought a heel down on the surface, cracking the ice and clearing it away before letting his weight settle on the stone. With another held breath, he eased forward to test the next one in the dijk.

Frigid winds wailing in from the North Sea bit at his cheeks, making his eyes water from the cold. His pace down to the waterline was slow and tedious. Overly cautious out of necessity. He wasn't the ideal choice for a water-based job. Frankly, he shouldn't have even been selected for this job, but Rai was needed with the team in Ibiza, and after Hong Kong, Keir needed space.

So instead of hunting down a Green Witch on an island with beaches where the sun actually shone, and warmth was more than a wistful thought, he was picking his way down a seawall, shivering in his Enforcer Blacks and trying desperately to avoid falling into the Ijsselmeer.

"I could have been in Ibiza right now, you know," Toby called down from the roadside. Tucked snugly inside a peacoat, his white-blond hair glinted under the streetlights lining the road up to the overpass. "Drinking *Tinto de Verano* and eating paella."

"You'll forgive me"—Keir risked another step, the stone wobbling beneath his weight. Throwing his arms out for balance, he struggled to hide how his heart lurched into his throat— "if I dinnae give a bloody damn."

"Donmar said she was growing demons from plants, Keir. A new classification of desecrant," Toby argued back. "Cyrus named them *fameliars* —" a truck rumbled past on the road, drowning out whatever he said next and leaving Keir alone with his thoughts. Joking aside, the spalování's complaints were doing the Horned God's work in distracting him from the task at hand.

Another step. Another precariously balanced stone. Another little slip in the algae and ice. He worked his way down to the waterline, pooling shadow in his hands in preparation of working his Way.

"If you had cared to detain this desecrant in Köln, we could be tucked into a *Kneipe* right now. With a helles for me and an atrocious cocktail for you."

"Really? A *Kneipe*," Keir shouted over his shoulder. "One of these days, you will explain to me what it is, exactly, you have against bars and clubs where people actually go."

Pulling an arm free, Toby held his hand out and stepped into his Way. Cerulean flame burst from his palm and licked up his fingers, bright enough to make Keir squint. Toby's cheek wrinkled in a tight-lipped smile. "One of these days, you will explain to me what it is, exactly, that happened with Rai."

Keir threw an arm up, two fingers extended in a "V," and continued picking his way down the treacherous seawall. Considering all that he and Toby had been through over the years, he should not have been surprised that the spalování asked about Rai or why Keir had appeared in his hotel room on that last night in Hong Kong, barely able to keep foot in the mortal realm.

But lack of surprise did not equate to readiness to talk. The wound was still too new. Too confusing. Keir needed distance. He needed time away from the vinefica to clear his head before he could even begin to pick apart her words and discover the meaning within.

"It's simply too much, Keir," Rai had whispered, keeping the Dark Witch at a safe distance as she groped the door behind her in search of the handle. "I can't be involved in this; it's too much."

"*What* is too much?" He'd pleaded, the world graying out around him as the poison witch, the woman he'd loved — or thought he did — stood in the hallway, suitcase at her side. "I dinnae understand where this is coming from, Rai; please stay. Stay with me. Help me understand."

"I can't," she shook her head, deep brown eyes wide and wary. "It's not my place, talk to Lou. I just — oh, Keir, it's too much, it's too far to ask me to go. I'm not the witch for you. I'm sorry."

And then she'd left.

The room, the hotel, and him.

She had left a pile of herbs sitting beside his vape pen, and she had left him.

When the two jobs landed on Lou's desk, one in Ibiza chasing a Green Witch playing Frankenstein and the other chasing a lorelei up the Rhine, Keir had jumped at the chance to go north. Happily running headlong in the opposite direction of Rai and the rest of the team. Toby, of course, went with him. It was his job, after all.

As a Fine and Faire witch, and Enforcer in the Coven for the Regulation and Oversight of Witches, it was Toby's job to ensure that Keir stayed in line, Forbidden and Foule thing that he was. His job to be ready and willing to put Keir down should he do anything wicked.

"The sooner you two talk it out, the sooner we can take the warm jobs!" Toby shouted from the seawall. "Rumor has it there is a team being deployed to New Orleans during Mardi Gras."

"You hate Karneval," Keir hollered, squinting across the inky black. A hum rose from the east, haunting and hypnotic. Red and yellow lights flashed on wind turbines in the distance, blinking as a sea of technicolor stars captured beneath the firmament.

Breathing deeply, Keir toed the path of his Way, reaching for the Shades in the inland sea. There was life in the upper reaches of the water — eel and freshwater fish, each with a Shade of their own and none of them a desecrant. If the lorelei were here she was further in the depths, which would require Keir to also be further in the depths, and that was absolutely not an option.

Cursing, he called back the Shade and rubbed his nose, the tip frozen in the biting, late January wind. "Why would you be interested in Mardi Gras?"

"I am not," Toby answered. "But you are."

"Arenae wrong there, mate." Keir twisted at the waist to stare up at his friend, noting the easy smile lit by spalování flame. "Ken it would be nice to see Lightner again."

Toby snorted. "Unwise, I would think."

"What's the job?"

"Unsanctioned ritual," Toby stated, eyes lifting to the lights on the wind turbines. "Or so the rumors say."

"So they say." Keir followed his friend's gaze out across the water. A car turned onto the overpass, heading into the campground at Breezandijk, a safe harbor and caravan campground at the midpoint of the Afsluitdijk—the thirty-kilometer causeway connecting North Holland and Friesland. Headlights danced over the gently lapping waves, illuminating the water, and—there!

"*Hast du das gesehen?*"

"Aye," Keir scrambled down the rocks to stand ankle-deep in water. "A splash, six meters out." Stooping low, he thrust his arm into the sea, grimacing at the bite of the water's near-freezing temperature against his skin.

With little more than a thought, he shaved off a third of his Shade to dull the pain and quiet his fear at being so near the inky expanse, vulnerable as he was. Sending a spool of shadow out in the direction of the splash, he felt it trip over the spine of an eel, bubble through a school of fish, and reform, seeking out the creator of the disturbance in the lake. Too big to house any of the smaller Shades he'd felt, and as they were on the freshwater side of the Afsluitdijk, it was most certainly not a seal.

"Either some enterprising Soul is out for an evening swim through eel-infested waters," he called up to Toby, "or we've got ourselves a desecrant."

"Can you seize its Shade?"

"Gies a minute." He flexed his fingers against the biting cold, shearing off more of himself to send shadow through the dark. In the distance, he felt the Shade butt up against the potential desecrant and skate over slippery limbs. "Shite." Bending his fingers into a sigil, he called his Shade back and shot it out again, this time with a wicked binding hex for good measure. The Shade whipped around what felt like a limb, holding fast. Keir curled his fingers into a fist and yanked. Leaning back like a fisherman wrestling with his line, he reeled the Shade in hand over hand. "It's a fuckin' wallaper!"

"Flame?"

"Hold!" He grunted, muscles seizing in his arms against the strain. "Cannae have you burnin' through my binding hex." The creature in the water twisted and jerked, pulling the Shade taut between them. Its strength was equal at least to his, but where Keir was one witch braced on slick, uneven ground, the desecrant in the water was in its natural habitat.

Edging deeper, he set his foot down blind, slipping on a submerged rock covered in algae and nearly landing on his arse in the water. Releasing one hand from the Shade, Keir caught himself on a rock and lurched to his feet, arm thrown wide in a taunt. "'Mon then, ye wanker!"

"Stop teasing the desecrant, Keir!" Toby shouted over the hum from the wind turbines, stronger now. A resonant warble that vibrated the fine bones in Keir's ears.

"You hear that?" He slapped his free hand back onto the Shade, lowering into a wide stance, knees bent, and heaving with all his might.

"Hear what?" Toby's voice harmonized with the hum, the deep basso thrum dipping Keir's stomach.

"The turbines!"

"What?"

"The turb—" Keir turned to look back at the spalování and nearly lost his grip on the Shade. The lanky German had abandoned his peacoat and was picking his way down the seawall at speed, eyes fixed on the water and lit by his low-kindling blue flame. "Toby, what in the nine rings are you doing?"

His hands burst into flame and guttered out, blooming a caustic blue only to be dimmed again and again. Still, the spalování pressed for the water, slipping on a patch of ice and stumbling forward as the humming grew intolerable. Keir slammed a palm against his ear, muting the noise as best he could. The desecrant caught in his Shade tugged and thrashed, ripping his attention away from Toby and out across the water.

"Toby!" He hollered, shaving off more of himself against the flare of fright and the biting cold. "Tobias, you absolute tube, get the feck off the wall."

"*Es ist so schön*," Toby sang, his voice breathy and dreamlike. He stood at the edge of the water, gleaming eyes fixed on a point in the dark less than a meter off and absolutely not whatever it was Keir held in his grip.

He darted his gaze to the water where the desecrant still fought his hold, then back to Tobias, lowering himself into the surf. The humming sharpened, the notes wound together in a gentle harmony warbling out of tune. Distinct and discordant driving an iron spike into Keir's skull.

A series of rapid-fire decisions skittered through his brain. He weighed the odds of himself against the desecrant, countering Toby against whatever was calling him into the water, and the known creatures that inhabited the area: the *Kledde*, a canid water demon, the frog-like *Flodderduivel*, and the black water dwelling *Nøkk*, a humanoid desecrant similar to Czechia's *vodyanoi*.

Dismissing them one by one until a convenient, albeit terrifying, truth presented itself.

"Lorelei," Keir muttered. What color still existed in their midnight world grayed out as he dropped headlong into his Way. Shaving off the last of his Shade, he sent it flying out across the water, binding it to the whatever he held with his hex and directing the rest of his attention on Toby, now waist-deep in frigid waters. Raising his voice above the shrill screech of the desecrant, he shouted, "Lorelei!"

"Hear how she sings!" Toby grinned, reaching out into the inky black.

"Toby, plug your damned ears." He wound the tail of Shade around his waist, knotting the shadow to his very self, and began picking across the uneven terrain.

"She sings for me," the spalování sighed, shuddering as the water swallowed him up to his shoulders. His breath steamed in the night air, clouding in front of his face and frosting his lashes.

The shrill, steam-whistle song of the lorelei grew deafening, and one of Keir's eyelids began to twitch for the pain of it. In the water, Toby tipped his head back, scanning the star-strewn sky with a beatific expression. Blue eyes wide and bright in wonder. "She calls to me."

"Ne'er gonnae let you live this one down, ye flamey bastart." Keir stormed into the water, one arm outstretched, fingers forming a sigil. He worked his Way into Toby's Shade, the feel of it blessedly familiar.

Switching intents, Keir clawed his fingers, taking hold of Toby's Shade and yanking as he'd done with the desecrant in the water. "*Liomsa.*"

Toby lurched back, rising in the waters to his waist. He gasped and sputtered, shaking his head as if dispelling a hex. "*Nein!*"

"Toby, I promise, you will thank me for this."

The lorelei shrieked, rattling the gray matter in Keir's skull. He had no idea why the song wasn't affecting him, and that bothered the Dark Witch more than Toby's inability to block it out. They had studied the entries in their grimoires, sat with local covens along the Rhine, and collected as much esoteric knowledge on the desecrant as they could, yet none of the witches had seen fit to warn them that a lorelei could direct her song.

"I must go to her!"

"Stand down!" Keir yanked on his friend's Shade a second time. A third. Towing him up the seawall as the tether between himself and the desecrant out in the water grew taut. His head ached from the lorelei's song, and a disturbing warmth began trickling from his ears, but he was close now. Toby just out of reach.

In another step, with another yank, he'd have the spalování in hand and could smack him back into clear-headedness. Arms shaking, he pulled on Toby's Shade, jerking the witch within reach. Outstretched fingers brushed sodden wool, and Keir lurched forward to grab the spalování. Closing his fingers around Toby's arm as two talon-capped hands gripped Keir by the calves and hauled him into the Ijsselmeer.

TWO

Impenetrable black closed over his head. Keir released his hold on Toby's Shade to claw for the surface. The theory was sound: move arms, break surface, gain oxygen, but in practice, he was woefully unprepared to be submerged in a near-freezing body of water with a lorelei tugging him down.

Primarily for the unfortunate fact that Keir could not swim.

Fear ought to have had him struggling, but absent his Shade, he approached the ordeal with a sense of clinical detachment. Knowledge gleaned from hours of CineNet and watching bathers in the Firth of Forth had him pinwheeling his arms, but the desecrant's grip was sound, refusing him the freedom to kick. Terror flittered as a half-formed thought. A weak whisper telling him to open his mouth and scream into the cold, wet void.

He was no stranger to the dark, no stranger to the cold. Still, there was that tiny familiar piece of Shade, little more than a shadow, that told him he'd gone too far. A stubborn little shadow intent on dragging him out of the nothing, now spitting mad and lecturing him that the void he knew was a void he owned and this was something else entirely. A separate world from the ones he inhabited, belonging to the fish and the eels, the lorelei, and the *Nøkk*.

The lorelei jerked him to the left, the right. Talons dug into the meat of his legs as she clawed her way up his body and plunged them both down low, disorienting her prey. There was no light, no telling in which direction the surface lay, and Keir knew without a shadow of a doubt that this was it. His not-so-great end. Another Dark Witch subsumed by the inky black.

His lungs burned, eyes bugging against the urge to open his mouth and breathe. Breathing meant swallowing the Ijsselmeer, filling his lungs with water, and drowning. Still, he worked his arms and bucked his hips against the lorelei.

She wrapped her legs around his waist, and slick, muscular arms wove around his shoulders. A cold, heavy thickness pressed against his cheek, and the muted world exploded in a high-pitched scream. Keir angled his head to the side and rocked it back, knocking his temple into the lorelei's cheekbone.

Her song hiccuped, the grip on his shoulders loosening. He jerked an arm free and swung his fist, connecting with the lorelei's skull. She juddered back, startled by the strike, while Keir made the mistake of shouting at the pain warbling through the bones of his hand.

Water flooded his mouth, ice cold and gripping. It seized his tongue and spasmed his throat, forcing itself down, down, down into his lungs and burning as only extreme cold was capable.

He ought to have been scared. Ought to have been pants-shittingly terrified.

Keir had always imagined his death would be swift and near pain-less. An accident while tearing down the motorway on his Triumph. A misfired Soul Sunder from one of the many fae still lingering in the Highlands. A cup of poison from his vinefica ex-girlfriend.

Not this slow suffering in cold, shapeless black. Unable to be afraid without his Shade. Unable to be angry. Quietly accepting his fate as the water froze him from the inside out, settling in his belly like an anchor dragging him down, down, down...

The ribbon of Shade around his waist snapped taut, squeezing his middle and forcing water from his lips in a warm stream. His hands moved drunkenly to the shadow he'd forgotten, still bound to the desecrant splashing in the waves. Blinking, Keir shook his head to clear his mind. He worked his casting hand to undo the hex and release the creature lest it be dragged down with him. His fingers fumbled the sigil, and the Shade tightened and jerked again.

Again.

Frantic now.

He tried again, plucking at the Shade and looking up to see the lorelei spin out of the dark, her eyes blown wide and mouth opened in a wretched, jagged-toothed grimace. She swept a taloned hand at his face, and an arm like an iron bar snapped around his waist, jerking Keir back against a chest hard as stone. The lorelei missed by inches. A stream of bubbles left her jagged maw in a soundless scream. She clawed at the water, surging forward and earning a fist to the face for her efforts.

Before Keir could wrap his waterlogged brain around what had happened, he was dragged through the water. Legs kicked rhythmically behind his lifeless limbs, powering them to the surface. He craned his neck and squinted against the drag of water, barely making out the sweep of a long, muscled arm and moonlight glancing off of a pale hand.

They broke through the surface, gasping in tandem, and Keir was hauled onto his back. The arm at his waist moved higher, banding across his chest, and his head was nestled beneath his rescuer's chin. Overhead, white winter stars blinked down at Keir and the unknown at his back, their cold, unfeeling gaze mimicking his Shadeless state.

He went limp, letting himself get towed across the Ijsselmeer. Something about that annoyed his rescuer. A heavy fist came down on the center of his chest, and Keir bowed upright, one absurdly strong arm supporting his back while the other tightened over his chest. He coughed and wheezed, lungs seizing and expelling the water he'd swallowed.

"I am going to let you go," a flatly accented voice stated. The vowels were too round to be purely American, but Keir's ear wasn't sharp enough to place the exact where.

"Nae," Keir wheezed, clutching at the stranger's arm. "Cannae swim."

The stranger hesitated, bobbing with Keir in the water, and then he went preternaturally still. "Then stand."

Without warning, the stranger's arms slid away, and he stood. Keir sank, panic kicking out his limbs and throwing his arms wide. His chin dipped beneath the surface, and his boots came down on loose silt. Digging his heels in, he gained his feet and stood. The water lapped at his shoulders as Keir spun in place, coming face to face with an unnaturally pale, black-eyed humanoid.

He startled back, sinking to his chin, and the desecrant snatched his wrist beneath the water, steadying the witch. Keir froze at the touch, studying the stranger's face and trying to place it in his grimoire.

The man was moon pale, austere features cut through by a long nose that drew attention to a wide mouth and lips pinched together in a thoughtful frown. Black hair clung to his scalp like a helmet, wet and slick as seal skin, but it was his eyes that caught Keir. Impenetrable onyx, the likes of which he had never seen on another being — witch or otherwise.

"What're—" he began.

"Let me go," the stranger stated, releasing Keir's wrist.

"What?" Keir gaped.

"You have your ... thing on me. I would like you to release it."

"My thing," he paced out. "What thing would that be?"

The stranger's brows pulled together in a mockery of human expression. Keir translated it as confusion, mainly by how wide mouth pursed into a genuine pout. He turned his back and surged through the water, stopping when they lapped at his waist. Even in the low light, Keir could make out the powerful form that had hauled him from certain death. The line of his wetsuit stood out in stark contrast to his pale hands and face. Goggles hung around his neck, and the cowl had been pulled away, but otherwise, he had dressed appropriately for the water — which Keir most certainly had not.

Scowling, the stranger fiddled fingers at his chest and down one arm. He pinched the wetsuit. "Your thing, it has grabbed me. I would like you to let go."

"Ehm," Keir worked his jaw, his water-logged brain slow to follow. The stranger plucked at his wetsuit a second time, pulling it away from himself, and it clicked. "Ah, my Shade, shite. Apologies." Striding through the water, he stepped beside the stranger. They were of a height, and it was impossible not to note the broadness of his shoulders. Muscular arms flexed at his approach, the stranger unsure of what Keir intended to do.

"Shouldnae t-t-take but a moment," he muttered, flexing his hands and willing dexterity back into his fingers. The bones were nearly frozen, and his fingers trembled the longer they were out of the water. He tried a sigil, failed, and tried again. Unable to get his ring finger to the proper degree of bend. "Shite, th-th-this is embaras-s-s-sing."

A wicked shiver overtook him, clattering Keir's teeth and making it damn near impossible to form the sigil to release his Shade. He looked up at the stranger, noting how he studied Keir in kind, gaze lingering on the Dark Witch's tremoring hands before darting to his face. Black eyes locked on black eyes, a moment stretched beyond its bounds, and a pale, long-fingered hand closed over Keir's.

"Come." The stranger turned, gently pulling the witch through the water. His stride was determined and steady, where the witch shivered and stumbled. Enough so that the stranger pulled him to his side and worked an arm across Keir's lower back. A quirk of his head had Keir draping a shivering limb across those broad shoulders, and together they gained the seawall.

"Keir!" Toby's voice carried over the stones, harried and frantic. Keir jerked his head up at the sound, eyes narrowed as he scanned the seawall for the spalování. Determined tugging at the hem of his drenched wooly-pully dragged his attention down to the stranger's hands, now peeling sodden fabric away from his body.

"What are you doing?" Keir seized his wrist.

"You need to remove this," he stated. The cold bit at Keir's skin, and he twisted away, brushing the stranger's hands off. He huffed and crossed his arms. "I wish you were hot."

"Some would argue I've succeeded in the endeavor," Keir snapped. The stranger stared at him, face complacent, head cocked to the side. Waiting as Keir tried to keep from shivering and failed miserably. It began in his neck, the tendons tensing and twitching, then crawled into his shoulders, seizing the muscles and jerking his arms and fingers. His teeth clacked and he bit the inside of his cheek, realization dawning. "You n-n-need m-me to b-be warm."

"For you to work." The stranger gestured to Keir's hands, clenched into tight, trembling fists. Black eyes watched him, waiting, and the witch nodded, raising his arms and trying as hard as he could to keep still. The wool clung to his body, melding itself to the dips and swells of muscle. Keir tensed at the first brush of cold fingers against his skin. The stranger was gentle, freeing the fabric from his arms and letting it pool over Keir's shoulders as he paused to assess the witch.

"Hold onto me," he ordered. Keir obeyed, reaching out and gripping him at the waist. The trim, firm waist.

The stranger hesitated, his body almost flinching at the touch. He worked his hands under the wool, fingers skimming Keir's shoulders and slipping up his neck. The sensation sent an electric thrill drilling down into his gut, hitching his breath and raising even more goosebumps. Their eyes locked as he worked the collar of the wooly-pully up and over Keir's head. The move tugged the witch closer, enough to note the shimmer of moonlight on the stranger's pale features and the gentle dusting of freckles over his nose and cheekbones.

His arms lowered, resting lightly on Keir's shoulders and locking him in place. Though the wetsuit was damp, heat bled through the neoprene, teasing Keir and urging him to step closer. His grip on the stranger's waist tensed, and he pulled a trembling lip between his teeth to keep from saying something stupid. The stranger's eyes dropped, watching Keir's mouth with a keen, brittle interest.

"The pants are next," he rumbled in that broad voice.

"And th-then the w-w-wetsuit?" Keir grinned through chattering teeth. The stranger's eyes dropped further, a wet squelch sounded behind him, and he pulled his arms away, staring at Keir — no. Not at Keir, but the sigil on his chest. He glanced down, noting the familiar moss and mint shimmer of the triskelion brand when caught in the light.

"—oh, Luminescence," the stranger murmured, reaching out to trace the sigil. Surprise had Keir darting back. He tripped over his sweater and stumbled over the pile of rock that made up the seawall, catching himself with his palms.

"What did you just say?"

"Bioluminescence," the stranger repeated, black eyes steady on the Soul Sigil. "I thought only — no." He blinked rapidly, shaking his head. "What are you?"

"What am I?" Keir's brows flew up his face. "What are you?"

"Keir!" Toby's voice called out again, closer now. "Horned God *verdammt*, Keir!"

"Here!" He glanced in the direction of the spalování's shout, regaining his feet. "I'm here, Toby." Twisting back around to face the stranger, Keir froze at the sound of a splash and the sight of empty space where the impossibly pale apparition had been.

Rocks tumbled, and German cursing announced the spalování clamoring down to the waterline where the Dark Witch trembled half-dressed in the moonlight. A coat was thrown over his shoulders, smelling of wintergreen and mint. Toby's peacoat, he realized, eyes still trained on the water, now silent and undisturbed.

"Keir." Toby gripped him by the shoulders, turning Keir to face him. Hands worked at his arms, tugging the coat tight. Working his palms up and down Keir's arms, he scanned his face. "*Meine Göttin*, your eyes, what happened?"

"Lorelei," he stated. "She sang to you." Toby gaped at him, working his mouth open and closed long enough that he followed his statement with, "I'm assuming you figured that bit out."

"One assumes." Toby glared at him. "What happened? My E.R.I.E. scanner is going insane."

"It pulled me under." Keir shuddered at the memory. The encroaching dark and creeping death. "The desecrant we saw in the water, it fought her and hauled me to the seawall."

"The desecrant?" Toby scanned the Ijsselmeer, chewing his cheek as he sought any sign of a desecrant — lorelei or otherwise. The only sound was the gentle lapping of water against algae and ice-covered stone, and their own quiet breaths puffing as little clouds in front of their faces. Toby huffed and snapped his gaze back to Keir. "What was it?"

"Dinnae ken." Keir shook his head. "Wasnae a lorelei, or a *Nøkk*. Wasnae human, but it wasnae a witch."

"A *vodyanoi*?"

"In the Netherlands?" Keir balked. "They'd nae be caught this far from Czechia."

"So what then?"

"Dinnae ken," he repeated, "but I doubt this'll be the last we see of it." He began the trudge up to Toby's rented sedan, his only desire being to finish what the stranger had begun and tear off the rest of his nearly frozen clothes.

"And why is that?" His friend pressed a hand at the base of Keir's spine, helping him navigate the rocks.

"Because," he replied, "the wanker's got my Shade."

THREE

The words on the screen blurred into an incomprehensible collection of e-ink vowels and consonants, refusing to arrange themselves into anything resembling a coherent, written text. Keir tossed his e-grim onto the hotel desk and slipped fingers under his glasses, pinching the bridge of his nose and sighing for the fourteen-thousandth time.

"Still nothing?" Toby peered at him over the rim of a C.R.O.W. legal journal. The title on the cover declared it to be a treatise on the rights of existing chimera, and the thought of such dry material made Keir's aching brain beg for sleep.

"Still nothing," he confirmed, slouching down in the chair and dropping his head back. Heels planted in the low pile carpet, he swiveled side to side, studying the bold black and white striped wallpaper. "Cannae assign the attributes to any one desecrant. He didnae have webbed extremities nor the soggy, sagging appearance of a *vodyanoi*. Wasnae frog-like, so that rules out the *Flodderduivel*, no tail so that's the *lamia* and *melusines* done for—"

"*Warum nicht ein Nix?*"

"A *Nøkk?*" Keir eyed the flame witch in the mirror over the desk, then dropped his head to massage throbbing temples. "No violin, nor a place to hide it in that wetsuit."

"Right, the wetsuit." Toby closed the legal journal and set it aside. "A very specific piece of attire often attributed to the Staid."

"Never seen a mortal with eyes like mine." Keir pulled his face up, staring at his own reflection in the mirror. Black eyes like marbles shoved into his sockets stared back at him. Two bottomless wells on a pale face, the mark of a Dark Witch stepped fully into his Way. He ran a hand through his hair, the action a mimicry of frustration — which Keir knew he ought to feel. Without his Shade, it felt robotic, his body going through the motions and giving the performance of a man who was supposed to care.

Tearing his fingers free from orangey-red strands, he jumped to his feet, all too aware that with his tousled ginger hair and waxen complexion, he looked like a possessed candle pacing the tiny hotel room. "He wasnae human; neither was he a witch. That much I could tell, but none of the identifying markers are found on any one desecrant in our e-grims."

"You are ignoring the most obvious feature of your mystery man." Toby laced fingers over his stomach, a tiny smile teasing the corner of his mouth. "He is not a *Nøkk*, a *Flodderduivel*, a *vodyanoi*, or a lorelei."

Keir paused, eyeing Toby over a shoulder. "And?"

"And therefore, none of our business." He uncrossed his legs, sitting on the edge of the narrow bed. "We are here to detain the lorelei, and you have spent the last forty-eight hours holed up in this awful hotel poring over your e-grim."

"Whose fault is that?"

Toby frowned, lacing and unlacing his fingers between his knees. "You suffered from mild hypothermia, symptoms of which include confusion and the inability to process coherent thought." He fixed a blue-eyed stare on Keir. "Keeping you under surveillance was necessary."

"So lock me in the room," Keir countered. "I'm nae stopping you from hunting the lorelei."

"*Naja*, but neither were you breeding any confidence in your ability to be left alone." Toby rose, stretching his arms over his head. "It is late; I am tired and have a meeting with the Witch of the Demesne in the morning. Either cease your hyperfixation for the evening or take it elsewhere."

Keir scowled, shoving hands into the pockets of his joggers and stalking to the window. He eyed the boats bobbing in the harbor, the locals of Harlingen wandering the red cobbled road along the waterfront. "Ye ken, I cannae do much with the Shades without my own."

Toby nodded, his lips pinched tight and blue eyes trained on the Dark Witch. Keir's skin crawled, hating the direct weight of that clear, clean gaze as though the spalování could read the weight of his Soul. "*Ich verstehe*," he stated, his tone final.

I understand.

Keir puffed his cheeks and exhaled, dropping his chin. "I dinnae fancy this."

"I understand," Toby paced out, in English this time, "that you need to detain the lorelei to strengthen your position in the ongoing argument with your sister."

Huffing a laugh, Keir shook his head at the floor. "Have you ever been wrong?"

"Not lately."

"It's hoora obnoxious."

"I understand." Toby shot him a tight-lipped smile. "What will it take to retrieve your Shade?"

"Being able to form a sigil." Keir worked the exact one, pleased with the bend of his ring finger. "And proximity to the desecrant."

"He will find you." Toby nodded, terse but accepting of Keir's brief explanation. "We will drive out to Lorentzsluis first thing."

"The lock?" Keir startled, caught off guard by Toby's declaration. "Why the lock?"

"While you remained impervious to her song, the lorelei implored me to deliver a message," Toby admitted.

"To whom?"

"*Keine ahnung.*" The German witch shrugged. *No idea.* "What lives in the sea that a lorelei would wish to speak to?"

"A selkie?" Keir suggested. "The seal maidens are salt-worthy. Or mebbe an *each-uisce*?"

"*Gesundheit.*" Toby gestured with two fingers to the east. "The Witch of the Demesne messaged earlier — he's had no sighting of the desecrant. The wards I set at Muiderberg and Ketel still hold, meaning the lorelei is still in the Ijsselmeer. She will probably attempt to enthrall a sailor heading into the North Sea, unable to swim those waters herself. We will interview captains to glean information. We will try again. And again and again, until we lure her close enough, using me as bait."

"Hate it."

"Fair." The spalování dipped his chin. "But we now have three jobs to accomplish: the retrieval of your Shade, the detention of the lorelei ..." He paused, and the silence stretched on. Long enough that even Shadeless Keir noticed the awkward weight of words unspoken.

"And the third?"

Toby smiled up at him. "Convincing C.R.O.W. that this all went according to your plan."

"Easy, then." He forced himself to laugh. Toby was the planner, logical witch that he was. Their mission dragging on as long as it had was purely Keir's fault. Were the spalování in charge, they would have captured the lorelei south of Koblenz and been done with it. The Dark Witch was the one that pushed to detain the desecrant rather than destroy. He was the one who had argued for them to research the history of the lorelei and attempt to discern a motive, and now — here they were. Holed up in a hotel room because of *his* choices. Perhaps it was time to admit he hadn't the slightest idea what he was doing or how to do it and let Toby take the lead.

"It should go without saying, that the less your sister knows of the Shade and its whereabouts, the better."

"Cannae disagree there."

"We will continue focusing our efforts on the lorelei and hope our proximity to the water also regains us your Shade."

Keir scratched his cheek, eyeing the striped wallpaper and seeking a connection to any emotion. Any feeling beyond the austere detachment that had driven every word, every action since the moment the mysterious wetsuit-clad being had disappeared into the Ijsselmeer.

Finding none, he let his arm drop weightless to his side. "We head to the Lorentzsluis first thing. But for now, with your permission, I would like to leave this toaty room and go for a drink."

The breeze coming off the Waddenzee was tepid, warming the late January night and putting it firmly at risk of being considered pleasant. Fishermen, locals, and tourists mingled in the narrow pub and spilled out onto the street, lounging around tables set in a jumble on the sidewalk.

Keir half listened to their chatter from his seat at the bar, catching every fourth word with his minimal Dutch. His fingers spun the glass of rum in front of him while his mind wandered along the line of his Shade, trying to pinpoint where, exactly, it was. Not far. That much had been evident the moment he passed through Toby's wards around the hotel and set foot on the red cobbles. In truth, he half thought he had followed it to this pub, obeying the gentle tug webbing beneath his rib cage and circling his middle.

The sensation was disorienting. He'd joined his Shade with others before, although never to this degree of severance. In those rare instances where Rai was high enough not to balk at his Way, she'd let him tie their Shades together. Let herself feel *him* as he felt her at all times. She'd been one of two witches to allow him to do so, and Keir had cherished each moment, though he could count them on the fingers of one hand.

The other witch, well, he was a different story altogether and one that was still hard to dwell upon. Ezra Lightner had been hungry for Keir's Way. Curious to a fault and constantly pressing the Dark Witch about the Shades and their haunted realm, the Neitherworld, a world closed to witches and C.R.O.W., save for the Dark Witch could enter and traverse at whim. In the few weeks they were together, he needled Keir about his interactions with and manipulations of the realm, asking leading questions that, ultimately, had taken on a suspicious bent.

But even then, with his Shade entwined with Ezra's, Keir kept control of himself. He remained the master rather than the anchor to an ever-tightening line that reeled him into this bar, only to be lost among the crowd.

More proof that Keir needed to retrieve his Shade, detain the lorelei, and get out. Convince C.R.O.W. that he was a witch Forbidden and Foule, yes, but good. Trustworthy. The longer he stayed on his sister's team performing the tasks C.R.O.W. asked of him, the more he lost sense of himself. He needed to leave his role as an Enforcer behind. Maybe put his degree to use and help desecrants and Shades move on.

"One day," he muttered, plucking his rum from the bar and swallowing the sugar-sweet amber liquid. It burned going down, watering his black eyes.

"*Wil je er nog een?*" The bartender looked up from the glass they'd been drying, eyes flicking from Keir's empty glass to the witch. Setting the towel down, they reached for the bottle of aged Brugal.

"*Ja, graag.*" Keir nodded and slid his glass across the bar. He dug in a pocket for coin, but the bartender filled his glass and waved him off, jerking their forehead to the side. Following the gesture, Keir skimmed his gaze past a petite dark-haired woman at the end of the bar, spotting a lone man sitting at a table in the corner. Loose, dark waves framed a pale, grim countenance, and high cheekbones drew attention to eyes shadowed by the recesses of the bar and fixed on Keir.

He swallowed, mouth going dry, and turned back to the bartender. "*Hoeveel?*"

They smiled and waved him off a second time. "He has paid." With a whip of their towel at the man in the corner, the bartender slid Keir's refreshed glass across the bar and moved on to the next patron.

He studied the rum between his hands, discomfort brewing in his chest, which was ... impossible, considering his Shadeless state. Back straightening, he spun on his stool to study the stranger, mentally lengthening and flattening his hair, applying a sheen of moonlight to the features, and feeling a distracting curl of interest in his gut.

The stranger continued to stare, dark eyes burning like a voided flame while the hex-bound Shade called to the Dark Witch.

"Right," Keir muttered, convincing himself to move. "It's showtime."

He held the stranger's gaze, raising the glass to his lips as he slid off the barstool and slipped in a puddle of water. The dark-haired woman shouted something at him, but Keir ignored her. Cheeks heating, he maneuvered through the crowd.

The Dutch were a tall people, but where they were willowy and lean, the stranger was broad and muscular, slightly larger than Keir himself. Even seated, the Dark Witch could tell the man would shame every fisherman in this bar. His sweater was a deep blue cable knit and ill-fit to his broad frame; the sleeves stopped two centimeters shy of his wrist while the collar had notched cuts on either side to fit the man's large build better.

Just as Keir studied the stranger, the stranger watched him approach with an equally cool, studious expression — brows slightly raised, lips slightly parted. His eyes dropped to take in the Dark Witch, lingering on his broad shoulders, the sweep of his hair, and narrowing at the hoodie and joggers he wore. He kept still when the witch sat down. One pale, elegant hand rested beside an untouched drink on the table, the long fingers and muscular wrist giving the distinct impression of having been carved from marble. Keir's eyes fell to the curve of his fingers, wondering if that moon-pale skin was as smooth as the stone it evoked.

"I have walked these streets for two days and could not find you." His low voice had Keir leaning forward, straining to hear him over the din of the bar. "It was some time before I realized this *thing*" —he raised his other hand, previously hidden beneath the table, to pluck at the center of his sweater— "could be manipulated. I apologize for luring you like a fish on a line."

"While I dinnae fancy being equated to a fish, I have certainly had less alluring company when it comes to drinks." The witch cocked an eyebrow, leaning back in his chair and propping an ankle on his knee. He raised his glass and offered it in cheers. "Though I ought to be the one buying, considering you saved me from a certain drowning." The stranger stared at him. Keir clinked the rim of his shorter glass against the untouched cocktail and swallowed a mouthful. "The wards on the hotel," he wheezed through the burn. "They would have kept you from finding me. Didnae think to have Toby disable them."

"Wards?"

Keir nodded, offering nothing else and half hoping the stranger would ask. It was odd to be seated across from the one who currently held your Shade and not know them at all. He was tempted to sever the tie and walk away, but, as always, Keir could feel himself getting distracted by this man and drawn to the mystery. His Shade spoke to the truth of his interest, whispering its curiosity across the distance to twist the muted jangle of nerves into a curl of something sinuous and decadent.

The stranger shivered, cold mask melting as a corner of his mouth curled up. He took in Keir with new interest and settled back in a mimicry of the witch's pose. "It is interesting, this *thing*. I find it familiar, how the sensations flit across this" —he flicked a long finger from himself to Keir and back— "and altogether new. What do you call it?"

"A Shade," he answered, no need to lie. "Specifically, mine. I suppose you would like me to remove it now."

"You suppose correctly." He tapped a finger against the table before taking his drink in hand, fingers curling around the stem one by one. He brought it to his lips, taking a sip while holding Keir's eye. The movement was sure. Intentional. And unless the witch was mistaken, seductive.

"Shall we get to it then?" He cocked his head, turning his hand on the table in a gesture for the man to reach out and take hold. The stranger smiled a broad, toothy grin that crinkled his cheeks and warmed those coal-black eyes, shooting heat directly into Keir's belly. He dropped an elbow on the table and leaned forward, pointedly ignoring Keir's hand while doing *something* that tightened the Shade connecting them. The gentle thrum of decadent promise heightened to a warble. Keir edged closer to the stranger, breath hitching in anticipation of his next words.

"I suppose we can hold off," he rumbled in that low, odd accent, each consonant curling at the base of Keir's spine. Black eyes watched him adjust his seat as if he knew exactly what he was doing to the witch. Again, the corner of his mouth quirked up. "For now."

"For now."

The stranger nodded, eyes drifting closed. Everything about the potential desecrant was measured. Steady. But there was a curiosity there; in the way his attention drifted over Keir, how he sat back and studied the bar and the witch upon approach. The man drank in the room, filing away the bits and pieces for later examination. Keir, for lack of a better comparison, felt like a smear of bacteria under the lens of a microscope.

"I have something you want," the stranger began, still speaking in those low, rumbling tones. "As do you."

"What could you possibly want from me?" Keir matched his lowered voice, roughening the brogue that colored his words. He was rewarded by another of those puzzling little smiles.

"Now that I have you here?" Black eyes glinted in the low light, settling on Keir's mouth. "Much."

Keir blinked. He curled his hand into a fist, coughed into it, and pressed his palm against his chest. "Pardon?"

"Is that a protest?"

"More an exclamation of surprise," Keir wheezed.

The stranger raised two fingers from his glass, laughter dancing in that impenetrable gaze. "Finish your drink."

He did as he was told and downed the rum, wincing at the burn and setting his glass on the table with a quiet *clink*.

"Very good." The stranger did the same, the muscles in his throat contracting and dancing as he swallowed.

When the dregs of the cocktail were finished, he side-eyed the witch, the air crackling between them. Whatever he was, whatever had brought this stranger to the Ijsselmeer to be caught by Keir's Shade, whatever reason or explanation there may be paled in the face of sudden and electric *want*. It was all he could do not to reach out, clutch the cable knit sweater in his fist, and haul the creature and his infuriating little smiles across the table.

Again, the curl of decadence warbled and thrummed. Humming from his Shade, still bound around the stranger, whirring across the distance and settling in Keir's bones. From how the stranger looked at him, he also felt it. Patches of color grew on his cheeks, and he unfolded himself from behind the table, rising to his full height. "Let us take a walk."

Four

"The creature in the water was a … lorelei?" The glow from the street-lamp silvered the long line of the stranger's nose, casting deep shadows under his cheekbones and jaw. They stood shoulder to shoulder on the pedestrian walkway overlooking the harbor. In the distance, boat horns bellowed through the clear winter night, and further out a lighthouse winked.

"Aye." Keir picked at the rail with a fingernail. "Ought to have bagged her near Düsseldorf, but I wanted to see how far she would go. Wouldnae have guessed she'd make it this far."

"And why are you chasing this lorelei?"

"Why am I chasing the lorelei, or why do my employers wish me to do so?"

"Are the reasons not the same?"

Looking out over the water, Keir pulled his lower lip between his teeth. "No," he stated after a moment. "No, they are not."

"That is a relief." The stranger turned around and leaned against the railing, elbows propped and eyes on Keir. "I have a certain fondness for dwellers of the deep; it would be a pity to discover you hunted them for sport."

Angling his face to the side to gauge the stranger's reaction, Keir chose his words carefully. "There are many interesting and diverse beings out there only trying to live their lives peacefully. Who am I, as one of their number, to decide whether one should live or die?"

Black eyes regarded him, the stranger's face impassive. And then he brushed his fingers along Keir's arm.

The contact pulled a shiver from his bones, raising goosebumps as his bound Shade reached for its master. He dropped his gaze to the stranger's hand, watching those long, marble fingers trail the length of his forearm and linger at the hem of his sleeve. When he looked up, he met that onyx gaze with an obsidian stare of his own.

"What are you?"

"What?" Keir laughed, caught off guard.

"With your eyes, so like mine. You are not ... human?"

"Ah." Realization dawned, and he huffed. "Nae, not one of Staid. No."

The stranger frowned, his fingers still at the back of Keir's hand. The moment stretched, witch and otherwise held in parity by a Shade and two fingers. Swallowing the nerves jumping in his belly, Keir turned his hand, revealing his palm and biting his lip at the soft brush of the stranger's fingertips along the sensitive stretch of skin beneath his wrist.

"Do I have to guess?" He trailed his finger up the arc of Keir's lifeline, cutting back across the center of his palm. "Or will you be a good boy and tell me?"

"Depends." An eyebrow rose on its own. "Are you going to tell me what you are?"

The stranger smiled and dropped his chin, cheeks darkening. It softened his features, painting a sweet vulnerability on the not-man. Keir drank it in, enjoying far too much that he had put that expression there. The decadent curl heightened into something wicked unfurling across the tether of his Shade.

"I can feel that," the stranger rasped.

"Oh?"

"It has been a distracting few days. I was supposed to observe the parallax shift and axial variability in the polar star during the tidal moon. Instead, I find myself confused one moment and sorrowful the next." His finger traced to the tip of Keir's middle finger, pausing. "You do not laugh like the people in that bar. Sadness echoes everything you feel; even your smile is ebbed in darkness."

Keir opened his mouth. Closed it. The stranger lay his palm flat against his and dropped his gaze to their hands. Their fingers were of a similar length, though where his were elegant and straight, Keir's showed the marks of his years as an Enforcer. His palms were calloused, the knuckles swollen with scar tissue, and the ring finger on his right hand was slightly crooked from a break.

"I suppose now is the time to take my Shade back." He flexed his left hand, testing the ability to form a sigil. The stranger curled his fingers, trailing down the sensitive sides of Keir's own, the skin just as soft and supple as he had imagined it would be. Locking their hands together, the stranger gave a gentle squeeze.

"Or perhaps we see if I can erase that sadness for a moment."

Keir jerked his face up and was met by the press of soft lips against his own. Testing and teasing before the stranger pulled away, brushing the tips of their noses together. The witch chased his mouth, using their locked hands to tug him forward.

He gripped the stranger's upper arm with his left hand, keeping him in place and deepening the kiss. His tongue teased the seam of his lips until the not-man opened for him. He tasted of salt and sea air, smelled of it, even, and the muddling of senses drew an old, ancient memory from the recesses of Keir's mind.

A boardwalk in a Mediterranean village. Salt-damp air in the pre-dawn morning as he drunkenly stumbled back to the holiday rental his sister had secured. A happiness dragged out of the young witch after years of shapeless, endlessly gray days.

Heat shot down into his belly as the memory surfaced, urging the Dark Witch on. He brought his hand to the stranger's cheek, fingers tracing the sharp jaw before drifting back into his hair. A small groan left the man as Keir swept his tongue deeper, wanting to drown in the sense memory he evoked.

Not to be outdone, the stranger mimicked his hands, cupping Keir's cheek and sliding his fingers behind his neck. He angled him back against the railing and pinned him in place with his body. Chest to chest, hips to hips, working his thigh between Keir's legs to bring them flush together as he met each sweep of his tongue. His broadness was a match for the witch, the weight of him caging Keir against the railing. The sensation was distressing and wildly freeing all at once.

Keir was a witch of control. Restraining his Way, leashing his emotion, and hoarding his battered and bruised heart. This stranger, this not-man was the sea during a storm. A tsunami of passion and sensation trapped at the point of the curl, crashing against Keir's mouth again and again and again.

It made his head spin for want of oxygen, for more of this stranger. His heat and his hunger.

Keir's hands dropped to the hem of that ill-fit cable knit. His fingers slipped beneath the fabric, palms sliding up marble-smooth, taut skin. The texture varied, suggestions of scars on an athletic body, and the thought of tracing those scars with his tongue surged a groan from the depths of his throat. The stranger pulled away, letting Keir catch his breath only to have it hitch in a gasp as lips trailed along his jaw. He tipped his head back, pressing the stranger to his chest as the man kissed down his throat. Soft brushes and the flick of a tongue in the hollow at the base.

A pleasurable shiver overtook him, and he hissed through his teeth. It made the stranger chuckle, a rumble in his chest that released a gust of warmed breath against Keir's skin.

He lifted his head, pressing another soft kiss at the corner of Keir's mouth and murmuring against his lips, "You have a habit of dressing poorly for the weather."

Curling his fingers and pressing them into the hard muscle on the stranger's back, Keir rolled his hips forward, swallowing the stranger's ragged breath with a kiss. He pulled away to whisper in his ear, "I'm nae shivering from the cold."

He grazed the man's lobe with his teeth, and the stranger shuddered against him, a large hand sweeping up Keir's spine.

"Yes," he breathed, "just like that."

So Keir did it again. A little harder this time, earning a sharp gasp before he kissed away the pain, tasting the salt of the man's skin with his lips and his tongue. Tugging the split collar of his sweater away, he gently nibbled on the sensitive skin where neck met shoulder. The stranger stiffened, hands dropping to Keir's waist and digging in. Almost to the point of pain, urging the witch to do more.

He crooked his fingers, picking at the strands of his Shade, working through the binding hex to take hold of the stranger's own. Lifting his head just enough to watch the not-quite man's reaction, he plucked the strands of *him*. Wanting to tease out desire and want. Euphoria and need. The emotions tied to their actions. Intending to bring them to the forefront and knot the strands in with his own.

Except his fingers slipped, the stranger's Shade shying away and hovering just beyond his reach.

Keir growled his frustration into the stranger's ear, trying again — only to miss. *Again*. It was maddening, and before he could stop himself, he fed his frustration across the tether of his Shade. Muddying up the heat and lust and overwhelming *need* this creature stoked in him. The not-man shuddered, worming his fingers into the witch's hair and tugging his head up and back.

His mouth fell on Keir's. Each sweep of his tongue deeper and hungrier than before, locking the witch in a tidal pull and drowning his senses in salt and sweat and the aether before a storm. Their hands flew over one another's forms, grabbing and unable to grab *hold*. Their kisses heightened with the sense of free-falling through a space with no gravity as the world spun lazily around them, and when it became too much — when Keir's lungs burned for want of air, the sensation all too much like drowning — he pulled away. Gripping the stranger's waist and staring dazedly into his eyes.

Chests heaving, breaths coming in stilted, staggered pants, they stared at each other with matching black eyes, seeing and not seeing the truth of *them*.

"What are you?" The stranger whispered, his wide accent canted with awe.

Keir's throat bobbed, the answer rising to the tip of his tongue only to be swallowed down by that old, trained fear, readying himself for the inevitable shudder and immediate backing away.

The stranger cocked his head to the side, eyes dancing over Keir's face with the question poised again on his lips. When he didn't pull away, when instead he brought his face closer, that wide mouth pursed for a kiss, Keir let himself exhale.

"Show me yours" —he stole the kiss the stranger would have given, fingers trailing the weave in his cable knit— "I'll show you mine."

He was answered by a maddening quirk at the corner of the stranger's mouth. His nostrils flared slightly as his lips parted, but a gust of wind blown down from the north stole whatever he was about to say. Below freezing, it ripped through Keir's hoodie and the fabric of his joggers, making the witch shiver in truth. The stranger tensed, his hands dropping away.

"You should return to your hotel."

Disappointment had Keir backing away, and the stranger darted out a hand, catching the pocket of his hoodie and keeping him from leaving.

"It is too cold for you to be out here, dressed as you are."

Keir scanned the too-tight sweater and thin pants. The lightweight shoes and absurd lack of socks. "Your attire is hardly better."

"True," he agreed, "but I am far more acclimated to the cold than you."

"I live in Edinburgh," Keir scoffed. "Am nae stranger to the cold. Though if you are so concerned, we could take this elsewhere." He hooked his fingers in the belt loops at the stranger's waist. Tugging him close until they were chest to chest. "Are you staying far from here?"

The stranger tensed, his attention drifting out over the harbor before snapping back to Keir. "Not in a manner of speaking."

"Good," he grinned, the one that drove a dimple into his cheek. "Lead the way."

Shaking his head, the stranger dipped his chin, looking up at Keir through thick, dark lashes, skin all but glowing in the lamplight. His hand drifted up to toy with the drawstring on Keir's hoodie, winding it around his elegant fingers and tugging gently. "How long will you be in Harlingen?"

Stomach dropping, Keir sighed. "Until we corner the lorelei, or my employers call us back."

"You will be out near the water again?"

"Tomorrow," he answered. "My ... colleague was enthralled by her song. He thinks she will be hovering near the Lorentzsluis lock leading out to the Waddenzee." Something clicked into place at his words. Keir blinked, scrutinizing the stranger. "Her song did not affect you."

"Nor you," he answered plainly. "Which again leads me to ask, what are you?" Keir only grinned and slipped his hand up behind the stranger's neck, drawing him closer for a kiss. A tender, lingering embrace to seal their interlude in sweetness. As he pulled away, he watched the stranger's eyes drift open, committing the way desire softened his dramatic features to memory. "Tomorrow, then," he whispered, startling Keir.

"Aye?"

"The casemate, at the Lorentzsluis lock." He jerked his chin up, catching the tip of Keir's nose with his lips. "Considering that you do not know how to swim, I do not like the idea of you so near the water without proper supervision."

"Well, I —" His cheeks heated, and a wicked flush crawled up his chest and neck. "That is to say—"

"Not a personal failure, but it does make one wonder about your capacity for survival." The stranger slipped out of his arms, trailing fingers along the railing as he backed away.

Keir stammered, bit his lip, and reached for him with his left hand. "Ken I'll take my Shade back now."

The stranger took a large step out of his reach. "No."

"No?" Keir arched a brow.

"You kiss so well; it is a pity your listening is so poor." The stranger grinned, broad and toothy, and Keir felt a troubling quake in his knees. "Having this attached to me is a useful tool and makes you easier to find." Moving quickly, he darted forward and kissed Keir on the cheek. "Tomorrow, dark one. Look to the sea."

He stood on the harbor walkway long enough for his teeth to start chattering and his fingers to turn blue. Watching the stranger walk away until he was little more than a silver flash of skin in the lamplight and then nothing at all. Strolling the cobbled streets back to his hotel with something like hope fluttering in his chest, Keir opened the door to the shared room as quietly as he was able. Toby had left the curtains open, and orange-gold light from the harbor bled into the room, faintly silhouetting the furniture.

Toeing off his shoes, Keir winced at the unnecessarily loud drag of zipper teeth and creaky bedsprings. He let his mind wander back to the stranger only once he was settled. The kiss. Dragging his lower lip between his teeth, he tasted the hint of salt and sea air. It had been ages since another being — witch or otherwise — left him feeling light and free. Not even Rai had managed to do so in the end, and yet, here he was: sprawled over his narrow hotel bed with half an erection and the memory of marble smooth skin beneath his palms.

Flustered, he rolled onto his side and stared out the window. Barges and tall ships bobbed in gentle waves, and a seal or a bird dove beneath the water, churning up a white, foamy splash gilded by the lights on the bridge. An all too suggestive curl of desire withered across the tether of his Shade; licentious thoughts echoed back at him from a distance.

Pinching his lips to keep from smiling outright, Keir worked his legs under the duvet and let his eyes drift closed. He was tiptoeing the edge of sleep when a heavy sigh sounded from the other bed in the room. Toby's weight creaked the springs in his mattress, and Keir felt the heat of the spalování's flame-licked gaze.

"Tobe." He greeted his friend, hugging a pillow tight to his chest.

Toby sighed again, his words colored with laughter as he said, "You kissed another desecrant, didn't you?"

Five

"Get out of the water; you are scaring her away."

"Am nae," Keir adjusted his footing in the silt, stiff neoprene creaking as he did. Though thankful for the rubbers and wetsuit bottoms, he was not too proud to admit that he should have worn more than a v-neck and track jacket. He stared glumly at Toby, clad neck to toe in the last wetsuit left for sale in Harlingen. "I was the one she towed in last time, lest you forget."

"How could I, when the result of your near drowning has had you staring off into the middle distance all morning with *ein dummes* smile on your face." Toby grinned back at him.

Keir shot up two fingers in a "V," but he turned and trudged back to the tumble of rocks beneath the casemate. Clamoring up to the shrub-covered earthen jetty, he settled against the three-meter tall, green-and-white striped lighthouse. He scavenged in the dry bag Toby had loaded with food and supplies and retrieved an apple, biting off a mouthful and scanning the water for any sign of the lorelei ... or other parties.

Tomorrow, dark one.

The memory of that rumbling voice crawled down his spine, raising goosebumps on his neck at the promise in those words and the memory of that kiss.

Look to the seas.

He felt foolish, doing as he was told with little more than the promise of a stranger. But that stranger held his Shade, and Keir felt the truth and intent behind those words. A truth which helped him ignore that he and Toby had been out here for hours, paddling around in the tandem kayak the spalování had insisted on buying, wading waist deep into the water, and generally making an obvious nuisance of themselves.

Beyond bribing the Witch of the Demesne to keep an eye out for any suspicious activity, this was the extent of what they could manage without Keir's Shade.

So he looked to the water, tugging gently on the tether between himself and the stranger.

And he waited.

The Ijsselmeer was still today, stretching to the east as a vast mirror reflecting a bright blue sky. Kayakers paddled near the sandbar to the south of the casemate while boats sailing for the lock sent quiet ripples lapping at the stones forming the foundation of the jetty. Behind him, the concrete pillbox of a World War II machine-gun casemate loomed, creating a square of cool shade should the sun prove too much. Still as it was, the winter day soon grew too warm for a witch in neoprene and a black jacket. Holding the apple in his mouth, Keir peeled off his jacket and laid it down as a blanket, lying back to soak in the weak sun while he finished the fruit. His shirt rode up, exposing a stretch of taut abdomen as he folded his arms behind his head, confident that the lorelei's song would be a heinous alarm should she decide to try lulling Toby again. Birds gulled in the distance, and the water lapping at the stones soon had him dozing off.

He woke in shadow, sensing the dark behind his closed eyes. With a dismissive flick of his fingers, he grumbled, "Get oot mah sun, ye tadger."

"Tadger." The stranger's curious accent tried out the word. His amusement trickled across the Shade between them. "Are we giving each other nicknames?"

Keir opened his eyes wide, then wider still at the sight of an Olympic form looming over him. Clad in form-fitting neoprene shorts and nothing else, his broad shoulders and muscular body were on full display to great, mouth-drying effect. He gripped an 8-liter, rescue orange dry bag in one hand, the other propped on a hip as he smiled down at the witch. Even backlit by the sun, Keir could make out drops of water running down the swells and dips of muscle. More dribbled from the loose, black tendrils of the stranger's hair to gather on the tip of his nose, where they swelled into one fat bead that fell free and splattered between Keir's eyes.

It jarred him from his painfully obvious study of the stranger but Horned God, look at the man. He was built for the Men's 200m Freestyle at whatever Olympics was next up, and Keir was a red-blooded, pansexual witch who knew with startling clarity how well the specimen looming over him could kiss.

"Holy Horned God," he breathed.

"I thought it was 'Tadger'?"

"Ehm," Keir cleared his throat, curling his legs into his chest and rolling back, only to thrust them out and hop to his feet in a gross display of athleticism. He turned, running a hand through his hair and dropping it to the back of his neck. More than a little pleased at how the stranger licked his lips, dark eyes trawling from head to toe.

He smiled, dropping his dry bag with a *squelch*. "You did not answer my question."

"Tadger isnae really a term of endearment."

"Not that one." The stranger took a step, bringing him close enough to touch. "Are we giving each other nicknames?"

Keir worked his jaw, trying to come up with something witty and failing to answer long enough that the stranger's brows pulled together.

"Am I using the word incorrectly? Nick" —he clicked the consonant in the back of his throat— "name?"

"Aye," Keir croaked. Cleared his throat. "I mean nae. No nicknames. Although you are the one who dubbed me 'Dark One', which is terrifyingly close to the mark."

"How so?" He quirked his head, a damp tendril of hair falling free.

Without thinking, Keir brushed it from his forehead, blushing furiously as he held out that same hand. "My name is Keir."

"Kee-ear." The stranger eyed his hand.

"Old Irish name, despite the accent." He tried a shrug and a laugh, the latter coming out more as a pant. "Means dark or black."

The Stranger angled back, eyeing Keir's hair glinting copper in the sunlight. "And you are certain that you are not a human."

"Is shaking my hand contingent on the answer?"

"No."

"Then I am fairly positive I'm not a human, though also a fool for freely giving my name without knowing what you are."

That earned a smile, and the stranger pressed his palm to Keir's, elegant fingers gripping tight. Instead of shaking, however, he tugged Keir by the hand, closing the last of the distance and kissing him on the cheek. "Names are not a given title among my kind."

"Carefully put." He returned the kiss on the stranger's cheek, cursing the daylight as he fought the urge to do more. Releasing his grip, he eyed the man before him. "What am I to call you, then?"

He shook his head, clicking his tongue. "So good at kissing and so poor at listening. Take off your shirt."

"Pardon?"

"Is that still not a protest?"

Cheeks burning crimson, Keir reached over his shoulder, bunching fabric in his fist and whipping his shirt up and over his head. He dropped the garment onto his discarded track jacket, never looking away from the stranger. Keir knew he was fit. Horned God knew he worked hard enough to be so, but watching those dark eyes widen ever-so-slightly and seeing that pink tongue dart out to moisten his lower lip was a reward and a confirmation all its own.

"Nae a protest."

Black eyes burned as they skated up his torso, lingering on the faint shimmer of the Soul Sigil before boring into his own. "And the boots."

"Why my boots?"

The stranger kept silent, prowling past Keir and heading for the jutting rocks at the edge of the casemate. The sun caught on the collection of scars shimmering over his torso as he descended into the sea. "Because I am going to teach you how to swim."

"Arms out."

"They are out."

"Like a stingray."

Keir angled his head back, squinting up at the stranger. "How am I to ken what a bloody stingray looks like?"

He dropped his hands from Keir's shoulders, and the witch started sinking in the still waters. "Use your imagination."

"Like a bat," Toby supplied. He stood a few yards off, keeping a polite distance from the pair. The introduction had been awful, for Keir. For the stranger, it had been polite, while for Toby, it had been the source of no small amount of snickering and side-eyeing as he took in the potential desecrant. Keir knew he was assessing the not-man, looking him over for any hint of his true nature. He also knew that the spalování was coming up empty-handed in his attempts, considering the varied themes of his questions.

"Do they not have bats where you are from?" He tried again.

"No."

"But they have stingrays," Toby pressed. He waded through the waist-high water and loomed over Keir. "I had thought stingrays and bats to both be temperate creatures."

"I suppose they are." The stranger sent him a tight-lipped smile. "But I do not have cause to spend much time in caves on land." He gripped Keir by the arm and hauled him up to his feet. "Legs out, arms up." With a smile that was more of a showing of teeth, he looked Toby dead in the eye as he finished his instruction. "Engage your core and keep that magnificent backside raised."

"Oh, Horned God," Keir muttered into his palms, unable to look the chortling spalování in the eye.

"Do not be embarrassed, Keir," Toby hollered, wading back into the depths to continue being bait. "You worked hard on that magnificent backside."

The stranger's imitation of a smile vanished, his expression darkening. He bit his lower lip, eyeing the witch in the water. It was enough to send Keir sinking lower if only to hide the blush crawling over his bare chest. "Ach, just let me drown."

"Not while I am here." Again, he gripped Keir firmly by the elbows and eased him into the water. "One leg at a time ... good." His tone warmed, putting a faint smile on that distracting mouth. "Very, very good."

He flattened his palms and slid them down Keir's arms as he spread them wide, the touch sure and steady. Sensual in how his fingers curved around Keir's wrists, thumbs pressing lightly down on pressure points as he held the witch splayed out in the water.

Then they slid away, and Keir fought the urge to panic at the absence of touch and the vulnerability of his position and circumstance. Adrift in the sea and unable to swim. Unable to call on his Shades. Unable to do anything but drown. His body tensed, he felt his legs dropping, his middle began sinking, and the instant his muscles tensed to begin thrashing — the stranger was there. His palms pressed against the base of Keir's spine, right over his hips. Forearms braced his back, and he brought his face low, right beside his ear. "You did so well, Keir."

His tone was unmistakable, and the feel of his lips against Keir's temple had him biting his lip at the praise.

"I dinnae ken what to call you," he managed after a moment. The stranger did not move, but his arms tensed, fingers splayed across Keir's back. "It's bloody awkward."

"My folk do not —"

"Have names, so you said." He turned his head, watching the stranger as he adjusted his stance. His hands slid to the center of Keir's back as he rose enough to look down at him with a puzzled expression. "You must call each other *something*."

"Do you remember when I said this ... Shade of yours was familiar?"

"The sensations you feel. My emotions."

He nodded. "Our language is not so different, though it is manifested as thoughts conveyed, coupled with the emotional intent of the phrase. Our names are similar in an abstract sense. We claim each other by our attributes. Our characteristics. Those titles represent the individual but are not bound by the rigid structure of an oral name."

Keir narrowed his eyes at the not-man. "And how should I think of you then?"

"In whichever way makes you look at me as you did when I arrived."

Keir sputtered, kicking his legs out and sinking in the water. He caught himself with heels in the silt and stood, sweeping hair out of his eyes. "You keep saying things like that, and it willnae be a problem. Although I'd rather not refer to you as 'Tasty Snack.'"

The stranger blinked, his chin tucking as he took a half step back in surprise. "You want to eat me?"

"In a way." Keir spread a broad grin across his face. "Though I dinnae ken you'll mind so much."

"Good Goddess," Toby balked from ten feet away. "I am going to swim around to the other side of the jetty." And he did, his blond head bobbing in the water as he disappeared around the land wall.

Keir watched him go, stomach clenching uncomfortably now that he was left alone with the stranger. Drifting his fingers through the cold sea, he watched ripples form in the wake of his lazy movement, nerves jangling this close to the stranger and his Shade. It was easier with an audience there to bear witness as Keir slipped into a character and hid behind a clown's mask. Alone, however, it was just him and the not-man who held his Shade captive.

"You are nervous?" The stranger stepped behind him; his body heat a welcome brace against the tepid air.

The temptation to lean back, to press skin against skin and feel all of that heat and strength envelop him drowned out all reason. It was rare, large, lanky witch that he was, to feel small next to someone. Keir's partners tended to be slight and Shade-like. Narrow enough that he could wrap his hands around their waist, lift them from the ground, and toss them onto a bed. Small enough that he could exert gentle, physical control in a world that refused to allow him any at all. Pliant enough to mewl and whimper at the pleasure he relished in giving them.

Everything about this stranger and this circumstance set Keir on edge and left him teetering between dread and desire. Waist deep in water that could kill as easily as nourish, feeling small and vulnerable beside a not-man who looked like he could lift Keir with one arm and sling him over his shoulder. A not-man that *kept* looking at him.

"No."

"I believe humans call that a 'lie.'"

"True," he conceded, scanning the horizon. "But I'm nae quite human, am I?"

"That you are not." The stranger took that last step, pressing his chest against Keir's back. Fingers drifted lightly down his forearm, and the witch tensed, hitching a breath as he closed his eyes. His Shade shivered and writhed in delight, and the stranger chuckled beside his ear. "But I know something that you are." He nipped Keir's lobe, earning a strangled whimper for the effort. "This distracting Shade of yours is very forthcoming."

"It's not the only thing," he panted as elegant fingers teased across his middle, toying with his waistband.

"Not the only thing to what?" The stranger sounded genuinely confused, and something about that settled the shaky ground beneath Keir's feet. He reached back, gripping a solid handful of muscular thigh.

"Be forthcoming."

He spun to face the stranger, and a foot caught behind his ankle, sending the witch flopping onto his back. Before he could panic, strong arms braced him at the shoulder and waist. He blinked up into a pale, amused face.

"You think too much." The stranger smiled, turning Keir as liquid as the lake. "Swimming too deeply in your head and unable to simply" — his arms drifted away— "float."

It took him a beat. A blink to realize that he was lying on his back, unsupported in the water. And then he thrashed and promptly sank. His heels caught in the silt, and he lurched to his feet, spitting and shaking out his hair. "You dropped me."

"You were floating." The stranger crossed his arms, settling back on his hips. "Not for long, but you were doing it."

"You cannae just drop people in the water."

He gestured with two fingers to the inland sea. "Again."

Keir's jaw dropped, his mind reeling. These demands were his game, and having the tables turned on him was unnerving, exciting, and ... dangerously arousing. He bent his knees, lowering in the water and willing the heat in his veins to cool so he could regain his composure. "I ought to take my Shade back, just for that."

"You can try." The stranger mimicked his plunge, the sea swallowing him to the shoulders. His arms stretched out in a fluid movement that pressed up against the water without breaking the surface tension. He drifted a few feet away, grinning widely. "But you will have to come closer."

Keir chewed his lip, testing the ground beneath his feet before moving deeper, knees bent and arms thrust out as if he could brace himself on the nothing.

"That's it." The stranger nodded, encouraging. Keir took another step. Another, until he was face to face with the maddening creature. Hands gripped him at the waist, thumbs drifting over the curve of muscle at his hips. The stranger's eyes darkened further. "Look at you, out here with me."

Despite the cold water, Keir's body flashed hot, pink crawling into his cheeks. He dropped his eyes, bashful this close to his Shade, and the stranger raised a hand to his cheek, lifting his head and demanding, "Again."

Keir fought to hold that gaze, to hold onto himself, feeling both slip away like water through a sieve and dragging his aching heart down into the comfort of the abyss.

"Again."

SIX

Keir let himself be maneuvered onto his back, spreading his arms and staring into dark eyes. Their liquid depths silenced the panic in his head, drowning his fear at losing control.

The stranger adjusted his arms, his legs, pressing gently against the base of Keir's spine to get him to raise his middle. Fingers cradled his skull to angle his face in the water just so before bracing Keir's shoulders. All the while, words poured from his lips.

"When I was young, my name was not who was, but rather what I was. My appearance, nothing more. Of course, that is all I ever needed to be amongst my folk. As I grew older, I discovered a world beyond where I was born. A wide world full of wonders, but none so magnificent as the stars."

"The stars?"

He nodded. "I traveled to the north, where the lights dance in the sky."

"The Northern Lights," Keir supplied. "On a clear night, you can see them from Arthur's Seat." A quirk of the stranger's head had him clarifying, "A promontory in the city where I live. Large, craggy edifice as hard and unyielding as the Scots themselves."

A wrinkle formed between his brows, but that curious little smile remained. "Is this city near the sea?"

"The Firth of Forth," Keir answered. "Loads of bathers, and the strand is less than a kilometer from my flat. Come visit; we could continue these lessons."

An inscrutable expression flitted across the stranger's features, his wide mouth pinching in a way that made Keir think he was hiding a smile. "I study the stars," he finally stated. "That is why I am here."

"To study a parallax shift," Keir remembered his off-hand comment from the night before. "Something to do with the polar star."

"That is the one."

"The one what?"

"The one you would call me by."

"Parallax?" Keir angled his face in the water, feeling disassociated from his body, his mind wholly engrossed in this conversation. "That's a mouthful."

"Says the one who called me a 'Snack'."

"Have you seen you?"

"Have you?" The stranger's face went still. His hands began to drift away. Keir turned over in the water, gaining his feet and gripping the not-man by his arm.

"Dinnae," he rasped. "Dinnae pull away before telling me your name."

"Keir—"

"It has to do with the stars?" He tried, skimming everything he knew of astronomy and coming up with astrology instead. "The-the polar star, the North Star?"

The stranger gave a hesitant bob of his chin.

Panicked and not quite knowing why, Keir caged the center of the other man's chest with his casting hand, intending to summon his Shade as he'd done the night before. He grunted his annoyance when the attempt again failed and grappled with his own Shade instead, letting the truth of his sentiment bleed through the bond and hoping the stranger understood.

"*Réalta Thuaidh*." He named the polar star in the language of his intent, magick surging to the surface of his skin and humming in his ears. He took the essence of the words, the title, and all it stood for in all of the tongues and attached it to the being. "Réalta Thuaidh," he repeated. The stranger looked down at Keir's hand, the fingertips digging into his chest and then into the Dark Witch's eyes. The name settled between them as a truth. "North Star."

"Réalta Thuaidh," he tried it out with the broad, flat accent, tasting the words and savoring their feel. "Another mouthful."

"Promises, promises," Keir murmured, slipping his hand behind Réalta's back and splaying fingers wide between his shoulder blades. He pressed them chest to chest and seized Réalta's mouth in a hot, wet kiss.

Despite the freshwater, Réalta still tasted of salt and sea air, stoking Keir's thirst. The witch knew he would never be sated even as he drank his fill. This being, this not-man was welding closed the fracture in his heart that Rai had left behind. Healing it with a kiss, a stroke, and a gentle word of praise to remind Keir that he was worth being cared for. Treasured.

Keir thrilled at the way this absolute specimen made him feel delicate. At how those powerful legs surged through the water, bringing them into the shallows for Keir's sake. All to put the witch at ease when he was so out of his depth.

When the water was at his navel, Réalta ceased his march. His hands slipped over Keir's arms and chest, his back, following a nearly identical path as the night before. Only this time — this time, there was no cotton or cable knit between them. This was skin on skin, their bodies slick and heated by desire.

Keir traced the pattern of scars on Réalta's chest and waist, blood humming in his ears as he pulled away to eye the irregular, circular pattern of silvered skin shimmering against his pale hue. Réalta allowed him to do so, muscles bunching and dancing at his light touch. When Keir met his eye, a question forming, the other man dragged his finger over the topmost whorl of the triskelion brand, lingering over his thundering heart. A devilish light gleamed in dark eyes, and he brushed Keir's nipple with his thumb.

The witch yelped, jerking in Réalta's arms. He laughed, hands gripping Keir by the thighs to keep him in place.

"Such a wonderful response." Réalta kneaded his hamstrings, laughter in his voice.

Keir scanned the water, calming himself enough to behave like a normal almost-human being. He spotted Toby in the distance, chatting with another bather — a woman, from her curves and slight form. Her dark hair hung slick and free, cascading down her back as she gestured broadly. Toby nodded, pointing in the direction of the lock. With a wave, the woman dipped beneath the surface, reappearing a few feet away to catch a breath as she swam.

"Have I lost your attention so easily?" Réalta mused.

"What was it we were doing?" Keir smirked. "Ken I might need a reminder."

"You are a puzzle among humans." He brought his face close, brushing the tips of their noses together.

"Lest I remind you—" Keir started, and Réalta lurched forward, tipping the witch back. He tightened his arms around the other man's neck and scowled into a grinning face.

"Do not make me dump you again."

"Oh, please," Keir clenched his thighs tight around Réalta's waist. "Anything but that."

He grunted, powerful body going taut a heartbeat before splashing the witch in the water. Keir shot his arms up, reaching for the surface, gasping out a laugh. He expected Réalta to let go, but that iron-strength grip dug into his thighs. The pain of it jerked Keir's face down. Skin blue in the watery light, Réalta's pale features were haloed by a dark mass of hair, his onyx eyes wide with shock. Keir had just long enough to register the genuine fear before they were jerked deeper.

The pock-marked surface of submerged rocks grated his back and shoulders, and then there was nothing but the broad, depthless expanse of the Ijsselmeer spreading wide and terrifying around them. Keir cried out, his fright escaping as a bubble of precious oxygen. Réalta kicked and bucked, fighting against whatever had caught him by the legs. He tightened his grip, squeezing Keir's thighs in quick succession to call his attention. When the witch looked down, Réalta released one arm to point to the surface. Keir shook his head, heart slamming as his panic rose.

Large hands skimmed down his calves, gripping his ankles and prying the witch free. Cupping him by the heels, Réalta thrust his arms out, using all of that brute strength to shoot Keir upwards.

A bubbled protest of "No!" left his mouth as Réalta was dragged into the depths. His head broke through the surface, and the witch gasped, windmilling arms and seeking purchase where there was none. One breath and one teasing view of the dijk and jetty was all Keir gained before he sank.

But the singular breath was enough.

This far from his Shade, fright was a distant thing. Keir peered through the water, his training taking over. Logic told him to think, assess, and act. Not dwell on his mounting terror and the anger that he'd disregarded the humming in his ears, again mistaking it for arousal and not the threat it was.

This was why he needed to catch the lorelei and strengthen his position with his sister: to prove that while he was capable, he needed *out*.

He was too easily distracted. His heart was too easily wounded, his head too easily turned, and one of these days, it was going to get him, or one of his teammates, killed.

Keir wasn't built to be an Enforcer. He was not cold and calculating like his sister. Wasn't driven by the white knight need to save the world like Toby or steadied by the hard-won experience of his brother-in-law.

He was a lone Dark Witch hidden among the weeds of C.R.O.W., clawing for the light when what he needed was his Shade.

Squinting, he spotted a blurry shape writhing in the murk, the struggle between Réalta and whatever had grabbed him, kicking up silt and muddying the water.

Keir held out his left hand, the fingers bent to form a summoning sigil, and barked the intentional phrase. Thick Irish bubbled at his lips, but it was enough. The tether of his Shade snapped taut, twanging against his ribs. He curled his fingers around the invisible line, pulling arm over arm over arm to drag himself closer to the watery wrestling match.

Terror rose with each inch he gained. He narrowed his eyes, ignoring the bands of light growing thinner and thinner as he pulled himself further into the depths and closer to Réalta. His lungs burned, the urge to open his mouth and breathe in the water rising, but he kept on. Deeper and deeper until Réalta's powerful form rose into stark, furious clarity from the shifting shadows. The curtain of water pulled aside to reveal the not-man swinging an arm and twisting away from the jagged-toothed maw of the lorelei.

She swept a taloned hand at Réalta, surging through the water to snap piranha-sharp teeth at his leg. He tucked his knees to his chest, pushing them out forcefully and catching his heels against her shoulders. His kick sent the lorelei spinning into the dark, and the not-man readied himself to give chase.

Keir grabbed Réalta by the arm and jerked him around. Those dark eyes widened further, darting from Keir to the distant surface and back. Determination slammed his brow, and he wrapped the witch in his arms. Thick legs snapping together at the knees, he bucked his hips, the motion rolling down his thighs and calves, propelling the pair through the water. Keir startled at the speed with which they ascended, clawing at Réalta's shoulders and back as he fought to free himself from that piston-strength grip.

They burst through the surface, gasping as one. Réalta flipped Keir onto his back, an arm again banding over his chest. Dragging in a deep breath, Keir slipped free and dropped beneath the waves, bending his fingers into a sigil and slamming it against Réalta's chest.

"*Scaoileadh agus filleadh.*" The intent-laden words jetted from his lips, releasing the Shade from his binding hex. It slammed into Keir like a rubber band released at its breaking point. He juddered back, shaking his head to clear the onslaught of emotions as they settled in his body. Nervous energy and bashful flutters, fright and unholy terror, rage and boiling anger at the lorelei who interrupted what was proving to be a *delightful* afternoon.

Incensed, he snapped his legs together and let his body fall like a stone, slicing off enough of his Shade to send the fear packing off into the Neitherworld so the witch could get to work. Shadeblades, cruel weapons formed from a smoke-like shadow made tangible, formed in one hand, and he summoned the obsidian hilt and blade of his athame to the other. Waiting, Keir drifted beneath the water, ignorant to all but the Shade of the lorelei tearing through the depths.

She was near and drawing nearer. Furious and wild, hungry for the Dark Witch that kept upsetting her plans. He gnashed his teeth in a fierce grin, whipping around to face her fury dead on. A current preceded the desecrant, and he shot out a hand, sending shadeblades flying. He felt them catch, searing through her Shade and tearing pieces free. Bubbles announced her veering off course, and she lashed out a hand, catching Keir by the arm and dragging him untold feet through the water before letting go.

He sliced off a bit more of himself to better ignore the burn in his arm, the subconscious twitch of muscle and tissue in his chest, and how Horned God damned cold it was this deep in the Ijsselmeer. Pushing it all away save for what he needed to perform the task at hand:

Detain the desecrant by any means necessary.

He would lose a little of himself in the process but gain ground with his sister. Earn her approval, her trust, her *belief* that he could be unleashed and left to his own devices.

The swell of a Shade at his back had him spinning in the water. More shadeblades formed in his palm, the intent on his tongue halting as he came face to face with Réalta.

The not-quite man, the *desecrant,* scanned him head to toe, stopping when his eyes caught on the obsidian athame in his hand. A blade that had been nowhere on his person during their little swim lesson. Eyes nearly bugging out of his skull, he grabbed Keir's wrist and hauled him up, up, up to the surface. Roaring when they broke through, "The lock!"

"Aye?" Keir shook his waterlogged head, pointing his blade across the water. "The fecking *lorelei!*"

He tried to wrench his arm free, but Réalta held firm. "No, Keir, the lock is closing; I need you to let me —"

Razor-sharp points dug into Keir's ankle and jerked him below the surface. Réalta went with him, caught in the lorelei's other hand. Sweeping his leg, Keir connected a heel with her skull, earning a sharper grip that pierced the skin around his ankle. Warmth burst from the wound, his blood spoiling the water. He kicked again, this time striking her shoulder, but she held firm.

A pity.

For her.

Keir bent at the waist, sweeping his athame in a wicked arc and slicing across her arm. Spilling blood for blood before vanishing his blade and gripping her bicep. Her shoulder. Upside down in the water, he crawled up the lorelei's body as she had crawled up his and surged a clawed hand at the center of her chest. Soft, spongy skin burst beneath his nails, her Shade a twisted, mottled thing rotted by a lifetime submerged beneath the Rhine. He snarled, black eyes narrowed as shadows seethed up his back, feeding their master with their strength and wickedness. Fueling the thing Forbidden and Foule until he forgot his name, his purpose, his intent. All he knew was his rage at this desecrant and the desire to make her Shade bend to his command.

It would be so easy. After all, he was a Dark Witch.

Something heavy buffered against his side, knocking his hand free. A thick fist came down on the lorelei, pommeling the side of her head and sending the water wraith drifting unconscious into the depths.

The Dark Witch snarled, whipping his face up to the desecrant who *dared* and stilling at the sight of deep, onyx eyes. A wide mouth shouted a name, his name, and the desecrant's long, powerful arm thrust in a point to their left. Then up at the surface. The Dark Witch followed the gesture, his shadows wisping away at the sight of boats overhead, the central chamber's steep walls, and the lock gates groaning closed.

He startled, swallowing a mouthful of water that had Réalta's expression softening. Caught up in the lorelei and lost to his Way, Keir hadn't realized how far she had dragged him down the channel. Right through the sluice and into the space where sweet water was exchanged for salt.

There was nowhere to surface without being seen. To surface meant having to explain his presence. It meant alerting C.R.O.W., bribing more mortals, and suffering his sister's not-so-gentle disappointment. A ripple in the water turned his head to the right, and he saw the gates to the Waddenzee crawling open. The light blotted out over his head, a silver gap tightening to a seam as two boats bumped together, sending a gust of current downward, pushing both witch and desecrant deeper in the water. Keir's feet came down in the silt, and Réalta gripped his arms, wearing a pained expression as he mouthed something that looked like, "I'm sorry."

He pushed off of the chamber floor, hips pumping, lower legs snapping in tandem through the water. Head on a swivel, Réalta tore for the surface, scanning the walls and sighting what he needed. He aimed for a row of metal bars laid into the stone, breaking through the turbulent waters and all but slamming a coughing Keir against the ladder.

Shouting at the impact, the witch tasted salt on his lips — ocean meeting the sea in a man-made liminal space. Hands shaking, he gripped the rails, hauling himself out of the water. He wrapped an arm through a metal loop, reaching back for Réalta.

"Give me your hand," he panted.

Réalta looked up at him, defeat dragging at his features. His lips were a dark blue from the cold, skin following suit. He shook his head. "I am right behind you," he winced. "Go, I am right behind you."

Keir frowned but did as he was told, hearing one weary utterance of "Good boy" as he climbed.

That absurdity forced a burble of disbelief, urging him up the walls and escaping as full-blown laughter when he collapsed on the grass and dirt lawn running the length of the central lock chamber.

He lay there, waiting for Réalta to tumble beside him, lifting his head when alarmed shouts in Dutch cried out over the groan of the lock and wailing of a siren. Lurching to his feet, Keir spun and gaped at the emptying chamber, the boats drifting out to sea.

"Nae," he breathed, frantically scanning the brackish water for any sign of Réalta's broad-shouldered form and finding none. "Nae, it cannae — no!"

He dropped to his knees, gripping the edge of the concrete wall, ready to fling himself into the water, searching for the strange not-man. A shadow darted for the Waddenzee gate, and Keir threw out his arm, reaching for the Shade of an eel or a seal or the Horned God-damned lorelei. His Way buffeted against something all too familiar and altogether strange, unable to grab hold.

"What." He staggered back, withdrawing his Way and watching the water as that shadow darted and twisted, bunching smaller before exploding through the gates to the sea. Keir followed, legs churning over the grass and gravel. He hurdled over a fence, landing on his right foot at an angle. His knee screamed; he staggered in the grass and then kept on, pushing himself as fast as he was able.

Across a service road, under a bollard, and through the tangle of cars waiting to continue their drive across the Afsluitdijk. Horns blared, his breathing rasped and burned, but Keir pressed his speed, a witch used to crossing insurmountable distances in a matter of steps and far better on land than in water.

Focusing on the end of an earthen jetty stretching out into the water, his left hand worked a sigil as he cried out a word of intent. Color and sound winked out as he ran headlong into his Way. The world drowned in the darkness of the Neitherworld. Winds howled, the Shades tore at his body and then the dark exploded into a riot of color and sound.

He skidded to a halt, squinting at the bright greens, blues, and browns. The Waddenzee stretched out before him, the Frisian Islands to the west little more than a smudge on the horizon. Gentle waves tumbled against a loose stone shore, and in the distance, a midnight black tail fluke slipped into the sea.

SEVEN

"I ken what I felt, and what I felt was impossible!" Keir threw his arm wide, cider splashing over the rim of his glass. Toby lurched over the table, a napkin ready in hand to wipe away yet another mess made by Keir Simmons, Overall Shite Witch. "What sort of creature has a Shade that I cannae grasp?"

"You need to control yourself, Keir," the flame witch advised. He tossed the sodden napkin into the trashcan with a wet *splorch*. "I understand it is difficult to restrain your emotions when your Shade is returned, but you have spilled more of that cider than you have drunk."

Keir raised the glass to his lips to prove a point, downing the contents and slamming it to the table. "Happy?"

"Are you?" Toby sat back, arms crossed and legs stretched out. "Do I need to visit a coffee shop to help you calm down?"

Keir dropped a fist to the table, rapping his knuckles twice against the surface and shoving his hand into the pocket of his joggers, fingers itching to feel the smooth lines of a vape pen. "Nae."

"No one could blame you—"

"Am done with that shite." He stood in front of the window, shoulders hitched and body tight. "Spent too many years hiding behind a high, Toby, and see what that got me."

Deep in his throat, the spalování made a noise that Keir thought sounded like approval. "Even so," he paced out evenly, "your story makes no sense; worse, it matches nothing to be found in our e-grims."

"I know what I felt and what I saw."

"And what did you see?" Toby countered. "A man in the water and a seal disappearing into the sea."

"Too big to be a seal."

"An orca, then."

"Too small."

"*Gehörnter Gott, verdammt*, Keir!" Toby slammed the heel of his palm against the table, rattling the bottles of beer and cider they had picked up from a nearby market. He seethed at the Dark Witch, blue flame twisting in his eyes. "I am trying to help you prove your point. I am trying to help you leave all of this behind, but how can I do that when you refuse to see logic?"

"Am nae witch for logic."

"*Deutlich.*" Toby splayed his fingers in the air and curled them into a fist as he regained himself. "Clearly, and no one should expect otherwise, but Keir — how will I explain this to C.R.O.W.? To Lou? We should have detained the lorelei days ago, yet we linger at the continent's edge, and now you are claiming that a — what, exactly, are you claiming?"

"A new desecrant." Keir twisted the cap off a fresh bottle of cider and refilled his glass. "Saltwater based, related to the *melusines* and *undines*. Potential kinship to the *lamia*, but new. Different. Other."

Like me.

"Like you," Toby stated. Keir swallowed the lump in his throat, simultaneously loving and despising his friend for knowing him so well. The spalování pinched between his eyes. "I cannot work with that, Keir. Goddess knows I wish I could, but there are too many unknowns." He looked up at his friend, flames guttering out and leaving only the clear sky blue to stare back at him. "We need to bring in the lorelei or put her down. That is our task, and that is what will gain you ground with your sister."

"I ken, but— "

"But *what*, Keir?" Toby stood, snatching an unopened bottle of beer from the table. He pinched the neck between his fingers, pointing it at the Dark Witch. "This has gone on for far too long. You know that, and what is worse, you want to present the possibility of a new desecrant to C.R.O.W. without doing the necessary anthropological work while *also* putting the anonymity of your new friend at risk."

"I dinnae—"

"Do you not?" Toby grabbed the bottle opener from the table, jerked off the cap, and took a deep swig. "I will not pretend to understand how difficult it is to return to yourself. Our Ways are different, and we travel in vastly different directions, but I know you, Keir, and you are not a hasty witch." He drank some more, setting his bottle down with a quiet *clink*. "This is not you, this is fear. Take a moment. Think, sleep, eat, make a plan, or let me make one for you. In fact, I will: all you should be concerned about right now is the lorelei. Detain her, turn her in to the Lowlands Coven, and wash your hands of this distasteful job once and for all. Until then, keep your mystery desecrant far, far from the attention of our employers."

Keir studied the table. The carpet. His feet. Weighing Toby's words against what he knew to be true of C.R.O.W. and his status. Again, loving and despising how much his friend knew. Sallow-faced and thick-throated, he looked up. "If I'm wrong, it means he's still down there."

Toby's fingers slipped free from the neck of his bottle. "Goddess."

"He saw me, Toby. He saw it all, and he pulled me to the surface. Set me on those rungs, and he didnae follow." Keir's throat was tight. Choked by the fears he'd kept strangled. "Did I leave him there to die?"

"Keir—"

"Am I imagining what I saw? Am I convincing myself that I couldnae grab his Shade because I cannae bear the thought that my actions—my Way—"

"Keir, *no*." Toby reached out, gripping his knee. "Let us say that you are correct. That you saw something impossible or unknown. I trust your judgment, for the most part—"

"Pardon?"

"—and agree all of the traits point towards what you suggest, but even then—even if he is what you believe him to be, it is impossible."

"Improbable."

"*Impossible*. If it is probable, C.R.O.W. will either hunt him and his kind down to a disastrous degree, or they already know." Keir straightened in his seat, staring at Toby. The spalování, for his part, kept his composure, silently willing him to see reason. "If they already know, then there is a reason they have kept the truth quiet or distorted it to a degree that we recognize *melusines*, *undines*, and *lamia*, but not what you suggest."

"Goddess." He breathed, reaching for his cider and giving up halfway to the glass. "Would C.R.O.W. do that?"

"They did it to you," Toby replied, far too soberly for the amount of beer he'd drunk.

Toby humored his need to talk through the jumble of thoughts bouncing around in his skull, but even the world's most patient spalování had his boiling point. It was well into the small hours of the next day when he threw up his hands and informed Keir that he was going to bed.

The Dark Witch sat for a while, listening to Toby snore while replaying the encounter with the lorelei over and over again, wondering what all, *exactly*, Réalta had seen and how badly he'd frightened the puzzle of a not-man by revealing his true nature.

Wondering if he really was too much.

The green and yellow lights bobbing on their prows offered no answer. Nor did Toby when he murmured nonsensical German in his sleep. Near dawn, Keir pulled on a long-sleeved tech shirt, laced up his runners, and stepped out onto the cobbles, determined to run until his mind was too exhausted to think.

Though the largest settlement on the Waddenzee and boasting nearly eight hundred years of recorded history, Harlingen was compact in the way of most fishing villages. Meaning a full loop of the *oude stad* along the canals totaled less than two kilometers, hardly far enough for Keir to outrun his thoughts. He loped over the bridge crossing the Zuiderhaven, taking the stairs to the elevated harbor walkway two at a time and rushing past the spot where he and Réalta had shared their kiss. A kiss that even now sent heat coursing through Keir's veins.

Frustrated, he aimed for the Zuiderpier—a seawall jetty curving into the Waddenzee—and opened his stride. The pinching in his right knee kept his focus on there, rather than the memory of marble-hard skin beneath his palms or the feel of a hot, slick tongue thrusting in his mouth as he was cradled in strong arms. Better to focus on the pain of an old injury than the remembered feel of hands kneading his thighs with the promise of—

"Ach!" Pain exploded along his left thigh. "Fer fuck's sake." Keir caught himself on the u-bend of a metal bollard, catching his breath and rubbing the ache away. Hissing, he prodded his leg and eased into a slow walk. The collision would bruise. One more mark to go with the scrapes on his back and wicked scratches on his arm and ankle. Minor injuries when compared to drowning. Or being crushed by a closing sea lock. Or being torn limb from limb by a lorelei.

"Nae doing much to ease your mind, Simmons," Keir muttered, gritting his teeth as he broke into an easy jog. As early as it was, fishing trawlers still lined the wharf, the men on board undergoing preparations to make way. At the far end of the pier, a striped lighthouse spun its warning, each revolution of the lamp paired with a low, sonorous klaxon.

Keir fixed his eyes on the lighthouse, shearing off pieces of Shade to move beyond the pain and outrun his demons. Still, he was unable to escape the niggling thought that if he had just been *better*, more discerning, more attentive, he could have detained the lorelei and spared Réalta whatever fate had found him.

The pier branched to the left at an absurd little fountain of a whale or a narwhal — Keir wasn't really sure which — jutting out into the sea at a curve and ending like most things in the Netherlands tended to do: with a low profile.

A rounded cap of octagonal stones lay like a tiled quilt beneath the lighthouse, dusted with loose gravel and bearded by seagrass too stubborn to recognize that it was winter. The Dark Witch slowed his jog to a walk and then a standstill as he took in the Waddenzee stretching gray and deep blue out to the horizon, the lighthouse standing stoic, and the hunched figure rolling an 8-liter rescue orange dry bag.

"Réalta?" He whispered, the word caught by the wind and pulled to the not-man's ears.

He jerked his face up, staring unblinkingly at Keir for a beat.

Another.

Then those powerful legs had him exploding upright and surging over the pier faster than Keir could recall all the severed pieces of his Shade. One large hand caught him at the waist, the other sliding along the stubble of his cheek and back into his hair. He held himself a breath away, dark eyes searching Keir's as if Réalta needed to assure himself that the witch was hale. Whole. Here.

"How are you—"

The rest of Keir's question was silenced by Réalta's mouth crashing against his in a hard, unrelenting kiss. The sort that turned his knees to goo and sent his stomach into a plummeting freefall. He dug his fingers into the ill-fit Henley the not-man wore, tugging it up and away. Desperate with the need to feel the heat and hardness of the being in his arms to convince himself this was real. Réalta groaned into his mouth as Keir pressed the tips of his fingers hard into that muscled back. He dragged them down the ridge of his spine and up again, each vertebra, each swell and valley of muscle proving to him that Réalta was here. Unharmed.

Unearthly.

Unknown.

The thought pulled him away from the kiss. Réalta surged forward, his hands traveling Keir's body as though he were also driven by a need to know this was real. They braced him by the shoulders, pressed against his lower back, cradled the side of his head, and cupped his rear. He jerked Keir's hips into his, letting the witch feel the stiffness that swelled between them.

Heat surged, Keir's blood boiling even as a thousand questions and concerns sprang to mind.

"How?" He managed to rasp between breaths, fingers of one hand working beneath Réalta's waistband.

"I saw you leave the hotel," he whispered against the witch's lips, black eyes watching him beneath heavy lids. "Followed you along the canals."

"The canals?" Keir's hand stilled. "Cannae have, I was alone."

"I came here to change where I would not be seen." Réalta cradled his cheek, fingers diving into sweat-damp hair. "You found me."

"A happy accident."

"It seems we keep finding each other." He gripped Keir's hair by the roots and dropped their foreheads together, peering at him with such genuine softness the witch felt vulnerable in the wake of it.

"Aye, well," he chuffed. "The stars align and all."

Réalta loosened his grip and lifted his head, staring at Keir for a beat before craning his face up to the sky. "Which stars?"

"Oi." Keir let go of the not-man to snap his fingers. "There's a stellar body. Right here."

His snark was met with a mystified expression. The heat of the moment trickled away, lost to the changing tides and pulled out to sea by a gentle breeze. The two stared at each other, recognizing the absurdity of the last few minutes. Days.

Arms dropped away, and they drifted apart. Réalta to his dry bag and Keir to study the ground, a hand taming the mess of his hair and pinching the back of his neck. When he looked up, Réalta stood disjointedly, a shoulder hitched, one hand curled into a fist, watching Keir as if he were a shark circling an unarmed diver.

"What happened?" Keir forced the words up and out of his throat. He moved for the not-man, cringing when Réalta backed away. "You threw me on that ladder; you said you would be right behind me. I thought you were dead. What *happened*."

"I let this go too far."

"Bollocks." Keir spat, long legs closing the distance and bringing him nose to nose with whatever Réalta was. "Take it further. What are you."

"I have the same question for you."

"I am *other*. Outside of a human but not a desecrant. I am me, and you have seen it with your own eyes else you wouldnae be shying away as you are now."

"Shying away?" Réalta's brows rose. "So good at so many things, yet self-preservation is not chief among them."

"How is this self-preservation?"

"As you stated so succinctly, you are Other. Outside of human, and yet you walk among them. Live among them. You are like *them*. Humans are *nothing* like me." He waved a hand, letting it linger in the air as his shoulders began to turn. Keir snatched it, shoving his fingers through Réalta's and tugging the not-man around to face him.

"You saw me," he seethed. Nostrils flaring and eyes narrowed to slits. "What I am, what I am capable of. You have worn my Shade and learned me through it." Réalta dropped his eyes, and Keir caught his jaw, gently forcing the not-man to look at him. "I am only asking you to extend that same courtesy to me."

His jaw went iron-hard in Keir's hand, black eyes searching for any hesitation, any fear, and finding only the confident demand of a witch face-to-face with someone like him. Réalta's chin dipped in the tiniest nod. He gripped Keir's hips, turning the witch so his back was to the Waddenzee.

"As usual" —the wide accent dropped into a deep rattling bass as he crowded Keir, forcing him to yield a step to the sea— "you have dressed poorly for the cold."

"I was on a run." Keir scowled. "I'm a sweaty mess, likely look hoora trash and smell even worse."

"I disagree." Réalta dropped his face to the crook of Keir's neck, inhaling before pressing lips to his skin. His tongue darted out, followed by the briefest nibble. Keir went stock-still, every nerve in his body standing at full attention. "You taste of the sea." Réalta grazed the skin with his teeth a second time. A testing pass, though for what, Keir had no idea beyond, "yes, please," "more," and "Daddy." His knees quaked as Réalta dragged his lips up to his ear. "I would have you in it."

EIGHT

"Hold on to me."

"What?" Keir balked, glancing over his shoulder at the water. "You cannae be serious, the water's freezing. I cannae float!"

"You were so good at following instructions," Réalta countered. His eyes twinkled with mirth as he edged the witch closer to the sea. "What happened?"

"Am nae goin' in the water." Trying to plant his feet, Keir slipped on the seagrass and gripped Réalta's arms to keep from falling. "What about my clothes?"

Réalta dropped his gaze to the hands on his arms and smiled. "Good."

One burly arm slid around Keir's shoulders, holding the witch to his expansive chest. The other wrapped around his lower back. He pressed Keir's hips to his, fitting them together like puzzle pieces while his smile sharpened into a mockery of true delight.

"Do not let go."

"What about your clothes?" Keir flinched as the water soaked through his shoes and socks.

"I have more." The not-man hoisted Keir from the pier, powering into the surf. Goddess, he made the witch feel so small, manhandling him in a way no one else ever had. Ever *could*. It was enough to wash away his trepidation and the fear that he was too much. That they would go too far when, in truth, they were destined to go further.

Lazy waves crashed against the back of Keir's calves and thighs, curling around his waist as an icy embrace. He shivered, and Réalta pressed a soft kiss at his temple, slipping his arms beneath Keir's.

"Grip your wrists behind my neck," he demanded, voice strained. The witch obeyed, eyes scanning the surf for any hint or suggestion as to what was about to happen. There was no tell-tale surge of Way. No electric crackle of energy rising in the air. There was only the Dark Witch and the desecrant watching him with those keen, black eyes. "Despite how it may appear, this does not hurt as much as one would think."

Keir snapped his eyes from the water to Réalta. "How is that supposed to help?"

The not-man opened his mouth, closed it, and winced. "Your eyes are green."

"What does that have to do with anythi—" The rest of his complaint was cut off by an emasculating shriek as Keir and Réalta plunged into the water.

Réalta buried his face in the crook of Keir's neck, his strong arms holding onto the witch as the sea took them both. They tumbled in the waves, tossed in a barrel, and dragged further into the Waddenzee. Keir's heart lodged itself firmly in his throat, the old fear of drowning surging to the forefront and tempting the witch to scream.

Before he could process the urge to act on the desire and inhale the brine, Réalta bucked against him. A quiet noise escaped as a bubble, his arms tensed further, and his mouth clamped down on Keir's neck. Not a nibble. Not a playful snagging of teeth, but a proper bite that had Keir finally crying out. Sound burbled from his lips. Réalta bucked his hips again, and the pain ebbed, replaced by a bubbling warmth as Réalta kissed the ache away. He alternated tiny nibbles with kisses in silent apology, stroking one large hand up and down Keir's back to soothe

the witch. A gentle sense of pleasure drifted through his thoughts, the idea that he'd somehow done something *right*. Warmth fanned across his chest, dribbling down through the viscera as a deep, primal heat that vanquished his fear and replaced it with something else altogether.

Réalta bucked his hips again, the movement slow and sinuous, practiced and maddening. A roil of muscle rippled against the ache that all that heat had stoked. Keir felt his arms weakening, going boneless with the surprising rush of desire, even as Réalta's warning echoed in his mind.

Do not let go.

But how could he keep hold when the desecrant, the not-man, the whatever-he-was kept writhing against him in a manner meant to drive a man mad? An arm slipped off of Réalta's shoulder. His head lolled back as desire drowned out wisdom. Through slitted, hazy eyes, Keir caught sight of an impossibility in the moment before the world became a blur.

Pushed to the surface for a breath, another, and then Keir was dragged back into the depths. Unable to make sense of what he was seeing, unable to swim away, and held entirely at the mercy of Réalta and all he was.

Another breath, and he was back in those arms, one large palm cradling the back of his skull as they rocketed through the Waddenzee at an impossible speed. He kept his eyes closed after that first drugged glance. Kept count of his heartbeats, never making it past thirteen before the creature that held him surged for the surface, rolling onto his back long enough for Keir to raise his head, drink greedily of the air, and nestle back against the safety of Réalta's chest.

Again and again.

A score of times before the mind-melting pace slowed to something more fathomable. The water around him rose in temperature, the chill from their initial plunge warming to bathwater tepidness, and then he was pressed against the edge of a low, floating dock. His hands were guided to rungs on another ladder; his body braced by an impossible heat sheltering him from the world.

"Hold on, Keir," Réalta's voice advised, wet-sounding and worried.

Panting, his head heavy enough to topple off, Keir adjusted his grip on the ladder and angled his face to the side. The not-man was low in the water, submerged to his nose and watching Keir with fright straining those beautiful, onyx eyes.

Keir blinked, freeing a hand to rub the water from his eyes. He dropped his forehead against a rung and mumbled, "Shouldnae left my glasses."

Knuckles brushed his leg, a plea, and a question. Gripping the rails, he worked himself around and braced his feet on the bottommost rung, planting his ass on another and staring at the wonder in front of him.

Because what else could it be but wonderful?

Though he knew it was Réalta, though his mind could quantify that he himself was a witch and the world was full of vast and diverse creatures only trying to live, he could not help but be amazed by the watery Shade staring back at him.

The onyx eyes were the same. The dark hair, the voice, the heat of him, and the comfort of his arms, but the rest of Réalta was different. Changed and altogether the same.

His skin was a shimmering dark blue. A midnight sky cast in stars, haunting and beckoning at once. Keir reached out, brushing his fingers along Réalta's cheekbone and trailing his jaw line to pinch his chin. He angled the not-man's face to the left, the right, catching it in the weak bands of light just now breaking over the horizon. As he did, the shimmer danced and swirled over the strong bones and planes of his face, not unlike the Northern Lights the not-man claimed to love.

"*Álainn*," Keir breathed the word, feeding it with his intent and pressing his hand flat against Réalta's cheek.

Beautiful.

The not-man leaned into the touch, eyelids lowering as the tension eased from his face. A faint smile curved his lips, and he drifted closer.

Keir swallowed. "What are you?"

That faint smile grew, and eyes closed, Réalta placed his hand over Keir's, bracing the witch before a long, powerful tail of fine scales and thick muscle wrapped around his legs. Keir startled, jaw hanging slack as he peered down through the water. He drank in the sight of an obsidian fluke rising to a slick, silken black tail that faded into the curve of muscle at Réalta's hips. A squeak of disbelief escaped. He jerked his face up, working his jaw, looking back down to the tail—the *tail*. That was a tail with fins and dorsals, and that man had legs, but that was a tail.

"Nothing witty to say?" Réalta tested, his voice quiet. Hesitant. At his throat, nestled in the tendons, gills fluttered in the open air, struggling against their very nature and wanting to be submerged.

"Have to admit, you've caught me at a disadvantage," Keir muttered, eyes still on that glorious tail. His inability to speak or act in the face of this impossibility stretched the silence too long, taking it from something fragile and precious and tainting it with doubt and regret. The trailing edge of Réalta's fluke drifted away, and his hand slipped free of Keir's. The witch thrust an arm into the water, fingers brushing delicate scales.

"Urk." The tail darted away.

"I'm sorry!" Keir jerked his hand from the water, staring back at Réalta in horror. "That's not—I mean, Horned God, I didnae just cross a line of consent, did I?"

Réalta's tail drifted in the water, allowing the ... him. Allowing *him* to bob in front of Keir. "A line of consent?"

"Isnae like the wings of the Fair Folk, aye?"

"Of all the questions to ask, that is your first one?" A brow rose on that midnight face. Keir pouted. "That I am a merman, that you now see what I—"

"You've nae idea the things I've seen."

"The things you have seen," Réalta paced out, drifting closer. The steady movement of his tail wafted a warm current over Keir's legs, and a knuckle brushed the length of his thigh. "Only seen?"

His breath shallowed at the gentle caress. Réalta's hand lingered at Keir's hip, awaiting his next words.

"More than seen." He pushed off the ladder onto Réalta, wrapping his legs around the merman's waist and clasping his head to bring the not-man's mouth to his. Impossibly strong arms braced his torso, large hands cupping the curve of his rear. His finned tail undulated between Keir's legs, rhythmic and slow. As drugging as the creature's kiss and stoking the kindling heat burning low and weak in wait for this moment.

Réalta met Keir's mouth eagerly, opening to the sweep of his tongue and plunging deep enough to steal his breath away. Locked in the deep abyss of a delayed kiss, Keir did not fear drowning. He let himself tip fully into the moment, refusing to deny the swell of emotion he felt in Réalta's arms. Safety, security, trepidation, and the fear of the unknown. A heady equation that amounted to desire and a need to know, to feel, and be felt. To truly connect with this not-man in the only way he knew how.

Clenching his thighs, Keir raised himself against the merman's hips, rolling his pelvis and groaning into the kiss at the delicious friction. Heat throbbed, his cock hardening at the feel of all that power between his legs. A strength at odds with the sensual sweep of Réalta's tongue and the plush cushion of his lips. Thoughts drifted through Keir's mind, things he wanted to do, the things he *would* do to this creature, all centered around that wide, plush mouth and talented tongue. Each thought was more decadent than the last, manifesting as a near-painful throb in his groin. He pulled away, panting for air, for solid ground, for sanity to come roaring back in.

But Réalta was not done.

Lips trailed Keir's jaw, his throat. His tongue swept saltwater from his skin, and teeth grazed his ear, making the witch shudder in his arms. Réalta rumbled his approval, sending an intense warble of sensation dribbling down Keir's spine like water running down a glass. He writhed against the merman, dropping his head back as that *mouth* trailed lower, revisiting the vanishing ache at the crook of his neck.

Réalta sucked on his pulse until the witch moaned, bucking his hips for want of more. The hands cupping his rear drifted to his waist, fingers digging in and bracing the witch as he was pushed back and lifted onto the dock in one swift, sure movement. Réalta loomed over him, deep blue skin shimmering in the dawn. He lowered Keir onto his back and eased that glorious body and Shade-black tail alongside the witch, looking down at him with softness and awe. Something behind Keir's ribcage stretched beyond its breaking point, snapping free with a burst of aching warmth that coated him from within. He shivered, gazing into Réalta's deep black eyes, hips rising of their own accord.

A tiny, barely audible whimper escaped, and the merman cocked his head. That inquisitive smile deepened and darkened. He raised a hand, sweeping taloned fingers through Keir's hair, trailing the sharp tips down the side of his neck and along the broad line of his shoulders. The move perfectly reversed that first touch when he pulled Keir's sodden wooly-pully away.

"Do not let go," Réalta repeated his advice, hardly giving Keir enough time to parse out the meaning before deadly talons scored down the front of his shirt, tearing the fabric away. Cold puckered Keir's flesh, hardening his nipples in the instant before Réalta grazed the tip of one with a razor-sharp nail.

The witch gripped the edge of the dock to keep from bowing upright, his overly sensitive flesh beyond ticklish. Réalta studied the response, slipping partially off the dock to submerge his tail. An elbow propped for leverage, he placed a kiss at Keir's hip, swimming around his legs to match the effort on the other side. He trailed the waistband of the witch's sodden joggers with his lips, nibbling flesh and tonguing his navel. Heat surged and boiled, the ache in Keir's throbbing cock becoming painful for want of touch.

He must have whimpered because Réalta peered up at him, black eyes heavy with desire and his deep, blue skin at beautiful odds with the taut, pale expanse of Keir's torso. Talons prickled at his waist, sliding down to his hips and the outside of his thighs. They sheared through the cotton weave and tore his joggers away, exposing him to the cool morning.

"Please," Keir hissed, desperate for any touch, heat, or sensation on the part of him that had been ignored until now. He shifted on the dock, urging Réalta to ease the strain. A throaty sound escaped as wicked talons slipped between his knees, spreading his legs wide enough to encompass broad shoulders, the witch now splayed and vulnerable before an obvious predator.

His hands skimmed over Keir's thighs, gripping him by the hips to keep the witch still, even as he actively worked against the demand. His pelvis twitched, muscles bouncing in anticipation. He propped himself up on his elbows to watch, needing to see with his own eyes the moment this beautiful creature took him into his mouth.

A taloned hand gripped the base of his shaft, slipping up the length as Réalta's brow twitched near imperceptibly, the only outward show of what he was thinking. Ringing Keir's cock in his fingers, Réalta thumbed the head and slid his hand down, rumbling his approval at the keening he wrung from the witch.

"I am so proud of you," he stated, voice crackling with heat. "Out here in the water with me." His tongue darted out, tasting the tip, and Keir's hips damn near left the dock. His head fell back on a groan, and his hands gripped the edge, every muscle in his arms flexing and straining. He needed more, wanted more, knew he would die if he didn't get *more*.

"Please, Réalta," he moaned. The not-man swirled the head of his cock with his slick, unbearably warm tongue. "Please."

"You do not need to beg," Réalta mused. His fingers curled around Keir's aching cock, pumping once. "Not when you have been so good."

His lips closed around the head, tongue swirling, and then Réalta swallowed him whole. The heat of his mouth enveloped Keir, body and soul. His arms went boneless from the pleasure, and he stretched out on the dock, eyes rolling back in his head, pelvis pumping, hands reaching for Réalta.

That talented tongue worked with expert efficiency, swirling and stroking, wrapping around Keir's girth and flicking over the ridge at his head, probing the slit and tasting the salt that escaped. He could feel Réalta wriggle at that first taste, fervor rising as a hand clamped down on Keir's hip. Talons pinched soft flesh, tugging the witch closer to the edge of the dock. Closer to his release as that fucking *mouth* worked him to euphoric heights.

Water lapped his legs, disturbed by the rhythmic pumping of Réalta's tail. His hand slipped from the dock, plunging beneath the water. He groaned around Keir's cock, and the sound surged his tongue in a rolling swell up his length.

"Ach, Goddess," Keir cried out, gripping Réalta's hair and guiding his head as the heat built, slow and steady. A rising tide with ample warning. Goddess, it was too much, too fast, and he wanted to go further. "Réalta," he panted, knotting his fingers and jerking the merman back. "Réalta, please, I'm gonnae—"

All of that glorious heat pulled away, and wintry air skirted up Keir's cock.

"Not yet," Réalta stated, the warmth of his breath a cruel tease. His hands slid under Keir's hips, and the tips of his talons prickled bare flesh. Keir shuddered at the sensation, biting his lip and gazing drunkenly at the creature between his legs.

"Tease," he hissed through his teeth. Réalta beamed, dipping lower in the water as he lifted Keir's ass from the dock and dragged him into the depths. He braced his hands against the merman's shoulders, fighting the urge to rut against all of that solid muscle. He ached for friction, for heat and warmth. For *touch*.

"I told you once; need I repeat myself?" One mighty pump of his tail had Keir shivering, the move brushing something thick and lengthy between his cheeks and curving up the base of his spine. "I would have you in the sea."

NINE

Keir straightened. Fingers digging into muscular shoulders and mouth drying out.

"What?" He croaked.

Another pump of his tail had Réalta's engorged cock thrusting along the seam of Keir's cheeks. Submerged in unnaturally warm waters, his cock rubbing against the sculpted, textured plain of Réalta's body, it was all too easy to imagine that he was still in the merman's mouth. Rolling his hips as that tongue lapped and licked, those plush lips puckered beautifully around his girth. So easy that, when Réalta caught his mouth, Keir blinked dazedly back at him.

"May I?" Réalta whispered against Keir's mouth, kissing him deeply before the witch could reply. He pumped his tail, punctuating his question. Keir reached back, closing his hand over what he could of his girth.

Slick and heated, the merman's cock was a surprise and delight. It slid easily through Keir's palm with the feel of running his hand over silk sheets. His heart lurched, the implication of that request having core muscles in his body going taut. He didn't enjoy being put in such a position, not necessarily. Not often. He enjoyed giving pleasure to his partners. Enjoyed watching them writhe under his ministrations and hearing his name whispered as a prayer and a plea. Relishing in the consensual control and knowing that he was trusted.

That *he* was wanted.

The whole of him valued and desired for being *him*, not just the parts that C.R.O.W. saw fit to acknowledge.

To turn that tide, to relinquish the control he harbored so greedily ... he needed a moment to think and assess where he was in this. Swept away, deluged, drowning in everything that Réalta was, and yet fear played no part in his assessment. Fear was hardly even in the same realm as Keir at the moment.

There was a power in being asked, a control to be had in someone requesting the same trust Keir so desperately worked to earn.

He shivered at the realization, rolling his hips against the merman and teasing his thumb over the head of that intimidating piece. Clenching his thighs and flexing the muscles in his legs to gain leverage, Keir returned the kiss, lips traveling the bones of Réalta's face, the thick set of his jaw and curve of his ear, all the while stroking his cock with the same fervent hunger the merman had shown him. A deep rumble built in that broad chest, vibrating against Keir's sternum and humming against the lips he trailed down Réalta's throat.

"Keir," he rasped, voice thick with arousal. One of his hands left Keir's ass, darting between them to take his cock in hand. He returned each stroke the witch gave him, tail undulating in a matched tempo.

Scraping his teeth at the center of Réalta's throat, Keir sucked on the pebbled flesh, eyes drifting lazily to the curious lines of his gills. He owed his merman an answer, yet he had so many questions.

He angled his head, fisting Réalta's cock as his tongue darted out along the fluttering membranes.

Réalta's tail shot straight, a snarl of outrage tearing out of the merman. He gripped Keir's hips, spinning him around and bracing him against the dock in a brutish display of strength. Keir gasped, hands scrabbling at the rungs. Talons pricked his hips, and the length of Réalta's tail settled against Keir's legs, cock thrust between his thighs. That broad, strong body pressed him flush against the dock, curving around the witch in absolute threat.

"That was naughty of you," he growled. A predator teasing its prey and making the lanky witch feel weak in a way that thrilled him to his very bones. The prick of Réalta's talons eased as a hand left his hips, rising from the water to pin Keir's wrist on the ladder. The other teased his lower abdomen in feather-light strokes before drifting down to take Keir in hand. His hips pumped, sliding that thick cock between Keir's thighs as he stroked the witch. They both groaned. Keir dropped his head back against Réalta's shoulder. "And you were being so"—another pump of his hand and roll of his hips—"very good."

"Horned God." Keir flexed his hands, bracing himself against the ladder to keep hold of something solid as Réalta pulled him into a whirlpool of desire. Deep groans were dragged from his throat, and one especially hard thrust had Keir's hand slipping free. He dropped lower in the water as Réalta dragged his length along his taint and teased the seam of his cheeks.

"If I have to look at this tight body for one more moment ..."

The rest of his words were lost to the water as Réalta dipped his head, sucking on the side of Keir's throat. He let go of his cock to trail talons down the length of a pale thigh, under a knee, and up the underside of his leg.

The light touch sent ripple after ripple of ticklish sensation up Keir's leg and into the base of his spine. He pressed against the merman, whimpering when Réalta pulled away. A finger slipped between his legs, massaging the sensitive stretch of flesh just behind his scrotum. Réalta's tail kept them high enough in the water for Keir to breathe, to moan his name, for Réalta to hear his adulations. With each stroke of his fist around the witch's cock, and each roiling pump of his tail, Réalta matched with the press of his finger, seizing control of the lower half of Keir's body. Muscles flexed and bunched against his back, the merman panting in his ear, and when it was too much, when he toed the edge close enough to fall, Keir forced the words from his throat.

"I want you."

Réalta made a choked sound, hands slipping away while his body and tail kept Keir pinned. He started at the fine-point brush of talons across his cheek, sweeping his hair back and away so the merman could see his face. Panting and writhing, Keir nudged his ass back against the crux of Réalta's hips.

"You said you would have me in the sea." He adjusted his grip on the ladder. "So have me."

Réalta rumbled his appreciation. As if to remind the witch what he was agreeing to, the merman pressed the slick length of his cock against Keir's cheeks. He splayed a hand across his abdomen, rocking gently. "You want this?"

"Yesss," Keir hissed, voice hitching as Réalta spread his cheeks and pressed the pad of his thumb against puckered flesh. Fright flashed, too little, too late, at the thought of those talons anywhere near *any* vulnerable part of him. Shoulders tensing, he turned his head, and Réalta met him with a soft, gentle kiss.

"I will not hurt you," he promised. "The last thing I want to do is cause you harm." Working his thumb to loosen the muscle, he showered Keir with more praise. "You are doing so well, Keir; let me reward you."

The thumb vanished, replaced by the tip of his cock, gently testing his entrance.

"That's it," Réalta purred in his ear. "Hold on and do not let go," he championed. Stroking a hand down Keir's arm and threading their fingers together, he pushed infinitesimally beyond the puckered ring. Keir grunted, bit his lip, and exhaled in a burst through his nose. "So very good." His praise never ceased, urging Keir on as he relaxed him with his words and soothed the aching muscle behind his ribs. Measure by measure entering the witch. Measure by measure tearing down his defenses and flaying open his chest to cradle that broken heart. "That's it."

Keir gripped the ladder, dropping his head forward and panting through pain so acute it curdled into pleasure. A feverish sweat broke out across his shoulders, his neck, kissed away by the merman slowly stretching him, filling him, drowning him in need and want and *now*.

More.

Now.

"Réalta."

"Take it for me." Lips fluttered behind his ear. "I know you can." Keir adjusted his hips, more of the merman sinking within him. Slow, so slow as to be torturous. Réalta slipped back, losing an inch and regaining that distance and more. Again and again until his hips were flush with Keir's rear. He seated himself with a final surge that sent Keir's belly into a swooping plummet. His eyes flew wide as rapture lit up every nerve, shooting like static down to his very Shade.

At the first pump, they groaned as one. Keir sought out Réalta's mouth, needing to feel the adoring stroke of his tongue as the merman moved inside of him. Slow at first. Gentle and tender. Easing Keir's body into pliancy before he twitched that magnificent tail, ramming into the witch and earning a ragged, bestial cry.

"Oh, Goddess." Stars burst in his eyes, the world graying out and snapping back into bright, vibrant colors. Keir's Shade pulsed and throbbed with every thrust, intensifying the sensations that had him slipping into Irish to hail the stars.

"You take me so well," the merman panted. He swallowed a deep groan as Keir worked his hips in counterpoint, rocking against the merman until he had to brace the witch by the hips. He was taut as a bowstring pulled back and ready to release, riding the thrumming edge as Réalta's pace increased. His thick heat slid out of the sensitive flesh and thrust deep, again and again. The water frothed from their motions, whitecaps rising between them as gulls and herons winged oblivious overhead. "Good, Keir. You are so good."

"Réalta." His voice didn't sound like his own, pitching high with a whimper of pleasure. A whine threaded the words as his body begged for more.

"Faster, Keir. I know you can do it."

He gripped the ladder, knuckles blanching and biceps straining as he braced himself to keep from being fucked into the abyss. Keir's Irish devolved into guttural cries and moans as Réalta slammed home. Again and again, the merman railed his witch hard enough to bruise. His tail snapped and thrust until suddenly it was too much, too far, and Keir was set to shatter.

"Réalta, fuck. I'm gonnae—"

"Ssh," he soothed. "Hold on, Keir. Hold on for me."

Scales slid against Keir's thighs, his calves. That powerful chest rubbed against his back, pressing into him as the merman joined Keir on the edge.

A particularly deep thrust made Keir's jaw hang slack, and he lost control. His Shades rippled free in the water, darkening the blue depths as his Way entered the world. Heat built all over his body, and his teeth began to buzz. "Cannae—"

"You have been so good." Réalta took Keir's cock in hand, gripping as he thrust into him again and again. He caught the witch's mouth with a brief, reassuring kiss and savored the strangled cries and whimpers. The way the witch twitched and shook against him, trying to hold on as he was instructed. Wanting to please the merman and earn his praise. "You feel so very, very good."

Réalta pumped his cock, gripping the head and tugging just ... so.

"Ach, fuck!" Keir shouted as he came. Wave after wave riddled his body, surging from his hips and shooting out through his extremities. He threw his head back, moaning loud enough to frighten away the birds.

The sound of his pleasure tipped Réalta over the edge. The merman came with a cry that roared like the surf, crashing against Keir and dragging a ribbon of pleasure through his body as the thrusts turned drunken and slow. He bit his lips, chest rising and falling in deep bellows as sensitive flesh puckered around Réalta's girth, teasing out lingering whispers of pleasure that curled his toes.

Eons later, when Keir's hands slipped away from the ladder, Réalta hoisted his torpid body onto the floating dock, crawling beside the witch and curling around him as a warm cocoon. He tucked his glorious tail behind Keir's legs and held him tight against his chest, lips at his ear. The transition, or change, however it worked, which, truthfully, was a matter for *later*, was quick. It began and ended before Keir's sluggish mind could register that the scales had been replaced by muscular legs tangling with his own.

He angled his face to the side, searching Réalta for any regret or the tucked-away fear he so often saw in his partners when he lost control, and the Shades whipped out, finding none. Eyes closed, and that sensual mouth soft and plush, the merman relaxed into a boneless state. His breathing slowed while his arms held Keir tight and cherished against his chest.

Exhausted, he did the only thing he could think to do and drew a blanket of midnight over them both.

PAGE OF CUPS

TEN

The sun was high when he woke, alone on the dock and covered in a woolen blanket in place of his Shades. Mouth dry and skin crusted in salt, Keir pushed himself upright, knocking over a water bottle.

Scrabbling at the dock, he grabbed the bottle before it rolled over the edge, wincing at lingering pain that wasn't pain but a reminder. His gaze tripped over the ladder, and a shiver of remembered pleasure twitched his shoulders, drying the witch's mouth out further.

It had been … different. Not jarring or odd or off-putting. Quite the opposite, but different still. Keir was no stranger to desecrants, himself being Other among witches, but no *vodyanoi*, fae, or selkie had come close to wringing that much intense bliss from his body. Even now, remembering the powerful roll of muscle beneath his legs and at his back, a wicked curl swirled low in his belly.

"Get a proper hold of yourself," he muttered, unscrewing the water bottle cap and draining it in four lusty swallows. Crumpling the plastic in his hand, he tossed it over his shoulder, crooking his left pinky.

A sliver of the Neitherworld opened to catch the trash. Keir shoved his arm into the seam of shadow, rummaging around until his fingers brushed silken cold and soft cotton. With a grin, he pulled a pair of joggers free and tugged them on. His shredded clothes were nowhere to be found, but his shoes and socks had been laid out to catch the winter sun. Both were still damp, so he stepped barefoot onto the tiny island, eyes scanning the low, sandy rise and coastal scrub. A wooden tower rose in the center of the glorified sandbar, and stilted, unmanned lighthouses dotted three points on the horizon. Spinning in a slow circle, Keir squinted across the water, spotting ships in the distance and nothing else.

"Stranded on an island in the middle of the Waddenzee." Hands on his hips, he scowled. "Am nae gonnae live this one down."

"I would not consider you stranded." Réalta's voice had Keir jumping and kicking up a cloud of dust.

"Get tae—"

"Unless you wish to be stranded here with me, though I would not recommend it."

The witch stared at the merman in the water. The merman stared right back, looking inordinately pleased with himself.

"Since I am a fool," Keir intoned, "I find myself having to ask why, exactly, you would not recommend it."

Réalta tossed his orange dry bag onto the low-lying floating dock. Folding his arms on the black composite, he rested his chin and gazed up at Keir. "There is a storm coming."

The witch took in the sun and unseasonably warm weather. "Is there."

"This afternoon," Réalta clarified. Flattening palms against the dock, he effortlessly pushed himself out of the water. Keir marveled at the strength of the not-man. The way his muscles bunched and jumped, the finely toned taper of his waist below a broad ribcage. He rubbed a hand over his mouth, darting eyes from Réalta's form to his face, then finally to the sleek, obsidian tail shimmering in prismatic ribbons like a sheen of oil over water.

The length of his tail was on par with his legs, and then some, stretching across the deck in all its muscular glory before fanning into a dangerous and delicate fluke. The deep blue tones of his skin shifted and shimmered, drawing attention to the scars Keir had noted before. Gleaming silvery in the winter sun, the odd circular patterns were striated with the historical markings of ancient wounds. The merman was liquid night, sinuous and sinful. Out of place in the daylight in a way that had Keir imagining him adrift in the Neitherworld, at one among the Shades.

Réalta saw Keir looking and rolled onto his back, crossing his arms beneath his head to better put his body on display.

"Horned God, man." Keir breathed, adjusting himself as he drank in the sight. Shadows pooled in the swells of muscle, the deep blue hue enticing the witch to kneel beside the merman and stroke all of that soft, supple flesh. Réalta grinned, purposefully tightening the muscles in his stomach as he eyed the witch in kind. His gaze dropped to Keir's midsection, and his grin widened.

"I see you are well rested."

"Aye." He stood over the merman, ready to straddle him where he lay. "I like you down there, splayed out beneath me." He kneeled, halting between a stoop and a crouch as the scales lightened. The black grayed like a puddle of water drying on concrete, fading to the pale white of Réalta's skin. "Get tae—" he repeated, eyes goggling as human limbs appeared, legs snapping apart.

It was simultaneously horrifying and mesmerizing. Keir did not know where to focus his attention: at the magic of a merman gaining legs or the scales and blue skin paling to near colorless white, returning that magnificent body to its Renaissance marble-hewn physique. So he settled his gaze somewhere in between, cheeks burning as the last of the tail faded away, and Réalta lay revealed before him. Naked as the day, dark eyes burning into Keir's, and fully erect.

"Do you still enjoy what you see?"

"Oh," Keir cut a slashing grin. "Aye."

He straddled the merman and bent forward, planting his hands above Réalta's shoulders and capturing his smart mouth in an eagerly returned kiss. Réalta's palms spread up Keir's back to hold him in place as their tongues danced. The merman's hips bucked, rutting that impressive erection against the witch's thigh. The feel of it clenched muscles in Keir's gut. He snagged Réalta's lower lip in his teeth, tugging as he pulled away. The move pulled a moan from the merman, a tiny little sound lodged in the back of his throat, and Keir marveled at the flush of desire coloring his pale cheeks.

"And you do not care what I am?" A tiny wrinkle formed between Réalta's brows. He stared at Keir as if the witch were a puzzle.

"The only thing I care about" —Keir nipped the merman's ear, relishing the gasp it earned as he kissed his way down Réalta's jaw— "is earning more of those little moans."

The merman opened his mouth to reply, and Keir swept in to steal his words. He refused to dwell on the implication of what Réalta was. The impossibility and the questions his existence raised. Why was his kind not recognized by C.R.O.W.? Was the omission intended or accidental? As an Enforcer, did Keir have a responsibility to report him?

That last one bothered him the most, so he backed away, tonguing the hollow of Réalta's throat and enjoying the desecrant that was his for the morning.

He skated his fingers up the sides of the merman's neck, letting a bit of his Way slip free. Shades drifted from his hands to tease Réalta, lacing around his neck and along the knife-sharp cut of his jaw. Flesh pebbled beneath Keir's lips, and the merman gasped, lifting his chin at the sensation and giving the Shades more space to play.

"Cold," he stated. It wasn't a complaint. Keir knew enough of the reactions to his Way to note the difference between complaint and observation. Encouraged, he sent the Shades shivering into Réalta's hair and down his torso, teasing over his hips and around his legs. Reaching between his thighs, Keir took the merman in hand, and his Shades followed, coiling around that magnificent cock. The sensory chaos of silken cold and the heat of his palm had Réalta arching into the witch, hips rolling as Keir stroked him from base to tip.

"This is ... different." Réalta sucked a lip between his teeth, eyelids fluttering. His hips left the dock to follow the upward slide of Keir's palm. Smirking, he let the Shades slip under his hand, winding around Réalta's cock counter to his strokes. The merman made a sharp, keening sound, his eyes widening in surprise. "How—"

"You showed me yours." Keir slid down his body, fluttering lips along his breastbone and flicking his tongue over a nipple to gauge Réalta's reaction. The merman raised one large hand to cradle the back of Keir's head. Half holding, half guiding him lower. "Now it's my turn."

"I have never—" Réalta began. Keir tongued his navel and nipped the stretch of taut skin just beneath, stopping the merman mid-thought.

"Nae many have." He edged back, using a knee to work Réalta's legs apart. He maneuvered himself between strong thighs, working the merman's cock with a hand and his Shades. A dull *thud* announced Réalta's head dropping back against the dock, and Keir smiled to see all of that strength made powerless by his touch.

He flicked his tongue over the divot where hips met torso, working his way achingly slow to the base of Réalta's cock. Muscles danced and twitched under his caress and that of his Shades—little slivers of self he let free to explore the merman with their questing strokes and velvet slick feel. Every glance, brush, and slide reverberated back along their length and fed into the witch, heightening his arousal as he allowed himself to explore Réalta's body in full.

He sent one Shade cascading over the tip of that erect member, skating down the shaft to tease his scrotum. Réalta's hand fisted in Keir's hair, gripping him by the roots and pushing him lower. A silent request that the witch quit, quite literally, dicking around.

"Needy," Keir hummed against his shaft, licking the swell of a throbbing vein.

"And you called me a tease," Réalta rumbled, loosening his hold on Keir's hair. The witch smiled, sending a wisp of Shade to trace the merman's plush lower lip as he ran his tongue up the length of his cock. Réalta made a strangled sound, his hand flexed, and Keir wrapped his lips around the swollen head, nearly groaning at the taste and feel. Salty, like the rim of a margarita glass, smooth as the velvet of his Shades. Different in length from the merman's piece in his oceanic form, but just as large and thigh clenchingly thick. Réalta moaned, bucking his hips to urge Keir onward, downward, and pleasure radiated down the line of his Shades.

He swirled that thick head with his tongue, savoring each whimper and pant. Forcing that glorious cock deeper down his throat, Keir closed his lips tight around the base. It had been years since he'd last had a male partner—since before Rai. He knew what he liked and how he wanted to be pleased, but every lover was different. Keir glanced up at the merman, watching his face as he circled Réalta's cock and stroked him with hand and mouth, learning what earned the keens, whimpers, and moans he hungered for, and then doing them again and again, reveling in the pleasure he wrung from the merman's Olympian body.

A pink flush stained marble-pale cheeks. Réalta's chest rose and fell in sharp, staccato pants. He alternated between biting his lips, arching his neck to thrust his hips against Keir's mouth, and eyeing the witch outright. Black eyes followed the slide of his cock between puckered lips. The swirl of the Shades against his most intimate parts. Seeing the thing that Keir was kneeling between his legs.

Their gazes locked, both witch and merman halting on a breath, waiting for the other to move. To address the reality of this impossible circumstance, the implication of their acts on this dock. Réalta moved first, threading his fingers into Keir's salt-crusted hair and brushing the ginger mess away from his face. His expression went soft, and he gently thrust in Keir's mouth, eyelids growing heavy.

"Like fire coral," he whispered in awe.

Fingertips pressed against Keir's scalp, and the bubble of hesitation burst, unleashing the witch from his restraint. Hitching up for a better angle, he swallowed Réalta to the hilt, shoving a hand into his joggers to relieve the building ache. He stroked himself in a matched rhythm, imagining it was Réalta's hand, Réalta's mouth causing the ripples of heat to waft up his spine and shoot back low in his belly.

He gripped the head of his cock, pursing lips tight around Réalta, sucking and swirling his tongue over the ridge. Réalta's hips bucked, his grip in Keir's hair tightening to hold the witch in place as he asserted more force, more control. His free hand fluttered from Keir's shoulder to his face, fingers brushing his cheek before falling away with a groan.

The Dark Witch sent his Shades to grace the merman's scrotum, cupping and cradling the sensitive sack as his mouth was fucked by rutting hips, the tempo bordering on frantic. He groaned at a particularly deep thrust, feeling all of that heat thrown against his tongue. Fingers dug into his arm. His scalp burned from the grip Réalta kept on his hair. The merman's body went tight beneath him, thick thighs clenching, torso becoming more defined as he tried to hold on, hold back.

That wouldn't do.

Keir wanted to hear his name as a groan in the back of Réalta's throat. Wanted to hear the demanding merman beg for his release. Wanted to control every reaction of that powerful body with his Shades, his mouth, and his hand.

He released Réalta's cock, sucking hard and deep as he cupped the merman's scrotum, slipping a finger between his cheeks and pressing against the flesh. Réalta made a sound that was half-growl, half moan. His legs jolted as a tendon strained in his neck, hips rutting even harder.

Pressing deeper, Keir worked Réalta's cock with his mouth. Pumping harder and harder at his member until the head was sensitive to the brush of his joggers, his thumb. Until his thighs trembled and Réalta's nails dug into the meat of his arm.

"Kee-ear," he finally groaned, the name separated into two distinct syllables and spoken by a tongue unused to the feel. "You are—this is—"

The witch swirled his tongue around Réalta's head, working his finger deeper and crooking it in a simple summons. "Let me taste you."

"Please, I—"

"Let me taste all of you." He took him whole, rolling his tongue and urging the merman with his finger. Gripping himself almost to the point of pleasured pain as Réalta went taut. His cock throbbed once in warning before the first burst of salt hit the back of Keir's throat.

The cry that escaped Réalta made the witch's balls tighten with urgency, the sound almost enough to send him tipping over the edge. Ragged and breathless, it was a shout that evolved into a deep groan drawn up from the merman's newly formed toes. Burst after burst of thick heat emptied into Keir's mouth, coating his tongue with the merman's bliss. As that groan faded into a whimper of pure, absolute pleasure, Keir tipped over the edge.

Slipping his hand away from Réalta to brace himself, Keir came with a shudder and a moan. He popped off of the merman's cock, kneeling upright and dropping his head back. Wave after wave of orgasmic heat radiated out from his hips. The Shades whipped free, blotting out the sun as Keir lost himself to the sensual thrill. He fisted his cock in languid strokes, not caring that his spen stained the joggers and coated his palm. Not caring that he was being watched. Keir was lost to the revels of intensity that followed in the wake of his orgasm, letting the drag of his hand at his cock pull him forward, bending him low to swallow what remained of Réalta's erection. His seed. Salty and heady, more intoxicating than any drink.

The merman shivered as Keir lazed his tongue up the sensitive flesh. Hands clamped down on the witch's shoulders, pulling him up the length of his body to capture Keir's mouth in a deep, lingering kiss. Sliding a burly arm across pale, freckled shoulders, he rolled them both and settled a knee between the witch's legs.

His weight pressed Keir into the dock, the heat of the merman better than any blanket, and the taste—Goddess, the taste was enough to have his blood boiling and mind soaring higher than any weed had ever managed. He groaned into Réalta's mouth, not wanting this to end and knowing all too well how easily he could get lost in whatever this was.

Réalta ended the kiss, pulling away slowly, his onyx eyes soft and tender. He cradled Keir's cheek, and the two regarded one another. The truth of the witch and the truth of the merman thrown into sharp relief by the midday sun. A million questions waited on the horizon of their tiny little island as they each processed the moment, the draw they felt towards one another. The *ease* with which they came together and came together.

"You are—" Réalta started.

"—Other." Keir finished. He surged up to steal another kiss and murmur in the merman's ear, "And covered in salt and semen."

"Semen," Réalta stated blandly.

"Ach, aye, there is quite a bit of sea man on me." Keir grinned. He laughed when Réalta glanced down, froze, and glared at him.

"Human jokes," he grumbled, rolling off of Keir and rising to stand in one athletic move. Holding out a hand, he gripped Keir's wrist and hauled the witch to his feet. "You are coming dangerously close to exhausting me."

"In a good way, I hope."

"In a good way," Réalta quirked one of his tiny smiles. "Though I need to get you back to shore before the storm hits." He nodded to the water, and Keir followed the gesture, squinting in the noon-day sun and barely able to make out the darker swell on the distant horizon that he took to be Harlingen.

"Still dinnae believe this storm threat of yours." Keir hooked his thumbs in his waistband, tugging the joggers down and tossing them over his shoulder, right into another very specific corner of the Neitherworld. He braced his hands on his hips and angled his face towards the sun. "It's downright warm out here."

"That is the storm," Réalta explained with patient exasperation. "The front will pass. The temperature in the water is already dropping."

"Aye, so it's gone from sauna to bathtub."

The merman cocked his head, waiting for Keir to explain.

"The water. When we were ... in it." He pinched his lips into a button. Pushing them up under his nose as he widened his eyes. The sudden embarrassment at how they'd spent their day sent an altogether different flush to heat his torso.

"You mean when I had you in the sea until you cried for mercy?"

"Horned God, man." Keir muttered, eyes flitting over the specimen beside him before he amended, "Merman."

Réalta's nostrils flared with amusement, warming his gaze. "There is an ancient volcano beneath the sea. Much like in the caves of other merfolk, the vents warm the water, making this area suitable for habitation." He pointed to the wooden structure in the center of the island. "Others like me have studied the waters along the low-lying edge of your continent. They keep caches on land with clothes and bags to keep them dry while we swim to shore."

"That explains the cable knit and concerning pants."

"Why were you concerned with my pants?"

"I liked what I saw wearing them." Keir stretched his mouth wide in another grin. "Do you have any wetsuits in your hut, or am I to suffer the swim in my birthday suit?"

"You brought a suit?"

"Ne'er mind." He waved the comment away and scratched the back of his neck. "Dinnae suppose you have any goggles, then?"

"The glass lenses, for your eyes?"

"Ken I'd like to see that magnificent tail returning this time," he stated. "Salt water tends to burn the eyes."

The merman blinked, taken aback by the statement. His black eyes shifted to the sea, back to Keir, and he let out a disbelieving huff.

"So quick to put yourself in danger and face your fears, it is easy to forget how fragile you are." Réalta's expression softened. He reached out, brushing his thumb against Keir's temple. "How fragile all humans are." Sliding his hand behind Keir's head, he tugged him close and pressed a kiss between his eyes. "So brave and so easily broken."

ELEVEN

Though Réalta humored him by scrounging up goggles, he hadn't put on the sort of show Keir was expecting during the change. Instead, he approached the affair clinically, waiting until the witch was settled on the ladder, instructing him to take a deep breath and join him beneath the surface the minute the merman dove in.

The instruction, Keir soon learned, came with good reason.

It began with a faint ripple running the length of Réalta's legs, no more than shadows cast by disturbances on the surface. The merman flinched so slightly that Keir would never have noticed it had he not just been working to learn every tic and tell of his face. A flash of white teeth told him that this was when Réalta had bitten him after walking them both into the sea. He reached out, wanting to comfort the merman through what was so obviously a painful ordeal.

Réalta waved him off, and Keir's focus zeroed in on that hand, mesmerized by skin blueing like a corpse in polar waters. The tips of the merman's fingers lengthened to wicked talons, and between each digit, a membranous webbing stretched to the first knuckle.

Réalta swept his hand away, staring back at Keir with wide, gleaming black eyes. A transparent third eyelid winked closed. He pressed his lips into a line, and his legs snapped together, the ripple of muscle surging and pulsing as the skin fused and darkened. It took Keir a solid beat to realize that the obsidian scales were surfacing through the epidermal layers and climbing up his legs as the fine bones in his feet stretched and distorted, forming the tail and majestic fluke.

He let his gaze trawl up Réalta's shifted form, lungs burning as he took in the midnight tail and deep blue skin shimmering in the diffused light. His muscles bunched and flexed, working that magnificent tail to keep him hovering in the water, staring right back at Keir. The witch had the impression that Réalta expected him to dash up the ladder and run screaming or swallow a mouthful of water out of paralyzed fright.

A moment passed, the witch drinking in the sight of that beautiful impossibility, and then Réalta darted forward. His hands clamped around Keir's waist, and the merman rushed him to the surface.

"Breathe."

"M'fine—"

"Breathe, Keir," Réalta pumped his tail, swimming them away from the dock. He tapped Keir's chin with a finger when his head dropped below the surface to study the motion. "Calm yourself, or you will never make it back to shore."

"We're going *now*?"

Réalta angled his face up and waited for Keir to follow suit. What had been a sunny, temperate sky over peaceful waters was now a darkening welter of clouds blanketing the West Frisian Islands in shadow and surging east, pushed by a North Sea wind. Stunned, the witch scanned the water, noticing the churning whitecaps and the hasty flight of herons seeking shelter.

"You would not do well out here on this sand bar."

"And you?" Keir slipped his arms over Réalta's shoulders, gripping his wrists tight.

"Unlike you weak humans, I can breathe underwater." Réalta grinned, a wide stretched thing that could only be a mockery of Keir's sarcastic expression.

"Get tae—"

"Breathe."

He did, filling his lungs before Réalta plunged beneath the waves, rolling his hips and pumping his tail to speed them across the sea. His earlier words echoed in Keir's head as they swam, never louder than when the merman had to surface so his charge could breathe.

How fragile all humans are. So brave and so easily broken.

Though he wasn't technically human, the witch was weak in the water. Near defenseless and useless without knowing how to swim. If the merman chose now to let go, he would drown. Dying with a silent scream, surrounded by Shades clawing for a surface they would never reach. Though he felt sure in the knowledge that Réalta would never leave Keir to slumber in a watery grave, the truth was that Réalta was an apex predator at home in this environment. A thing of legend that C.R.O.W. either had no knowledge of or chose to ignore willingly.

He had to consider himself before forming a solid theory. Had to weigh his own Otherness as the Dark Witch that oughtn't exist against that of the desecrant cradling him to his chest.

In that, C.R.O.W. couldn't know. If the coven had known, if the Three Heads of the Tribunal had been aware, they would have sought to regulate the merfolk and bring them under their control. Just as they had with the lorelei, *melusines, undines,* and the *Nøkk*. Analyzed, categorized, and leashed.

Like Keir.

Therefore, it stood to reason that C.R.O.W. did not know and hadn't Réalta said enough to support the idea?

His kind had trawled their shores. They wore human clothes and sat in bars unnoticed as they studied humanity, walking among their kind, learning their language, and coexisting with a species they despised. In that, Réalta had been abundantly clear.

You are like them. Humans are nothing *like me.*

These thoughts kept him silent as they left the now frigid waters, Keir shivering in goggles and wetsuit bottoms, Réalta bracing his hands on the octagonal stones and waiting for his legs to return. Once they had, he rose and tugged on the dry bag still buckled to Keir's back, pulling out two sweaters, a pair of pants, and Keir's shoes. Réalta handed over a cable knit without a word, sensing the witch was deep in his head and drowning in thoughts as tumultuous as the waves.

Reality waited for them both on the Zuiderpier, an unwelcome presence after a morning spent learning each other.

"I will walk you to your hotel." Réalta offered, extending an arm along the pier. Keir studied the gesture. So natural, so *right*. Something uncomfortable burbled in his chest at the ease with which this merman passed as human and the quality of the deception. Ducking his head, he started along the path, thankful for Réalta's continued presence despite the unease and unsure of what it meant. Of what *he* meant.

Réalta seemed happy to let the silence stretch, and after a mile of walking, it occurred to Keir that silence was probably an old friend of an underwater being. That thought finally dragged a huff of laughter from the witch. He glanced over, noting the merman side-eyeing him, brows raised enough to open the door to Keir's many questions.

"You despise humans," he blurted, wincing at his inelegance. "If I were only human, would this have happened?"

The merman faltered in his step, recovering quickly. "If I were only human, would you have let this happen?"

"Well cast," Keir grumbled.

Réalta pressed his fingertips to Keir's spine, guiding him onto Haven-plein and across the narrow bridge. "My interest in a partner is not de-termined by whether or not they have fins or sentient shadows. Though it would be a lie if I said that your not being human did not work in your favor."

"Carefully put," Keir muttered. He stopped abruptly, grabbing Réal-ta's hand and forcing the merman to face him. "Stay. In the hotel. Can-nae bear the thought of you weathering out a storm while I wrap myself in a blanket sipping tea."

"And your friend?" Réalta countered. "Will he not have questions?"

"It will be easier to explain to Toby where I've been if he sees you with his own eyes," Keir admitted, his neck warming. "I'm nae suggesting we tell him what you are; it's only—I've a bit of a habit of wandering off, though usually, it tends to be into the shadows rather than a sandbar in the middle of a Dutch sea."

"He will not mind my intrusion?"

"Nae an intrusion." He gripped Réalta's hand tighter, knowing the statement to be the truth. Toby was many things, but territorial wasn't one of them. Conversely, the spalování shared his space and activities a little too freely if a weekend hunting dryads outside of Thessaloniki was anything for Keir to judge by. Which it was, as he'd seen *everything* and even taken part in some of it. "Though he will make fun of me."

"For what?"

Keir stepped forward, fingers worming between Réalta's as he brought them chest-to-chest. Lowering his voice, he dropped his eyes to the merman's mouth. "My proclivities."

Réalta stiffened, hand flexing as the meaning in his words took root. His throat bobbed, endlessly amusing the witch with how easily he'd caught the not-man off guard. "Ah."

"Ah," Keir repeated, "is not a protest."

"No," Réalta agreed. "It is not."

The first rain drops spattered fat and heavy on the cobbles as they approached the hotel. They rushed through the doors, Keir chuckling at the absurdity of darting away from a little storm when they had spent their morning in the water. He offered a lazy wave to the woman behind the desk, who called for him in reply.

"A woman came looking for you," she explained. "Earlier this morning."

Keir frowned. "Tall? Blonde?"

"*Nee.*" She shook her head. "Medium build, dark hair. Wet shoes."

"Wet shoes?" Keir shook his head at the non sequitur. "Did she leave a message?"

Another shake of the head. "*Meneer Sterne* spoke with her."

Mister Sterne, Keir translated with his minimal Dutch. *Toby.*

"Did you catch a name?"

The woman looked outright offended at that, scuttling behind her desk with a scowl. "I run a professional hotel, sir," she sniffed. "If a visitor cannot request a guest by name, we dismiss them outright. Meneer Sterne was kind enough to escort her away when she became upset. In the future, be kind enough to ask your acquaintances not to yell at my staff."

She sniffed again, glued her eyes on the computer screen, and dismissed Keir with a too-hard typing of the password to unlock the machine.

Keir scratched his cheek, watching the woman as he let loose a slip of Shade. It coiled around her ankle, feeding him a thread of confusion and stolid Germanic indignation. Nothing amiss there. He tugged Réalta up the stairs, faltering in front of the door to his room. Patting himself down, Keir frowned at the damp wetsuit bottoms and borrowed sweater. "Ehm."

"Is everything alright?"

He hunched his shoulders, sheepish. "My key now lives at the bottom of the Waddenzee. Along with my pants."

"The hotel overlooks the harbor; I could drop in and swim out to the island," Réalta offered, already stepping away from Keir. An unnamed fear prickled, the sense that if Réalta left now, that would be it. He would disappear into the waves and swim out to sea. Lost to the storm or distracted by the next interesting almost human he came across.

It was an ugly feeling, one brought on by the abruptness of Rai leaving him in that Hong Kong hotel. The sudden end of their relationship had become the manifestation of a fear fostered by years of having only his sister to trust. The root of his inability to place himself in the vulnerable position of being seen. Whenever he did, people tended to push him away ... or leave.

He saw it with his brother-in-law, Donmar. The lovable Kazakh had assumed the role of father, brother, and friend to the lonely Dark Witch after marrying Lou. Even so, he looked away whenever Keir separated that essential piece of himself and let it roam the Neitherworld unburdened. Just as the rest of their team scowled and gagged, making snide remarks about the sound of his Shadeless body hitting the floor or commenting on the distasteful nature of his Way when they thought he couldn't hear. All while smiling to his face and patting him on the back with a "Good work!" when he returned, never quite managing to meet his eye.

Toby tried and, to give the witch credit, he mostly succeeded. Keir had lost count of the times he'd groaned back into himself to find the spalování glowering at him from across the room, perched on a barrel in a cellar, or waiting patiently in the driver's seat of a car while Keir pushed himself upright in the backseat. Still, for all they had been through together, Toby kept him at arm's length. He accepted the Dark Witch and turned a blind eye to his antics and terrible plans but never spoke on Keir's behalf. Opting instead to run point and act as a barrier between the Dark Witch and his sister.

Keir was self-aware enough to recognize that this distance, the separation other witches kept between themselves and him, was why he grew far too attached to anyone who gave the barest suggestion of acceptance. Why he forced relationships and friendships too much, far too soon.

When he'd sought out Rai for the first time, needing an escape after dealing with the *bean sí* in the woods outside Droum Cross, she hadn't turned him away. Instead, the poison witch had offered him a little bit of kindness in the form of forgetting ... so he'd sought her out again when Ezra returned to the States.

And again, whenever the toll of his work became a too-heavy weight, happily smoking or swallowing whatever she offered to cope. The vinefica—new to their team and freshly excommunicated from her home coven in Kowloon—was all too happy to oblige.

The intensity of the highs lessened over time as the witches grew comfortable with one another in their self-induced isolation. Eventually, the nights he spent in a haze beside her evolved to nights spent in each other's arms. She still fed him pills and potions and still handled his weed when the world became too much, but Keir had convinced himself that Rai accepted the witch and his Way as a whole. Had even convinced himself that he loved her, only to learn that he'd been too much.

His palms prickled at the memory of sliding around her narrow waist, fingers twitching for want of touching her silken fall of hair. The merman in the hallway cocked his head, waiting.

"I'll be just a minute," Keir rasped, tearing open a seam and stepping into the Neitherworld before Réalta could react. Wind tore at his borrowed sweater, making his salt-crusted hair stand on end. The Shades pawed at their master, demanding his attention and guidance. Keir ignored them, stepping out into the center of his hotel room, smoothing his hair down, and storming to the door. Turning the lock, he pulled it open and grinned at the baffled merman in the hallway. "Would you like to come in?"

"Where did you—"

"In or out?"

Réalta stared at him, face devoid of expression. Keir's smile faltered, the old doubts creeping back in. He'd made a mistake, the *same* mistake, in trusting too soon and losing control of his Shades in a moment of passion, letting them free to enjoy the merman's magnificent body as much as he did. He'd torn open a hole between worlds and used it as a personal doorway, proving, yet again, that he was too much.

"Ink," the merman finally stated.

"What?" Keir's palm slid from the door, and Réalta pressed a large, bare foot against the base to keep it from closing.

"Squid ink." He flicked two fingers to where Keir had been standing beside him. "It was a cloud of squid ink blooming in the water." Something like surprise flitted over the stoic features, and the merman nodded. "Impressive."

"Thanks?"

Réalta shouldered past the witch, entering the room and standing in the center. Hands at his sides, eyes skating over the surface of the table, the chairs, the beds. Keir pressed the door closed, watching the merman take in the mortal space, and was struck by the inane idea that he had ever thought this being to be human.

He was too tall, too broad, too confident in a space designed for the antithesis of *him*. For once, Keir realized he wasn't alone in being *too much*.

Heartened, the Dark Witch crossed the room, stroking his fingers along the merman's lower back as he did. His mobile was where he'd left it charging on a bedside table. Beside it was a note from Toby, his handwriting as neat and orderly as the witch.

Meeting with the Witch of the Demesne. Stay in; a storm is coming.

"'Course a storm is coming." Keir set the note down. A tiny smile drifted as the pieces fell into place. Toby's meeting with the Witch of the Demesne, the dramatic swing in the weather. "Bloody Witch of the Demesne is a meteomantic."

"The what is a what?" Réalta turned his face from the window, the glow from the streetlamps gilding pale skin.

"Nothing." Keir thumbed the screen. He opened a message from Toby asking if Keir wanted him to bring back lunch and a second message admonishing him for leaving his mobile behind. There was one from his sister, consisting solely of the word "Status?" and another from Donmar informing him that Lou was concerned and asking if he could please call. "Just that the weather is about to get worse."

It was a good plan, one Keir should have thought of himself. Have the Witch of the Demesne on hand, enlist his aid to churn up a storm, and keep the lorelei sequestered. It was an obvious plan and further proof that the Dark Witch really and truly was not fit to be an Enforcer.

Sending a quick reply to thank Toby and beg another favor, he set the phone down and lowered himself to the edge of the bed, staring at the floor. Outside, the sky deepened from stormy gray to smoky black. The patter of rain began to hammer at the windows, rattling them in their frames as gusts of wind blew in the weather.

"Are you alright?" Réalta's voice jerked Keir from his absent thoughts. He blinked at the merman standing in the center of the room, no longer studying the furnishings. His black eyes were weighted on Keir, reading the witch in a way that left him feeling as open and bare as he'd been on the dock.

"Aye." He pushed his palms against his knees, rising from the bed. "Mulling over a reply to my sister."

"You have a sister?"

Keir nodded. "And a brother-in-law. They are concerned that this job with the lorelei is taking too long."

"What will you do?"

"In terms of assuaging their fears, or as it pertains to the lorelei?"

Réalta waited, letting Keir decide for himself which answer was desired.

"Dinnae rightly ken," he admitted. "As far as we know, the lorelei has yet to make contact or find anyone to deliver her message, and the storm will further delay that. She's attacked me twice now, which lends no confidence to my being able to sit her down for a cuppa and a long chat." He shoved a hand into his hair, tangling fingers in the salty strands and tearing them free with a swallowed snarl. It was infuriating how terribly he'd bungled this job and beyond obscene that he'd ever thought he could shave off enough of himself to be the Enforcer Lou and C.R.O.W. wanted him to be. "I would prefer to give her the benefit of the doubt, help her in her mission, and get her back up to her rock on the Rhine." He needed Toby to return so he could ask the spalování what he thought they should do. Toby would make a plan, nine rings, he'd even devise one that looked like it was all Keir's doing, but first, he would ask the Dark Witch what he wanted to do, but all he *wanted* was a distraction. "But short of that, I'd really and truly settle for a shower."

"A shower."

"Aye, water from the sky, only warm and with soap. Nae that dreich outside."

"Dreich?" Réalta angled his torso, gazing out the window with an inscrutable expression. "You have the most interesting words."

Keir smirked, toeing off his running shoes and kicking them beside the bed. The borrowed sweater was pulled off next, and his smirk sharpened to a dimpled, tight-lipped smile as he felt the merman's attention returning to him. Hooking thumbs in the waistband of the wetsuit bottoms, he tugged them lower, revealing the light dusting of hair that spread from his navel to his pelvis. Réalta's black eyes lingered on Keir's hands, heated like a voided flame. The moment stretched thin, ready to snap as the witch crawled his gaze down the merman's body. He dragged his lower lip between his teeth and jerked his head towards the bathroom. "Care to join?"

"Join you where?" Réalta's voice was the rough whisper of sand over stone. His shoulders rose and fell with each breath, and that black marble gaze remained firmly fixed on Keir's hands as he lowered the waistband further.

"Ken you'll figure it out."

Twelve

The shower was a Goddess-sent blessing of modern mortal engineering. Keir tipped his head back, letting the liquid heat pour over his hair and face and licking his lips as the last remnants of salt were washed away. He heard the floorboard creak and raised his head, wiping water from his face and turning his back as Réalta studied him through the glass.

It was absurd that he felt a rush of butterflies in his stomach, as though this were the first time the merman was seeing him naked and vulnerable. He'd had him in the Waddenzee, bringing the witch to the height of ecstasy while submerged in the source of his greatest fear. Keir had had the merman in his hand and mouth. Heard him keening with pleasure and begging for release, and yet he felt like a weak-kneed witchling beneath that quiet, intent study.

Cloth rustled and fell to the tiles. A cold breeze raised the flesh on Keir's legs as the glass door was tugged open. Keeping his back turned, the witch rubbed a bar of soap in his hands, building a lather to wash his face and neck. He skated the bar down his chest and stomach to clean away the salt and the sweat of their exertions. Réalta hovered at his back, not touching the witch though his silent presence was a caress, reminding Keir of the gravity surrounding the merman as he sat in the corner of the bar, summoning the witch with little more than a locked gaze.

He cleaned himself, fighting the urge to stroke the thickening erection brought on by the mere *thought* of the merman. It was too much. Finally, he was beginning to understand those damned words because his reaction to Réalta was too much and too far while being not enough and not *far* enough.

There was movement at his back, and Réalta's hand slid into the corner of his vision, grabbing the shampoo from a shelf. Keir nearly jumped out of his skin when fingers began massaging his scalp, fright immediately ebbing away and leaving a shivering coil of desire in its wake. He swallowed a groan as those strong hands worked lather into his hair. Tipping his head back, he pressed a palm against the shower wall to brace himself.

"I am aware of what a shower is," Réalta chided after a moment, amusement lifting that flat accent. "Though I have only taken one in my lifetime."

"Ken you've got the gist of it," Keir managed through clenched teeth. He hitched his shoulders as a tiny huff of laughter tickled his neck. Réalta's fingers pressed against his skull, guiding Keir's head to rinse the shampoo free.

Without a word, the witch plucked the conditioner from the shelf and held it back over his shoulder. The merman chuckled, exchanging the tiny bottle for the shampoo. Lavender filled the tiled chamber, floating on the steam and soothing the witch in ways he hadn't known he needed soothing. His shoulders dropped, a tightness in his back eased, and his fingers slid down the glass, leaving streaks in their wake. The merman massaged the creme into his scalp, and this time, the groan that escaped Keir's throat was audible.

"Very nice," Réalta commented.

"Again, with the praise," Keir muttered. "Not that I mind, ye ken, but I've noticed you're very sparing with it."

"I prefer to give praise when it is earned," Réalta answered. "Now touch yourself."

"What?" Keir sputtered, whipping around and slipping on his heels. The merman darted out a hand, lightning fast, to right the witch and drag him forward for a kiss. The hand on his arm slipped to his wrist, guiding Keir to the obvious swelling between his legs.

"I want to know how to give you as much pleasure as you give yourself."

Reddening, Keir fisted himself, eyes locked on Realta's. Again, there was that sense of being flayed and dissected, of being weak and helpless before an apex predator. And then he lay his hand over Keir's, guiding them both up the length of his cock. Slow at first, hesitant, as the merman learned his grip. Elegant fingers laced through his and they stroked together, the sensation of self and stranger enough to have heat coiling in his gut.

"Goddess," he panted, pumping into their joined hands. Sultry heat dribbled down his spine, puddling in the space between vertebrae and overflowing to pool between his hips. He gripped Réalta's shoulder, dropping his head in an attempt to keep control. "Fuck, that's good."

"Good," the merman crooned. He stroked Keir's face and swept the hair out of his eyes, his erection standing proud between them. Keir reached for the rigid member only to be stopped by fingers wrapping around his wrist.

"No," Réalta grunted, desire making that singular word throaty and coarse.

Keir jerked his face up, lips parting to protest, and the merman pressed a kiss to the corner of his mouth, his hand slipping away from Keir's cock.

He plucked the soap from its dish, dropped it in the witch's palm, and turned his back.

Keir stared at the nape of the merman's neck, attempting to work through the fog of lust and parse out what, exactly, had just happened. He followed a rivulet of water coursing out of dark hair and wending down the muscles bracketing Réalta's spine. "Ehm…"

"Is this your first shower?" The merman angled his face, eyeing Keir over his shoulder. He dropped his gaze to the soap in Keir's hand and back up to the witch. A wicked, sharp smile wrinkled his cheek, and Réalta reached back, knuckles grazing Keir's erection.

"Right," Keir rasped, trembling at the ripple of pleasure that shot directly into his balls. He shook his head, and confusion melted to wicked intent. Cupping the soap in one hand, he braced the merman with the other, pressing his soapy palm at the center of Réalta's back. Keir worked the muscles, massaging the heel of his palm into each swell and dip. A rumble formed deep in the merman's chest, rattling through the bones in his arm.

Encouraged, he worked his way up and down Réalta's spine, savoring each moan and groan the effort earned. The merman threw out an arm to steady himself against the wall, his head falling back in bliss.

Keir relished in the control their position gave him. Near two meters of muscle and bone stood between the merman and the door, his powerful form bracketed by the witch's lanky figure. With each sweep of his hands, Réalta grew more languid and loose, eventually pressing back against Keir's chest.

It was a reversal of the day, Keir now turning Réalta into a limpid, aroused thing. He grinned when the merman rolled his hips, brushing his rear against the witch's erection with a quiet little moan.

"Please," he whispered, the sound almost lost to the dull roar of the shower and the blood rushing in Keir's ears. "Touch me."

Keir replied by sliding his hands down Réalta's sides, gripping his hips, and skimming down onto his thighs. He lowered his head, mouth seeking out the sensitive flesh at the crook of Réalta's neck. Sucking and nibbling, massaging his thighs, cupping his glorious ass, and working the merman until he mewled, "You do that so well, Kee-ear."

Again, that accent separated his name. It was enough to drive a witch mad.

His hands skated to Réalta's front, sliding up his taut abdomen to feel each ridge of muscle. He hooked his arms under Réalta's and held the merman tight against his chest, fanning fingers up his throat and pressing the tips on the underside of Réalta's jaw. Keir turned the merman's head and captured his mouth in a deep, consuming kiss. Rocking his hips forward, he swallowed both of their groans at the delicious slide of friction. The brush of his swollen member against water-slick skin sent an electric jolt through his bones. He broke away from the kiss and thrust again.

"Goddess—"

"Touch me, Kee-ear."

"Ken that I am," he murmured into Réalta's ear, grinning at the shiver it sent down the merman's spine. Unable to reach back and take the witch in hand, unable to turn, he was held completely at Keir's mercy, trembling at the gentlest stroke of a finger across the plush pad of his lower lip. Snagging a lobe between his teeth, Keir rutted his hips against the merman and thrust that finger into his mouth. Réalta's tongue swirled, shooting Keir, body, mind, and Soul back to the dock. The memory of Réalta's tongue doing just ... that ... stroke around his cock.

It was enough to make the witch snarl, arousal testing the bounds of his control.

And then the merman begged one last time.

"Please, Keir." The rumble of that voice drilled into Keir's body. He released one of Réalta's arms, splaying a hand across his taut abdomen, fingers grazing the ridge of his Adonis belt.

"Now who's the good boy?" Keir demanded, each word laced with smoke and heat. The merman keened, hips twitching in a manner that told Keir he was trying very, very hard not to do so. He drifted his hand lower, dancing fingers over the marble-pale skin and reveling in each twitch and whimper it earned. Bypassing the merman's thick erection, he swept lower, fluttering fingers at his thighs, between his thighs. Dusting under and around his scrotum until the merman hissed and went rigid, pounding a fist against the glass wall.

"Touch me," Réalta demanded, hips rolling in search of Keir's hand. "Touch me as you touch yourself."

"Fuck, you say the sweetest things." He circled his thumb and forefinger around Réalta's girth. Not quite gripping. More of a promise for what came next. A pulse of his hand and he released the merman to trail one finger along the vein running the length of that glorious cock. Up to tease the ridge at his head and back down again. Réalta whimpered, shivering bodily against the witch. Again, he pounded a fist against the glass. With the arm still captured by Keir, he reached back, worming fingers into a sodden mop of hair and holding tight.

"Tease."

"I do try," Keir simpered, tightening the ring of fingers at the crown of Réalta's cock. Slowly, oh-so-achingly-slowly, he slid down the swollen tip. Right to the ridge and tightening as he withdrew. The merman hissed through his teeth, biting his lower lip, but he did not beg and that would never do.

So Keir did it again. Teasing Réalta with subtle strokes just this side of satisfying. His thumb gently grazed the slit. A finger sliding along his length. Tracing and trailing, grazing and never quite grabbing hold. All the while nibbling on his ear, kissing his neck, and scraping teeth over the tendons where his gills would be, rocking his erection up against Réalta's rear and driving himself into a mindless, needy state while he teased and taunted the merman. He played that glorious body until the merman was a tightly strung thing barely capable of forming words beyond "Keir," "tease," "fuck", and finally, "please, touch me."

And who was the witch to deny the merman who asked so nicely?

He fisted Réalta's cock, taking it firmly in one hand and stroking upwards just as he would stroke himself. They groaned as one—Réalta for the touch and tightness, Keir for the feel of that piece in his hands, nearly undone by the weight and the heat of him. He marveled at the difference between Réalta's human cock and the one that had pleasured him so keenly in the Waddenzee. Less slick, shorter, yet no less impressive for the length and thickness. Wholly human in all ways except that Réalta was anything but.

His Otherness was in the way he vocalized his pleasure. There were no adulations to the god of his kind or any other, and the mixed cries of Keir's name and curse words vanished into grunts, moans, and a strangled sound in the back of his throat. Animalistic and primal, unlike anything or anyone the Dark Witch had ever lain with.

"That's it," he crooned in Réalta's ear, grounding himself in the plea-sure of praise. "You like this, don't you?"

"Keir—"

He tightened his grip, twisting his wrist and stroking Réalta as he stroked himself, nearly slipping off the tip of that magnificent cock only to thrust back down. He rocked his hips forward with each downward slide, butting against Réalta so the merman fucked into his hand. The fingers in his hair spasmed, gripping and releasing, each flash of pain adding chills to the heat building in Keir's spine.

A fervor took over the witch. He rutted harder against Réalta's rear, wanting to give the merman as much pleasure as he had received. Stroking and thumbing, pulsing his fingers and bucking against him. His lips found Réalta's ear, and he whispered, "Do you want me?"

"Yes." He released Keir's hair and gripped the top of the shower stall. The witch grinned, slipping his fingers between firm, rounded globes. He sighed at the shudder of pleasure it earned. Pressing the tips of two fingers against Réalta's taint, he fisted his cock harder, faster. Forcing the merman to the edge of his restraint and working a strangled gasp from that thick throat as the arm braced against the wall began to tremble.

His pace slowed, and he slid his fingers back, beyond pleased with himself and distracted by the joy of controlling another with his touch and attention. So distracted that when the merman yanked the knob of the shower to "off," whipping around with a snarl and pitch-black eyes, Keir blinked dumbly back at him before he was shoved through the shower door.

Réalta's hand clamped at the back of his neck, jerking Keir forward into a kiss that was more teeth than tongue. A frantic, wild embrace that further fogged his sex-focused brain. The merman strode him back, back, back through the door and across the bedroom. Not letting him breathe or think, turning all that brute strength and *power* on the Dark Witch.

Keir landed on his back with a *whoompf*, propping himself on his elbows. Réalta glared down at him, chest rising and falling as if he'd run a marathon. His hands were fisted at his sides, eyes black as night, and that cock stood straight and rigid as a mast. The water clung to him like a second skin, highlighting every dip and swell. Keir's erection twitched in response to being merman-handled by such a specimen.

"I want," Réalta seethed. He advanced, knees brushing the top of the mattress, and bent low to press his fists into the blanket on either side of Keir's thighs. "I want to watch your face as I pleasure you."

"Holy Horned God."

"I want to wring the same sounds out of your body as you did with your hand." He crawled onto the bed, bracketing Keir's legs with those powerful thighs.

"Ken I might die."

Réalta brought his face alongside Keir's, his next words dancing as gentle puffs over his cheek. "I want to see what you look like when I fuck you into a boneless, helpless state."

Thirteen

"Ne'er mind, I'm deid." Keir dropped his head back, rolling it along his shoulders. Réalta dipped low, licking up the line of his throat, and the witch groaned. "Pure deid, this isnae Eternity, is it?"

Réalta spread Keir's legs with a knee, kneeling between them and bracing his hands on the witch's hips. He traveled that sinful mouth up Keir's throat, along his jaw, and flitting over his cheekbones. With his elbows still propping him upright, the witch was held in place by the merman, unable to do more than flutter fingers along muscular thighs as Réalta turned every one of Keir's tricks against him.

Every gentle brush and teasing touch thickened the haze of lust and want and need. The witch rolled his eyes in ecstasy, his hips leaving the bed in search of friction and heat. The merman chuckled in his ear, a deep throaty sound reverberating over the fine cochlear bones and shivering into his skull.

Keir grunted. A tiny little "unh," half a whine, half a plea. His cock ached, need building. This merman was going to drive him right over the edge. Too much, too far, and Keir was quickly losing hold of anything resembling care, worry, or fear.

"I see why you enjoy doing this so much." One of Réalta's hands left his hip to cradle the back of Keir's head, drawing him up and pressing the witch's lips against the base of his throat in a silent request. Keir obeyed, resuming the sucking and nibbling that before had earned such a glorious response. Réalta groaned, guiding Keir's mouth with the gentle pressure of his fingers. "Good boy," he sighed, turning his head to grant access to the sensitive flesh where his gills would be.

Keir licked and exhaled, his breath raising gooseflesh along the tendons. He reveled in the knowledge that this stretch of skin was as erotic and responsive to touch as he thought it would be, only — not in Réalta's true form. But as a human? Oh, as a human, Keir was far too happy to abuse this sacred knowledge.

He closed his mouth at the crook of Réalta's neck, sucking and swirling his tongue. The merman bucked his hips, the heads of their cocks brushed together, and Keir let out a moan that Réalta matched. He settled over Keir's legs and took them both in one large hand, gliding his broad palm up their lengths. The move sent jolts through Keir's buttocks, jerking his hips from the mattress.

"Fuck, that's good, *leanbh*," he panted. Blood thrummed in his ears, his thighs twitching and toes curling as Réalta stroked them again and again. The texture of his palm and the rigid silk of his cock tested Keir to his very limits. "I cannae, *leanbh*, please, *please*."

Réalta rumbled his pleasure at having brought the witch to pleading. He slid his cock free, tightening his grip on Keir while guiding the thick head along the seam of his cheeks. Keir tensed, fisting the blanket and biting his lip to keep from halting the merman. Afraid that if he offered instruction or interrupted him, he would stop and leave Keir dangling on the edge of release.

Réalta noted his tension and froze short of spreading Keir wide. "Forgive me," he murmured with a kiss. He eased the pressure of his grip, the cessation of sensation giving Keir the space to breathe. To think. "I forget that it is different on land, in this form. How do I make you ready?"

"The drawer." He gestured with a shaky jerk of his chin. "There's a bag."

Réalta kept hold of Keir, reaching into the bedside table drawer and retrieving the bag. He dropped it beside Keir's hand, still fisted in the blanket. It was an effort to relax his grip. His fingers fumbled with the zipper, digging among the toiletries to retrieve a small bottle. Réalta watched him closely, dark eyes taking in the label and darting up to Keir's face, awaiting instruction.

"I can do it myself if you wish."

Réalta snatched the lube from his hand, swinging his arm wide and taking the bottle out of reach. "Have you forgotten how to listen?" He chided, thumbing the lid and blinking when it flipped open. "Ah." Realization raised his eyebrows, amusement quirking the corner of his mouth. Upending the bottle, he squeezed a decent amount onto his fingers before slipping them between Keir's cheeks. A finger slid over puckered flesh and pressed in.

"Unh," the witch grunted, fire lighting up his bones as the damned merman spun his wrist and pressed down on exactly the right spot.

"Bad?"

"Good," Keir exhaled. His elbows slipped out from under him, and he flopped back against the mattress, burning beneath the midnight gaze of his merman. A drizzle of lube found its way onto the head of his cock, and Réalta collected it with his palm, stroking Keir as he fingered him. "Goddess, that's so good."

"Look at you," Réalta purred. He matched the slide of his hand with the pulse of his finger, and Keir arched his back as if he could will the merman to delve deeper. Stroke harder. His skin flashed hot, his teeth hummed. He knew he sounded wanton and needy, but there was no restraining himself, not when his body was being worked by a master. "So beautiful."

"Beautiful," Keir murmured, raising an arm to reach for the merman. His movements were slow, like he'd been transported to the ocean's depths by a single touch. His thoughts drunken and thick from the pleasure wracking his body. All of a sudden it wasn't enough. He needed to feel the weight of Réalta pressing him into the sheets and the swells and valleys of all that muscle. The pleasurable bite of pain that came with being filled and fucked. "I need you."

"That's my boy." Another finger worked its way in, forcing a gasp from the witch even as he raised his hips, allowing easier access for those probing digits. The intensity of being stretched and the dull throb of soreness that lingered from their morning had his nipples pebbling and gooseflesh rising down his arms and legs. Réalta saw that, and his smile sharpened enough to be threatening. He released Keir's cock and slid his hand down the length of a thigh, gripping behind his knee to hoist his leg and prop a lean, lanky calf on his shoulder. "You are so good to me."

"Good to you?" Keir laughed in disbelief. A sound that evolved to a breathy moan as Réalta fisted his cock and dragged the head along Keir's length, coating himself in the lubricant as he swept lower and lower, teasing the entrance his fingers still worked. "Horned God, *leanbh*."

"You and your gods." The merman removed his fingers, forcing Keir to suffer only a moment of their loss before he pressed into him. Slowly filling the witch and stretching him with his girth. They again groaned as one, the sensation overwhelming and stealing the air from Keir's lungs.

He gripped the sheets tighter, raising his hips to allow Réalta better access until the merman was seated to the base of his shaft. They held like that, Keir angled to perfection, his long leg poised on a broad shoulder, and Réalta gazing down at him through dark eyes brimming with warmth. He ran a hand down Keir's front, feeling the leanly muscled form for himself and tracing the divots at his hips. A plush lip disappeared between the merman's teeth, and Keir moaned to see him so close to undone.

"Your eyes are green," he whispered, thrusting his hips to roll those very eyes back into Keir's skull. "They were black when we met."

"My Way," the witch tried to explain, but multisyllabic words wouldn't form. His brain turned to mush by salacious need. "The Shades."

"Bring them back," Réalta demanded, thrusting again as his fingers wrapped around Keir's cock.

He hissed in reply, a sharp intake of breath at the way every nerve lit up from that touch. Goddess, it was new. He had rarely been ridden, rarely experienced the bliss he strove to give his partners, and the poor witch had no idea what to do, how to behave or react. It was thrilling and foreign, and the merman threatened to unravel him with each thrust.

"Bring them back," Réalta demanded a second time, bending low to press a kiss to Keir's chest. "I want to feel as you feel." Another kiss against his clavicle. "I want to know the sensations that put such a look on your face." Another on his lips before he rammed his hips forward, stroking Keir at the same instant in exactly the way the witch had shown him.

"Fuck!" The Shades exploded from the witch, lashing like ribbons in an angry wind and blanketing the room in midnight. He tried his best to direct them to the merman, but each Shade was an extension of himself, and he was coming undone. "Réalta—"

The merman's pace slowed long enough for the Shades to latch onto his arms, his legs, and his waist. Réalta shuddered at the onslaught of carnal pleasure throbbing through the connection from witch to merman and back. The sharp glint of his black eyes softened to a fuzzy haze, and when he looked back at Keir, the smile Réalta wore was lazy with bliss. "Perfect," he whispered, voice thick and heady. He settled into a slow, luxurious rhythm. "Ah, you use your power so well."

"You're so fucking huge," Keir replied. Blinking slowly and altogether uncertain if he meant the merman's cock, or his body, or the way he filled the room and the world, stealing all the air until Keir was drowning anew. Whatever he meant, the merman gleaned *something*. He bent low and licked up the center of Keir's chest, working his hips in an increasing rhythm. Their mouths met in a sloppy, sensual kiss, words devolving into grunts and moans and whispers of each other's names. With each press of his hips, Keir's cock slid against Réalta's body, captured beneath the ribbed torso and surrounded by the heat and the weight of the merman.

He whimpered, seeking to adjust his hips and ease the heightening sensation, but it was useless. He was delicate beneath Réalta's touch. Overpowered and loving every moment of feeling small and precious.

He propped a heel on the edge of the bed, lifting his hips higher so the merman could thrust deeper. And he did, pounding harder and harder still until Keir's toes went numb and his teeth buzzed. Until the sticky-slick slide of their bodies was all he knew. His fingers dug into Réalta's leg, his arm, reaching for his face to pull the magnificent creature down into a deep, drugging kiss while the Shades whirled around them as a maelstrom of emotion and feeling.

The threat of release rose like the tide, lapping higher and higher with every thrust and slide, each sweep of Réalta's tongue swelling Keir to the point of bursting. His skin stretched tight over his lank, too small to contain the sensation. A whimper rose in his throat, high-pitched and almost mewling. The sound, desperate and ragged, sent Réalta into a frenzy. He drove his hips against Keir, black eyes wild as he chased the witch to the edge. His hand slipped between them and took hold of Keir's cock, the heat and the roughness of his palm altogether too much. Every part of the witch cried out in reply, his spine snapping straight, the muscles in his legs seizing.

"*Mo bhandia!*"

It was all he could do to hold on as Réalta stroked him and railed him, the tandem motions slamming against Keir and pushing him over the edge.

A hoarse sound left his throat, the world fading to white as pleasure drilled into his bones and spilled as a sticky mess between them. His body pulsed and throbbed in aftershocks that had the witch twitching beneath his lover. His hands slipped over those broad shoulders seeking to take hold as the ring of muscle clenched around the merman's cock.

Réalta gasped, arms giving out. The weight of him blanketed the witch, and he buried his face in the crook of Keir's neck, grunting as his release powered through him. The sensation of being filled, coupled with the pulsing of Réalta's cock had Keir whimpering and frantically kissing his ear, his jaw, his forehead. Running fingers through Réalta's hair to see his face, wanting to memorize the way utter rapture softened the strong features into a cherubic mask.

However long they lay there, sticky with their own pleasure, Keir did not care. The wind raged beyond windows pommeled by rain, fat splatters, and heavy, rattling gusts crisping and sharpening into a battery of ice and sleet. The meteomantic Witch of the Demesne doing his best to corral the lorelei while within their hotel room, the witch held his merman. Long limbs tangled as tentacles while they floated in a hazy sleep without dreams. Their bodies came down from the height of euphoria and only moved when their mingled sweat cooled and pebbled flesh.

"I suppose we ought to bathe," Keir murmured after an eternity. He withdrew his Shades, running his fingers through Réalta's hair as he did. "Again." The merman rubbed his face against Keir's shoulder, burrowing deeper into the witch and the bed.

"I could sleep for days," came the muffled reply. "I abhor sleeping on land."

Keir pulled his head back as far as he could, tucking his chin to look at the merman. "How come?"

"Dreams," Réalta answered. He shuddered and raised his head. "Such twisted images." He screwed his face into a mockery of disgust. "Terrible."

"A dreamer who abhors dreams," Keir mused. He kissed Réalta's chin, earning a bemused smile. "You are a puzzle, merman."

"I could say the same for you." He traced the corner of Keir's eye with a thumb. A tiny line appeared between his brows, and it took the witch a moment to realize it was in response to the color having returned to its natural gem-bright green. "Other."

"Other." Keir flitted a smile and wriggled beneath the over-large merman, making a face at the squishy noises that earned. "Dinnae take this the wrong way, but as much as I enjoy being pinned beneath you,"—Réalta's smile broadened, showing off straight, white teeth that could almost pass as human, save for the too-sharp canines and pre-molars—"we're more than a bit of a mess and the hour I asked Toby for is about up."

"The hour?"

"May have broadly suggested he not return to the hotel with anything resembling immediacy." Keir's cheeks crawled red. "Perhaps a bit presumptuous of me, but I'm happy to have been proven correct."

Réalta rolled his eyes, reaching between them to gently remove himself. Keir winced, shifting his hips and quietly grunting at the ring of pain and ensuing emptiness. Réalta settled onto his knees beside the bed, cleaning him with a towel-covered hand. The care in that blossomed a warmth in Keir's belly, and he caught himself gazing down the length of his body at the merman, softness clouding his expression.

Réalta felt his gaze and glanced up, a smile on his lips. "Come." He rose and reached for Keir, drawing the witch from the bed. Lingering soreness had the witch wincing again. Réalta slipped an arm behind his knees, earning an indignant laugh.

"I can walk."

"Can you also accept help?" Réalta hoisted near two meters of muscle and lank into his arms as easily as if Keir were a doll. The witch snorted at the absurdity and then laughed outright when he caught their reflection in the mirror. Two large mostly-men, one carrying the other like a damsel-in-distress. Réalta angled them toward the bathroom, faltering when he, too, saw the absurd visual they made. Laughing, he carried his witch back into the shower.

Fourteen

The steady *chirrup* of an incoming call dragged Keir from a sleep so deep that he awoke not knowing where he was or why there was a heavy weight pressing down on his chest. He blinked in the darkened room, groggy and confused, bringing a hand down on the weight and smiling at the feel of silk-smooth tresses beneath his palm.

Réalta.

His gut clenched at the memory of the who and the what and the why of where he was. The events of the day rose and fell in his mind's eye like a die in the window on a Magic 8-Ball, each vignette bringing with it a shiver and sizzle of remembered bliss. Keir drifted his eyes closed, enjoying the replay and the weight of the merman who had fallen asleep — despite his protests — with his head on the witch's chest.

Their last shower had been utilitarian and somehow more intimate than the physically charged one that had led to the sweetest fucking Keir had had in a long while. The merman had set him carefully on the tiles, testing the water before allowing Keir to step beneath the stream. Then, he gently cleaned the witch, ordering him to towel off and dress. For his part, Keir was happy to be coddled and cared for. He returned the favor by calling the hotel restaurant and ordering a meal in his broken Dutch, demanding that Réalta try one of everything before they gave in to their mutual exhaustion.

His mobile chirped again, alerting the witch to a new voicemail. He opened one eye, sighting the device on the bedside table. Careful not to jostle Réalta, he stretched out an arm and grabbed his mobile, swiping through notifications—all from Lou, which wasn't entirely odd, but he'd expected at least some form of communication from Toby by now.

Brow wrinkling, Keir selected the first voicemail and held the mobile to his ear.

"I don't suppose you would care to explain," his sister's cool, lilting voice played through the speaker, "why the E.R.I.E. scans for Harlingen are pinging off the fecking charts for meteomantic activity, hm?"

The next one wasn't any better.

"*I* know that *you* damn well bloody know that the ritual to create a storm surge of *this magnitude* has to be filed through the proper channels within C.R.O.W., and I *also* know that *Toby* bloody well knows, so what in the *piss shitting hell* are you two gobshites playing at?!"

But the last one ...

"Keir," her voice was low and measured, never a good sign. "I will not pretend to understand the half-baked scheme you've concocted and managed to talk Tobias into, but one of you bloody wankers needs to answer your bloody mobile."

He tensed from shoulders to toes, pulling the device away from his ear to read the time. The movement stirred Réalta, who grumbled into Keir's chest, rubbing his face side-to-side before raising his head to stare bleary-eyed at the witch.

"Is everything alright?"

"Nae," Keir breathed. He tapped on the screen and held the device to his ear, listening to a call ring and ring and ring. "Nae, he always answers."

"Who?" Réalta popped up on an elbow. Keir noted the rumpled state of the merman's hair and how it had dried with a loose curl. His fingers twitched, wanting to reach out and brush the strands back from his face, but duty called, distasteful as it may be.

"Toby." Keir rocked forward to sit on the edge of the bed. On autopilot, his fingers tapped Lou's number, the call connecting as he stared at the screen. Réalta settled beside him, peering down at the mobile and then skimming Keir's face with those dark eyes.

"You had better be able to explain this." Lou's voice through the speaker was tinny and tight. Keir glanced at Réalta, reaching out to squeeze his bicep and trail fingers down his arm. "Keir?"

He rose from the bed and settled into his role in a fluid movement. "Lou."

"What in the nine rings is going on up there?"

"Thus far, the desecrant has proven far cleverer than reports would have us believe. In previous attempts to apprehend the desecrant, the lorelei has attacked both Toby and myself, as well as endangered the life of a passing, ehm" —he glanced at the merman in his bed— "Staid."

"Staid?" Réalta's brows lowered.

"Human," Keir mouthed.

Réalta straightened, nostrils flaring at the insinuation he was anything resembling a human.

"Endangered, how?" Lou demanded.

"We were able to ascertain his safety and well-being."

"Hm," Lou huffed. "Do you need me to run interference?"

"No!" Keir blurted. Too forcefully, but Lou's brand of interference was best avoided where the Staid were involved. He scrunched his face tight and pinched the bridge of his nose. "Nae, not needed; we convinced him it was a hallucination brought on by sunstroke."

"A stroke, certainly," Réalta muttered. Keir's eyes flew open, bugging at his tone.

"Perhaps I was wrong to let you run point on this," Lou sighed. "Given your history around aquatic desecrants—"

"The *vodyanoi* has nothing to do with this, Lou."

"And the storm?"

"The storm."

"Yes, Keir, the storm," his sister needled, her words crisp and clean lest they be misconstrued as anything other than an Elder Witch demanding answers from her subordinate. "The one setting off every E.R.I.E. on the continent."

"Aye, well, we thought—" he stopped, switching tracks. Toby would understand. He would corroborate Keir's claim even without prompting from the Dark Witch. Horned God knew he wanted Keir freed from his role as an Enforcer almost as badly as the witch wanted it for himself. "I thought it would be best to enlist the aid of the Witch of the Demesne in corralling the desecrant within the freshwater bounds of the Ijsselmeer, as well as ensure that no further Staid were placed in harm's way."

"And you thought freezing the bloody sea was the way to go about it?" Lou's voice sharpened and rose. Not to screeching levels, yet, but certainly trending in that direction. "This stunt of yours has brought the western edge of the entire continent to a literal fecking standstill. Did you even take into account the economic impact? Shipping lanes into Europe are frozen; they're having to re-route airplanes to bloody Iceland and the fishing industry, Keir!"

"I didnae ... fishing industry?" He met Réalta's gaze for a beat before spinning on his heels and striding across the room. They had drawn the curtains after that second shower, wanting the peace and calm of a cocooned space to rest in each other's arms, all too willingly ignoring the winter storm raging beyond the glass. Now, Keir gripped the heavy drapes and tore them open, revealing a world gone polar.

Frost crawled at the corners of the window, fogging the glass and close to obscuring his view of the world beyond. In another hour, the pane would be entirely sheeted in ice, but for now, what Keir could see dropped his stomach straight to Satan's frigid pit in the ninth ring of the Inferno.

Ice clung to the railing lining the harbor and canal, warping the wrought iron into twisted metal. Icicles hung heavy from street lamps, eaves, and awnings like stalactites while bulbous white formations threatened to snap the lines and masts on ships no longer bobbing at the dock. The cobbles were a glassy sheet, the gutters miniature luges and the drawbridge to Noorderhaven was in grave danger of becoming an immovable fixture.

Further down the canal, heavy winds had thrown the water up against the steep, reinforced walls, glissading the masonwork and freezing as an arctic swell over the Raadhuissteg. Below the narrow pedestrian bridge, a frozen wave strained against the gates of the Grote Sluis, warping the historic lock that led to the original canals of the city.

His breath fogged against the glass, and Keir blindly groped a chair-back for his long discarded wooly-pully, using the thick woven, hex-resistant fabric to clear the window. The rain had stopped, as had the hail and sleet, and what existed outside of their room was a snowstorm in stasis.

"It's cold."

"How very perceptive of you," Lou drawled. "Donmar won't stop griping about having to put on a shirt with sleeves for the first time in days."

"How cold?" Réalta stepped beside Keir. The witch was startled, though not from fear. Too late, he covered the microphone on his mobile, mouthing for Réalta to stay quiet.

"Keir?" Lou chirped through the speaker. "Is that Toby?"

"I'm sorry, please," Keir whispered, "please don't talk, I'll explain when she's—"

"Keir! Who are you talking to?"

"I'm sorry."

Réalta's face was impassive, his eyes a flat, unreadable black. He nodded, the slightest bob of his chin, and turned his attention to the window and the frozen world beyond. Though he did as the witch asked, it felt like a dismissal.

Swallowing a surge of bile, Keir tapped the speaker icon on his mobile, and Lou's voice flooded the room.

"—can be there in a number of hours, so long as you stay put in the hotel."

"Dinnae."

"Don't argue with me on this, Keir. You clearly weren't ready to handle the lorelei. I suppose I should have known better; I know *you*."

"Then you know I can do this," Keir snapped back. He spun from the window, and Réalta pacing the room. "My way."

"C.R.O.W. gave explicit instructions that you were to—"

"My *Way*, Luminescence," he snarled, an old anger flaring. "I can handle this with my Way, not C.R.O.W.'s, if you would just let me—"

"Extreme prejudice, Keir." Her tone dropped. Cooled. Each word as crisp and cold as the ice outside his window. "You were instructed to detain the desecrant and practice extreme prejudice in carrying out C.R.O.W.'s orders. Not laze about in the Netherlands convincing mortals they've had a bit too much sun in *January*." She sniffed. Lou's tell-tale tic that this conversation was far past over. "Handle the desecrant better than you handled the Staid."

"I would like to see him try," Réalta said, eyes still skimming the glacial landscape. Keir juddered to a halt, shoulders twitching up to his ears. He slowly craned his face from the mobile's screen, eyes large as saucers and jaw hanging slack. The merman slid hands into the pockets of his borrowed joggers and turned to face him, brows slightly raised in challenge.

"Keeeeeeir," Lou sang his name, treacle sweet. "When you say you 'ascertained the safety and well-being' of the Staid onlooker, that would not happen to include bringing said *mortal human* back to the hotel room with you, would it?"

"*Human?!*" Réalta seethed.

Keir rushed the merman; hand outstretched to cover that lush mouth so intent on talking. Réalta's shoulders broadened, hands curling into fists in his pockets, and the witch fell still a step away from him.

"Is he there with you? *Now*?" Lou nearly shrieked, her voice clanging against the walls and getting caught in the pitched slope of the ceiling.

Working his jaw, Keir tried to force the words. A squeak strangled free, and he cleared his throat. "Y-yes?"

"You utter, fecking, *gobshite*."

His thumb ended the call before Lou could continue her train of thought. He tossed the mobile onto the bed, rubbing his face with his palms and thrusting fingers into his hair. "Fuck."

"We did." Réalta glared at him. "And it appears this is not something you are proud of."

Keir tore his hands free, throwing his arms wide as he stared at the merman. Réalta stared back, hewn from marble and beyond offended.

"Is it because I am a, what was the word you used, a desecrant?"

"Nae."

"I am *not* a human," Réalta spat, "so what is it, then?"

Lanky arms dropped heavily to his sides. Keir sank to the bed, propping elbows on his knees, and, for once, let himself speak freely.

"I'm nae trying to hide what we did, I'm nae trying to hide *you*—no. No. That's a lie, and I need to be better than that." Raising his head, he gazed up at the merman. "Lou knows about ... me, my past, and the sorts of lovers I'm attracted to. She kens I'm nae one to turn away when there's a—a connection. A feeling." He scratched the skin over his heart where he felt the quiet roil of his Way at all times. The emotive pulse of the Shades feeding his inner turmoil with their turbulent nature. "I wouldnae want to hide you, or whatever this is for however long it's anything, only, it's more that you dinnae exist."

The merman crossed his arms over his chest, muscles bulging. His face settled into a mask of restrained anger. "I beg to differ."

"In my world, my employers, they dinnae recognize merpeople—"

"Folk."

"Merfolk. Nine rings, they hardly recognize *me*, and my sister, she—she's made her career out of upholding the letter of the law. If she suspected that you were anything out of the ordinary"—he jumped to his feet, appealing to Réalta with open hands— "and believe me when I say you are *extraordinary*, she wouldnae stop until you were detained and studied and categorized and regulated." The words left his tongue as a bitter poison, bringing back the memories of every test and trial he had endured. Every aural exam performed to assess how Forbidden and Foule the Dark Witch was trending. Every sneer and muttered remark that he was a thing to be controlled or, better yet, extinct. "I wouldnae want that for you."

"Why do they not recognize you?" Réalta asked. The anger softened enough to urge Keir closer.

"My Way, what I am, terrifies them," he admitted. The slightest effort had a slip of shadow blooming across his shoulders, one end draping down his front while the other curled possessively around his neck. "There are those who would have me erased, those who prefer me leashed. Every mention of my kind of Otherness is tied in with fairy tale monsters and nightmares, the sort of creatures my employers have spent the better part of half a millennia hunting and executing."

"Then how are you here?"

Keir clenched his jaw, fisting and flexing his hands. The urge to punch something made the muscles in his arms dance. The Shades latched onto his anxiety, prompting him with their whispers and fanning the fury that always came when he thought about his role on the team and how indebted he was to the witch responsible for keeping him alive.

Let it out.

Toby wasn't here to strap on focus pads and help him work through the anger. He needed to keep calm, keep talking to drown out the Shades telling him to let it out, let the anger ride him, let the darkness free to consume the witch and the world.

Let it out.

"My sister," he forced through his teeth.

Réalta's brows rose, his eyes widening as understanding erased the last of his anger. "I see."

"Do you?"

"The waters are murky, but shapes are becoming apparent." The tightness at his mouth eased, and he brushed a knuckle against Keir's cheekbone. A single swipe that settled the Shades. Keir's jaw relaxed, his lips parting as the anger was drowned by something akin to wonder.

He was so used to upholding the lies and existing within the narrow constraints of the world his sister had constructed. So used to swallowing his anger and pride until he could safely expel it on a casting range, in the Neitherworld, or a gym. The merman had managed to ease all of that strain with the swipe of a knuckle and words of understanding.

Keir's heart thudded in his chest, and another bruise healed as something upsettingly close to *hope* fluttered to life. The hope that he could be understood, that someone could and would accept all of him, and not just the carefully curated pieces. So long as he didn't fuck it all up at this moment.

"My folk have gone unnoticed for this long," Réalta stated, "and we will continue to do so until the time of our choosing."

"Even so, I'll nae be the one to out you or your folk. Even if this"—he pointed from himself to Réalta, letting his finger drag along the centerline of his chest—"is only a fleeting thing. You can trust me."

"If I did not, do you think we would even be having this conversation?" Réalta cocked his head to the side, eyes darting over Keir's face. "Your employers know of *you*; what makes you so certain they do not know about the merfolk?"

"Nothing," Keir admitted. "Either the merfolk are indeed hidden from C.R.O.W., or they know and have chosen to erase the merfolk from our history, which begs the question: why ignore your existence outright or, a step further, why hide you behind *melusines*, *undines*, *lamia*, and lorelei?"

"I assume it is due to their recognizing us for our threat."

Keir shook his head, spinning away from the merman. "If C.R.O.W. believed you to be a threat, they would have regulated your behavior with a very short leash or villainized you to the point of persecution." Bitterness soured his tongue. "Believe me, I would know." Swiping his hand at the bed, he collected his mobile and unlocked the screen. Lou had left three additional voicemails while they had been talking, finally resorting to screaming at him via text message.

"I AM ON MY WAY."

He dismissed the notifications, opened the E.R.I.E scanner, and tapped to the map function. A useful piece of coding the chronomantic that regularly worked on his team had built with a technomantic witch in London. Using the energy tracking functions of the application and cleverly triangulating the surges along with GPS coordinates and recorded signatures of the individual witch, the E.R.I.E. was able to work as a witchy Find My Fam app under duress.

The Ijsselmeer and Waddenzee appeared on his screen, separated by a thin line representing the Afsluitdijk. He zoomed out, bringing Harlingen into view, and opened the settings to adjust the scanner.

"Perhaps they ignore us due to our numbers."

"Hm?" Keir looked up, somewhat surprised that Réalta had turned his back to the witch. Hands crossed over the base of his spine, his broad figure filled the window. What light filtered in through the ice and snow gave his marble skin a ghostly glow.

"We are many," Réalta rumbled, turning his face enough to view Keir from the corner of his eye. "How many are you?"

"Legion," Keir replied, speaking first for the Shades and next for himself. "And one."

FIFTEEN

The shrieking E.R.I.E. alarm pulled Keir's attention away from the stoic merman regarding him from across the room. He read the screen, blinked, and read it again.

"Oh, Horned God."

"Keir?"

"No, nonononoo." He tapped and tapped again, willing what he was seeing, what the E.R.I.E. was reporting, to be a lie. A mistake, a grievous error in the programming. But it remained the same no matter how many times he refreshed the map and re-ran the scan he'd set for Toby's signature. A little red dot denoting the location of a spalování surge, blinking as steadily as a Christmas light on the Afsluitdijk. Right next to a blue meteomantic signature and — "Ach, I fucked up."

"This appears to be a theme with you."

"It is." The witch raised his hand to run fingers through his hair. He clocked himself in the head with his mobile instead. "Ow, fuck, it really is. Best you learn that about me now."

Hands shaking, he tossed his mobile to the bed and began scavenging the room for his boots and pants, needing to be active, not standing there like an overgrown hedge trying to justify its existence. Keir needed movement to keep his mind off of the truth: he'd fucked up. Again. Letting his emotions get the better of him, getting distracted, and assuming Toby would be there to clean up his mess. But he wasn't. He was elsewhere, and Keir ought to have known. He ought to have put the pieces together and predicted what would happen, but he didn't, and Toby was—

All his gear was where he'd left it the night Réalta pulled him from the water, laid out to dry across chairs and over a closet door. His boots were still damp, even with their placement next to the radiator, but his socks were thankfully dry. He dressed, ignoring the merman, the storm, everything save for the few pieces of vital information he had:

Toby was on the Afsluitdijk using his Way, right beside the meteo-mantic Witch of the Demesne and the signature of a known desecrant.

"What is this?" Réalta's presence in front of him stilled Keir's fingers. He looked up from his boots, mid-knot, to find the merman somewhat dressed and studying the mobile gripped in elegant fingers.

While the witch had been spiraling in his personal panic, Réalta had been following his lead, albeit with very different results. Where Keir's wooly-pully was fitted but comfortable, the one the merman had stolen from Toby's luggage was too small at the shoulders, too short in the sleeves, and just tight enough to be distracting. He still wore Keir's joggers, which mostly fit save for the blessed tightness around his thighs and rear. A running shoe and a loafer were set neatly against the foot of the bed, telling Keir that the literal fish-out-of-water had considered shoes and discarded the idea just as quickly.

"E.R.I.E."

"Is the outfit so bad?"

"Nae, E - R - I - E." He spelled out the acronym while pushing himself upright. "Energy Reading Investigatory Equipment. We use it to track different energy surges and determine where the threat lies." Pointing at the red dot, he clarified, "That is Toby, he's a, well, he's Other, like me. But in a socially acceptable way, and that" —a point at the black dot—

"is the desecrant." Réalta raised his head, staring blankly at the witch. "The lorelei."

"If the lorelei shows up so easily, why did you not use this the entire time?"

"Much like myself, mobiles dinnae work in water," Keir stated. "Though we did use the E.R.I.E. at first. It's how we ended up out at Breezanddijk the night you found me." He jerked his chin at the device. "Useful tool in my line of work."

"Which is?" Réalta tugged at the collar of his borrowed sweater, eyes dropping to take in the Living Shade standing before him.

"Hunting," Keir answered. "You dinnae have to do this."

"You do not know how to swim, and if this means what I think it means,"—he placed the phone in Keir's hand and grabbed the ends of the witch's belt, slipping the leather through the buckle and pulling it tight— "then someone must ensure that you do not drown. How embarrassing that would be for me."

"I cannae ask you to —"

"So good at following instructions." Réalta tapped the underside of Keir's chin with a finger and stole a quick kiss. "So terrible at listening.

"*Waar wil je heen?*" The OverAuto driver reared back in his seat, buggy eyes ready to pop out of his skull.

"The safe harbor, ehm, near the campground," Keir racked his brain, struggling to translate. "*De zuidhaven, bij Breezanddijk. Meteen,* please."

"In this weather?" The driver gaped at him. "*Ben je gek?!*"

"Crazy? It's highly likely," Keir responded, handing over a one-hundred Euro note and showing him two more. "*Meteen.*"

The driver clacked his teeth together, glancing at the large merman in not-large-enough clothes crowding the backseat, then back to the terrifying witch in the passenger seat. Keir knew his eyes were wholly black. He could feel the Shades aching to slip free as they pressed against the sclera and roiled in the vitreous humor.

Let ussss, they whispered, writhing behind his eyes and cajoling the Dark Witch to step into his Way. *Let us out, let us help, let us free.*

Keir fought the urge to scrub his palms against closed lids. He wished he'd worn his glasses, but contacts were the safer choice for what he was about to do.

"*Meteen,*" he repeated, dropping a hand on the driver's shoulder and easing his hold on the Shades to tiptoe into his Way. "Now."

A slip of black sighed free beneath his palm, flooding the man with a yearning, not unlike homesickness. The overwhelming desire to be somewhere specific. The mortal frowned, and his bug-eyed expression grew distant. Deep down, Keir shuddered in disgust at himself and his Way. The Shades he released took care of that for him, packing the self-hate into a tidy space where emotion held no bearing. This was his right, his *Way.*

"Now." The driver nodded, eyelids drooping with a wistful sorrow. He drifted his gaze out the window and sighed. "*Meteen,* yes. Yes, I can take you there."

"*Dank je.*" Keir settled in his seat, staring out the window at the polar landscape blurring past. Fear was a distant thing, regret nearly forgotten. He was a Dark Witch with a job to do; there was no room for angst and nerves. There was only the task. The goal. The result he desired above all else.

Detain the lorelei, act with extreme prejudice, and earn his freedom.

The merman wasn't one for excess speech, the driver was too focused on chasing his desire to be elsewhere, so they drove in silence down the N31 motorway towards the dijk. Outside of the city, the roads grew treacherous. The car skidded over black ice at every bend, jostling the human, witch, and merman within. The driver gripped the wheel, his knuckles blanching further with every slip and fishtail.

"Stop." Réalta slapped his large palm down on the driver's seat. His deep, wide voice filled the car, jarring the Dark Witch from the calm imposed by his Shades. Jerking into action, Keir clamped a hand down on the driver's wrist and sent Shades to ease the muscles and slow the vehicle safely.

As with all things, he was too slow.

The driver yelped, foot slamming on the brakes. The sedan's tail whipped out, and they skidded on the ice, spinning round and round and round. Someone shouted a panicked cry that could have come from any one of them. Keir gripped the handle on the door, bracing himself for impact as the auto spun wildly off the road. His shoulder slammed against the door, temple cracking against the window as the car jolted to a stop in a frozen snowbank.

The engine pinged and plunked. The mortal groaned and slumped in his seat, his head dropping against the steering wheel. Keir took that in, registered it somewhere in his Shade-drowned brain as "irregular," unbuckled his seatbelt, and jerked the door handle. It took three tries of yanking and slamming his shoulder against the door before the metal creaked open, scoring a muddied trench in the snow. Like the living Shade he was, the Dark Witch slipped out of the car, treading across the ice and climbing a low hill.

To his right, the Waddenzee shot out towards oblivion. To his left, lights shone in the wintry landscape.

The petrol station, a Shade whispered. *Zurich.*

Zurich, the little settlement on the Frisian end of the Afsluitdijk. Somehow more disappointing than the Zurich in Switzerland, if only for the fact that it was less than ten kilometers from Harlingen. Which meant they were still close to sixteen kilometers from Breezanddijk.

Do you seriously think you can make it?

"Quiet," Keir snarled at the Shade.

Rude.

He pulled his mobile out and studied the screen. The red dot was still blinking at the center of the dijk, next to the signatures of the Witch of the Demesne and the desecrant. That was good. He could easily reach them as long as he had a heading, a familiar Shade to latch onto in the dark.

If you don't get distracted first.

Which begged the question: why hadn't he just done this in the first place?

Aren't you forgetting something? The Shade asked, brushing up against his conscience with the sensation of laughter at him.

"Didnae summon you."

You never do when you decide to go all creepy, the Shade sighed, *but you should really let me out because I think you forgot something.*

"I said shut it." He raised his hand, fingers dancing as he formed the sigil to tear apart the world. The roil of the Shades increased, ready to welcome Keir into the dark, but the seam remained solid. "Shite."

Let me out, the little Shade demanded.

He tried again. And again. Crooking and bending his fingers, twinning his intent with his desire, but the flex of his pinky was wrong, and his index finger trembled in the cold.

Goddess, you're dumb. Let me out.

He was cold. Too cold to think clearly, shivering too hard to form the sigil.

A car door slammed at his back, shouts rose, an argument in what sounded like two languages broke out, and Keir—*No! Nononono, don't!*—shaved off more of himself to weather the cold. His shivering lessened and stopped altogether.

Better. Another Shade acknowledged, their voice lower than the first Shade's and slick with promise. *Now come, we will show you where to go.*

"Nae," the Dark Witch snarled. "I do not follow you." His voice was broad and endless, even to his ears. The Shades simmering beneath his skin went still, awaiting his command.

Which is why I keep having to drag you back out, the little Shade snarked, though her voice was distant.

"Keir?"

Arm held before him, the Dark Witch formed the necessary sigil with terrible accuracy and tore through the fabric of the world, opening a doorway between the mortal realm and his. Color leached from the world as billowing black clouds stained the stark white blanket of snow. The arctic gusts of the Neitherworld howled out of the dark, tearing up whorls of frost and powder and drowning out the sound of a name shouted by a distant voice.

"Keir!"

Snow clung to his arms and legs, chilling the exposed skin at his wrists and neck. In his boots, his toes curled against the cold, and still the Dark

Witch stepped deeper, shearing off more and more of himself to feed the Neitherworld and his Way.

The cold ceased to be a problem, and howling winds swallowed the voice yelling at his back. Snow crunched beneath his boots as he stepped forward, ready to enter the Neitherworld and chase down the Shade of a spalování.

Something heavy thudded in the snow, and iron-strong arms wrapped around his waist. Before he could manage even a step, the Dark Witch was pulled back from the torn seam. "Keir, it is too cold for you to be out here."

He glanced down, taking in the warbling Shade rising like smoke from a being that was neither human nor witch. With a flick of his fingers, needle-thin shadeblades shot out, sinking into the desecrant's forearms. The creature gasped in either shock or pain, and his hold weakened. The Dark Witch ducked low, slipping under his arms and sweeping smoothly through the snow. He straightened, stalking towards the gateway to his realm.

"I need to get you out of this cold." The desecrant grabbed the Dark Witch's wrist and physically hauled him away from the Neitherworld. A meaty fist manacled his casting hand, and the witch was pulled back against a broad, muscular chest. Warmth from the desecrant bled weakly through the thick wool of his sweater, the sensation at odds with the nothing the Dark Witch felt, stepped as deeply into his Way as he was. "You are freezing."

Those words clouded in the arctic air, blooming beside the witch's cheek and teasing him with the scent of the seaside. He snarled at the distraction and crooked a finger. A tongue of shadow lashed out from the void, wrapping around the desecrant's legs. Pulling it taut, the Dark Witch tripped the creature, and they both went down in a heap. He rolled off the desecrant, kneeling in the snow as more shadows answered his summons, whipping around the desecrant's arms, legs, and neck; restraining the Forbidden and Foule creature.

"You willnae stand in my way." The Dark Witch's voice boomed above the howling wind as he rose. Shadows pulled the creature to its knees, stretching its arms out to the side. Onyx eyes glared up at the Dark Witch, shock tightening moon-pale skin. A grimace revealed too-sharp teeth, the canines and molars meant for tearing. The desecrant was large and powerful. A predator, if those teeth and his strong form were anything to judge by, but it was *nothing* compared to the awful magick of a Dark Witch defied.

Clawing his hand, the witch held it inches over the desecrant's heart, seeking its Shade. Smoke curled from his fingers, ribboning over the slight distance and purling against ill-fit clothing. Black eyes glared at the Dark Witch, and still, the desecrant fought, jerking broad shoulders and straining the muscles in his legs in an attempt to stand. The Dark Witch tightened his grip on the Shades, jerking the creature's arms against his sides and binding them in place. Another Shade cloaked the creature's throat and jaw, forcing him to look his ruin in the eye.

The Dark Witch bent at the waist, bringing their faces level. In the depths of his mind, a piece of the witch sighed in awe at the chiseled bone structure and beautiful features of the creature, an artistic rendering of masculinity cast between a Michelangelo and a Botticelli, but the Dark Witch only saw a Shade that denied its master.

Take your due.

"Mine," he seethed. The tips of his fingers pressed against the desecrant's chest, caging his heart as he released the Shades to burrow deep. They slipped in easily, and the desecrant's groan was music to the Dark Witch. A soft keening that put a smile on his face. He let his eyes drift closed while the Shades worked, wending through muscle and bone as they sought that space where Shade and Soul resided.

He felt the claustrophobic grip of squeezing through a too-tight space before his shadows graced a boundless plain of being. They lapped smoke-black tongues against the desecrant's Shade — and slipped away.

No. More. Take what is your right!

Again, he sought to claim the Shade, and again, he could not grab hold or loop his Shades around that essential piece of the being. So he sent more. More of his Shades, more of his Way into the creature, but each attempt failed, his magick bouncing off with the feel of magnetic poles repelling one another.

Snarling, the witch withdrew with a ripcord gesture, tearing the Shades free. The act pulled a pained grunt from the desecrant and sent the witch staggering back. Hunched and panting, he glared at the creature braced on hands and knees in the snow.

"What are you?" The Dark Witch wiped spittle away with the back of a hand. The tightening of frost on bared skin dragged his gaze away from the desecrant to his hand. Crooked and clawed, the nailbeds were a deep purple, the skin itself tight and blue.

Oh no, Dark Witch, that little Shade whispered, her tiny presence coiled safely against the back of his ribcage. *What did you do?*

In a blink, Keir fell out of his Way. The sub-zero cold embraced him like a shroud, freezing in his throat and lungs, making him cough and inhale more of the bitter air while gaping in horror at his hand. The skin at his wrists and palms burned, but his fingers were dead to the cold, frostbitten beyond sensation.

"Please do not drown on dry land," Réalta muttered, head hung low. His shoulders heaved as the merman fought to regain himself.

"Oh, Goddess." The witch gaped at his hand. At Réalta. "Goddess, I tried to - to -"

"Keir," Réalta rasped, pushing himself upright and reaching for the witch. "You need to get inside."

"Nae," the witch choked. "I need tae get to Toby, I need tae—oh, *Goddess*, what did I do?"

Dumb question, he knew what he'd done. He'd gone too far, allowed enough of himself to be drawn off by the Shades that he stopped caring about the ice, treacherous roads, or the danger in which he'd placed the mortal driver. He'd stopped caring that Réalta was *Réalta*. Not a desecrant. Not a creature Forbidden and Foule to be brought before C.R.O.W. and judged. Goddess, he'd been trying to tear his Shade free, ready and willing to make a thrall of the merman and perform the odious task that C.R.O.W. demanded of him time and time again.

"Come." An arm fell over his shoulders, the merman's warmth doing its best to fight off the cold as he escorted Keir down the snowy rise. "I sent the driver ahead; there are lights on in the structures—"

"Nae." Keir locked his legs, causing the merman to stumble. "Toby is out here, I need to get onto the dijk."

"The car is stuck," Réalta argued. He swept around to Keir's front, raising a hand to press fingers lightly against his temple. Pain warbled out from his touch, reminding Keir that he'd cracked his head against the window in the snowy wreck. Réalta frowned at the wince his touch earned and pulled his hand away, the tips of two fingers darkened by blood. "I will not let you use your Otherness to persuade another human."

"Dinnae need to." Keir surged around him, charging up the hill and stopping at the grand altitude of four-and-a-half meters to examine the terrain. The Waddenzee stretched out before him, boundless in the dark night. He released his tenuous grasp on the Shades and they came rushing forward, eager to be once again set free. His hand formed the sigil as he raised his arm, and Réalta snarled. He stooped low, grabbing an item from the snow before charging up the berm. "Stay back, Réalta. Dinnae fancy fighting you again."

"Nor should you." The merman seemed to swell, muscles straining against the tightly woven sweater. He adjusted his grip on the item in his hand — a tire iron. "I would win."

"Would you." Keir let the merman see how the black of his eyes overtook the iris, bleeding across the sclera like a viscous oil until his face bore two lightless obsidian pools.

He'd been a fool to bring the merman along. A fool to think himself worthy of being protected or needing protection. He was a Dark Witch. *The* Dark Witch. The Master of Shades who called humans and witches alike to heel. Able to cross the boundless expanse in less than a handful of steps. A witch healed by the darkness he so readily ignored.

"Shouldnae brought you with me." It would have been easy to open up the seam from the safety of his hotel room. He could have stepped right through, located Toby, and ended this whole affair in less time than it took to drink a cup of tea, but no, he had wanted to feel safe. He wanted to feel protected; he wanted someone to stand beside him rather than looking the other way while the Dark Witch did C.R.O.W.'s dirty work. He was selfish and weak, and now an entire region of witches, mortals, and otherwise would pay for his failures. "This is nae place for you."

Réalta lowered his chin, opening his mouth to reprimand the witch when the E.R.I.E. app started screeching anew. Grimacing, the merman snarled, "What is that *sound*."

"A signature swell." Keir fumbled at a pocket, squinting at the screen lighting up in bright shades of red and caustic, neon blue. Bright light hurt when he gave over to the Shades, and the frenetic, seizure-inducing flashing was doing little to keep the Dark Witch from developing a migraine. "Meteomantic." He flashed the phone screen at Réalta. "Right next to Toby on the Breezanddijk. Whatever they're gonnae do, it is happening now."

On cue, a bright white and heart-of-a-flame blue flared far down the Afsluitdijk. A tower of pure, white steam raised by the metal-melting heat of a welder's torch. Even at their distance, the bright spalování flame painted a cerulean swathe across the water. Shadows dragged from swells in the Waddenzee, and it took Keir a minute to recognize what had happened.

"Ice." He rubbed an eye, blinking to clear the Shades and see clearly. At the sight, Lou's screeched condemnation made a hell of a lot more sense. "Holy Horned God, they've frozen the entire sea." Keir took a step that had him slipping on ice and skidding a few feet down the berm toward the glacial Waddenzee. "I thought she meant the Ijsselmeer, but this ... this is ..."

"You need to get indoors," Réalta repeated. Keir glanced up at the merman, jaw-dropping at the stretch of pale torso revealed by the upwards pull of a sweater.

"What in the nine rings are you doing?"

"One of us needs to get out there to stop your friend and the ... whoever it is with him," Réalta stated. The wooly-pully puddled beside his tire iron in the snow like a discarded seal skin. His hands went to the waist of his pants.

"Aye, one of us, which again has me asking: *what* are you doing?"

Réalta shoved his pants down around his ankles, revealing naked flesh. Another pillar of flame rose in the distance, painting his marble skin a vibrant blue. The streaks of scars shimmered silver as they were caught in the light. He watched, transfixed and too utterly stunned to say anything, as the merman stepped out of his borrowed shoes and pants. Bending at the waist to grab the tire iron and clothes, he marched down the slope, bare feet leaving potholes in the snow.

"I am fast in the water." Réalta shoved the wad of fabric into Keir's arms. A hand flexed, the fingers clawed, and Keir remembered the wicked tips of deadly talons that had so sweetly caressed his skin. In an absentminded gesture, Réalta brushed the line of a scar that ended in a circular pattern. "And have survived many terrible things. I promise I will not hurt your friend, but I cannot say the same for the lorelei."

"Dinnae care about the lorelei." Keir worked the clothing into his right arm and grabbed Réalta. "What I do care about is your decision to play the hero. This isnae any of your concern."

"And how will you get out there before your friend burns his way to the sea?"

"Leave that for me to worry about." Keir thrust the clothes at the merman. "And put your clothes back on, you cannae come with me. I trust Toby, but I dinnae ken the meteomantic. They might turn you in or mention you to the wrong person."

"Do not be absurd."

"Am nae being absurd!" Keir barked. "If you swim out there, if you are seen, C.R.O.W. might learn of you and your kind *if* they dinnae already know. You'll be hunted like I've been sent to hunt the lorelei. Réalta, I'm—" His throat seized, the words choked in the grasp of fear. With his left hand, he worked the sigil to open the Neitherworld. "I'm trying to protect you."

The world tore open before them, howling gusts of arctic wind shrieking into the mortal realm and kicking up the snow at their feet. The Shades snaked free, sweeping through Keir's hair and caressing his arms. They danced around Réalta, studying the merman with the same intensity as their master before coiling around his arms and legs, stretching up his torso to feel the merman. To *know* him.

Réalta held Keir's eyes, never shirking or cringing from the embrace of his Shades. "And who is going to protect you?"

Sixteen

"Focus on your task," Réalta had demanded, sealing the command with a kiss. "Do not look to the sea."

And Keir did not.

Not that he could. The moment he set foot into the Neitherworld, the Dark Witch took over. His softer emotions, his harsher ones, all of them winnowed away until only the Living Shade existed.

It was risky to step this far into his Way, but it was useful. Time spent in his boundless demesne was the Dark Witch equivalent of plunging into a hippocromantic healing sauna. The Shades flocked to his person the moment he stormed into the dark, wrapping around his fingers and soothing the frostbite, reinvigorating the witch as he charged across his midnight plain seeking the Shade of a spalování, a Shade he *knew*.

So long as he had a heading, an anchor point of emotional attachment—his sister, his best friend—Keir could find them in his demesne and use their Shade as a waypoint to keep from getting lost in the boundless expanse. So long as the Dark Witch was in control, finding Toby's Shade would be simple. Child's play among the vast array of skills he possessed.

In a quarter turn he felt the thread of the German witch, in a stride he had latched on, and in a handful of steps he emerged from the Neitherworld. Disoriented, Keir set foot onto the center lane of the Afsluitdijk, immediately slipping on the ice and falling on his arse.

"Ach, feck," he groaned, working his feet beneath him and throwing his arms out for balance as he rose. Ice coated the road in both directions—smooth and treacherous to his right, close to being as invisible as black ice were it not for the blue ribbon of light reflecting over the glass-like surface. The ice was thicker and less uniform to his left, rising in sloped walls that curved inward like a curling wave. The blue light played over ribbed features in the icy hallway, painting a history of flooding and freeze underscored by the sepulchral hum of the now-familiar wind turbines churning massive blades in the distance.

He shivered, unable to ignore the threat of the frozen seas on either side of him. Even the Shades recognized how vulnerable their host was. In the depths of his mind, they allowed the old fear to prickle — it would take only one surge of meteomantic-influenced water rushing over the masterful Dutch engineering to knock the Dark Witch down. One rogue wave to fill his lungs, and he would be drowned.

Witch of the Demesne. A Shade stroked his mind. *Take the Witch of the Demesne.*

The logic was cruel but sound. It was exactly what his sister would have done, which was what needed doing. Shades slipped from his hands, seething from his shoulders and surging from his shadow cast by the blue flame. He sent them crawling over the ice in search of the unknown, needing a location to which he could direct his next steps.

It would be quick work. Detaining a Shade was one of the easiest and wickedest things he could do. An act C.R.O.W. sanctioned when the words "extreme prejudice" were used.

He started toward the plume of cerulean steam, stalking forward two steps when another Shade threw herself against the Dark Witch, playing down the xylophone of his ribs.

Oh, Horned God, seriously? You really need to let me out; this is getting ridiculous. *Save your friend!*

"Friend." The Dark Witch stopped, blinking to clear the Shades from his eyes and scan the road. He glimpsed a lean silhouette within the steam, and his heart plummeted low. "Oh, Goddess. Toby!"

Closer to the steam, the ice shifted from smooth glass to a pocked and ribbed surface, allowing Keir's boots a better grip. White clouds billowed, blinding his path, so he pulled back the Shades he'd sent for the meteomantic, redirecting their course for the spalování and latching onto his familiar Shade. They tugged at the softest bits of the Dark Witch, guiding him through the dense, obscuring steam.

The temperature soared, and the air on the dijk grew humid and heavy the closer he came to Toby's flame. With a burst of eyelash-curling heat, the clouds parted to reveal the witch. Toby's mouth was stern, his body held tight. Though his goal wasn't clear, Keir saw immediately that his eyes blazed. Blue flames licked up the whites and drowned the color, leaving only the tiniest black pinprick of his pupils. Consumed by his task, Toby's skin had taken on a fevered pallor, the signature of a flame witch lost deep, deep within his Way.

Fire shot from his palms as liquid fury, melting the clear, clean ice from the Ijsselmeer as he slowly worked across the dijk. The steam billowed and clouded, swallowing the spalování and revealing the witch standing opposite his flame for half a heartbeat.

Short and stocky, the Witch of the Demesne was dressed as a fisher-man in heavy cable knit and dark, durable trousers. A meteomantic, he had the ruddy skin and scraggly bearded appearance of soft middle age, which, for a witch, meant he was upwards of a century old. Far older than Keir and deeply entrenched in his Way, in the heart of his demesne.

Toby's flames guttered out, the heat vanishing with the retina-searing light and dropping the dijk into subpolar cold. In a heartbeat, Keir's breath clouded in front of his face, the flash of sweat from Toby's flames freezing along his hairline and jaw.

Take him, the Shades demanded; *take the Witch of the Demesne.*

Keir hesitated, glancing over at Toby, then back to the meteomantic, weighing his options. Toby, or the Witch of the Demesne. He needed one of them freed from the lorelei's thrall. He would *prefer* Toby, for obvious reasons, but the Witch of the Demesne was a weather witch in the seat of his power, leaving him no other option but to obey his Shades.

He rushed past Toby with both arms extended, fingers forming the sigil he would need to grab hold of the meteomantic's Shade and rip it free. Water splashed with every step, dampening his rip-stop trousers and clinging the fabric to his legs. At the sound, the meteomantic jerked his attention to Keir. The flash of white teeth beneath a dark beard was all the warning he received. The witch swept an arm in a wide arc and a wave of water rushed up from the Ijsselmeer, cascading down a slide of ice at the end of the road and swallowing Keir's boots. He skidded to a halt, heart pounding and eyes narrowed at the floating cubes bumping against his shins.

This little water can't hurt us, the littlest Shade scoffed.

Mebbe nae, Little Shadow, he named his familiar, the closest thing the Dark Witch had to a conscience. Together, Shade and witch frowned at the frost crawling over the water and the handful of ice cubes. *But that ice is gonnae fuck us up.*

Spinning in place, Keir eyed the water and caught sight of the lane lines painted on the road. Just visible, they ran parallel to the arc of the pale moon rising overhead. Keir dragged his eyes away from the lane lines and the water, frowning at the moon as he chewed his cheek. Then back again to the rising water, the direction from which it had surged, the ice crawling from the meteomantic, and the fact that those lane lines were drawn in the wrong direction ... if he were standing on the dijk proper.

But he wasn't.

Realization struck him all at once.

The moon rose from the east, the lane lines ran east-to-west, but the dijk ran north-to-south. The rise obscuring the Waddenzee wasn't a man-made earthen structure; it was *ice*. A wall of solid ice, just like the berm serving as a waterfall for the Ijsselmeer to flood the overpass *at the end of the road*.

The Afsluitdijk was thirty-two kilometers in length. Toby's signature had placed him sixteen kilometers down at the halfway point on Breezanddijk. The water had come rushing *up* from the end of the road to the east, meaning Keir wasn't standing on the dijk. He was standing on a Horned God-damned overpass crossing *over* the dijk.

Goddess, he'd assumed Toby had been melting the water and creating a low passage for the lorelei to get to the sea and deliver whatever message she had.

He had *assumed* that the Witch of the Demesne was a meteomantic sharing an affinity with water, like his brother-in-law. A witch who had aligned his Way with manipulating humidity and condensation, honing his skills in calling storms and maintaining fluvial plains. *Not* aligning himself with *ice* like the Horned God-damned Disney bastardization of a beloved Danish fairy tale.

But ice is what the huddy bawbag of a witch had chosen. At least now the Dark Witch understood what his aim was. The meteomantic hadn't been surging the waters and calling a storm; he'd been summoning a freeze to drop the temperature and form the ice, using Toby to melt it so it could be reformed and melted again.

They were creating a freshwater bridge for the lorelei.

With an absolute shite sense of timing, Toby's flame roared back to life, aimed at the newly formed ice.

"Ach." Keir turned and ran, shouting Toby's name above the roar of magickal fire. He threw out his hand in the sigil to seize and grabbed Toby's familiar Shade. Clenching a fist, he jerked his arm back and dragged the witch off balance. The spalování faceplanted, flame sizzling and guttering out in an eyebrow singeing cloud of steam. He pushed himself up, red splotches darkening his cheeks, and blue eyes narrowed to gleaming slits at the Dark Witch.

"*Idioten,*" Toby spat, jumping to his feet. He stepped into his Way, palms sizzling as he worked against the nullifying effects of fresh water to bring his flame roaring back to life.

"Toby, I ken you're hoora pissed, but we need to get out of the water." Keir circled his wrist in the air, leashing the spalování with his own Shade. He dragged him through the cooling puddle toward the Waddenzee side of the overpass. Here, the salt-crusted ice formed a low curb that rose out of the frigid water. Keir released his friend, knowing that at any moment, he would be lobbing a ball of ruinous flame at the Dark Witch's back.

He ducked, covering his head with his arms as Toby did just that. The wool of his sweater heated and melted, scalding his neck. Keir whirled and dropped headlong into his Way, doing the only thing he could think of to get the flame witch to stand down.

"*Liomsa.*" Shades shot from his outstretched palm and collided with Toby. They wormed through the wool and wheedled into his skin, navigating the passages between muscle, tendon, and bone. Again, that sensation of squeezing through a too-tight space before the Shades expanded within the spalování, spreading like a parachute to enshroud the center of his being and sew the influence of the Dark Witch into the essence of Toby. Where he had failed with Réalta, time and time again, here the Dark Witch was successful. He gripped Toby's Shade and, with little more than the twitch of an eye, cleaved the witch.

Shadows whipped free from the spalování as Shade severed from Soul and body. He rattled out a gasp, eyes bugging and chest swelling. The Dark Witch absorbed the last tendrils of his Shade, and the German witch's body crumpled.

Another rush of water flooded the overpass, lapping over the toe of his boot to draw his attention to the ground. The spalování burbled at his feet, face down as he was. Any other witch would have been concerned with the poor sod drowning or succumbing to hypothermia and eventual death in the sub-zero temperatures.

The Dark Witch was not any other witch.

What did he care for drownings and death when he had a new Shade to master?

He inhaled deeply, feeling the warmth of the spalování flood his veins. He could not use the fire magick, but there was power in the Shade. Strength in the memory of wielding fire without fear of being burnt. Power in the memory of the pain and pleasure the witch had experienced, and oh — was there a muddled mess of it. Longing and homesickness, yearning, and a sense of fraternity. Love for a sibling lost and for ... the Dark Witch.

He blinked, shaking his head to dispel the fuzzy sensation. It was a well-practiced trick to remind the witch to care and a distraction he could not afford. There was a desecrant somewhere on this bridge and another witch with a Shade to claim. Stalking forward, he froze at a second burbling inhale. Angling his head at the sound, the Dark Witch observed the spalování's pallor paling as hypothermia set in. Ghostly strands of white-blond hair drifted in the water like sea grass caught in a faint current.

He frowned at the wrenching sensation of loss brought on by that still body.

Are you forgetting something? Little Shadow sang.

"This is *absurd*," The Dark Witch spat, crouching low to turn the flame witch onto his back. He worked his arms under the spalování's, straightening legs and hauling the witch up onto the rise of ice. Safely out of the water, he laid him out flat and stood, looming over the witch with a sour twist to his mouth and a puddle of midnight cupped in his left hand. "I suppose you'll be needing this back, aye?"

The spalování said nothing. Not that the Dark Witch expected him to. Witches and mortals alike were bloody useless in this state. No better than toy soldiers awaiting his command, his *permission* to feel again. Until then, they would lie as broken dolls or gloam about moaning without end.

Give it back.

A heavy sigh dropped his shoulders, and the Dark Witch begrudgingly released the spalování's Shade. It trickled between his fingers and dribbled onto the witch's chest, bleeding through damp wool and fevered skin to leak into those too tight spaces and coagulate as a whole.

A leg twitched, a hand jumped, and the spalování lurched back into being, scrabbling over the ice like a crab, bright blue eyes wild with fright. It took him a moment, one the Dark Witch was very annoyed to give, before the spalování calmed himself and rose on shaking legs.

"Shit," he said.

The Dark Witch's brows shot up. "Pardon?"

"Shift. She can *shift*." Toby stormed over, scanning the witch from head to toe, his face masked in fury. "The dark-haired woman from the casemates, you saw her?" The Dark Witch nodded, unable to speak around the rise of bile in his throat. "The lorelei can shift from one form to another; she's been hunting us as we hunt her. The *schlampe* grabbed me this morning; where have you been?"

"Swimming," he replied.

The flame witch stared blankly at him, working his jaw and muttering, "*Dummer verdammter Zauberer.*"

It was so clear. Clear and clean and *obvious*.

The woman sitting at the end of the bar staring pointedly at the witch as he followed the summons to Réalta. The woman in the water, chatting with Toby while Keir had been distracted by the merman's kiss, and the unnamed visitor described by the clerk at the hotel.

The Dark Witch slammed back into himself, name and desires and fears swimming to the surface.

"Wet shoes," Keir murmured, attention drifting to where the meteomantic worked the ice. "There was a puddle of water in the bar. Ach," he slammed his palm against his forehead and groaned, "'course she can bloody shift. Why wouldnae she be able to? Lorelei have haunted their rock on the Rhine for half a millennia; every classical depiction of them is of a beautiful maiden. Not an overgrown piranha that took it upon itself to evolve *legs*."

"Keir," Toby warned, "do not spiral; you need to focus."

He paced the ice, running through every encounter, every manuscript, every gobshite piece of marginalia he'd scoured during the weeks spent chasing the desecrant. None of them had mentioned shifting or even suggested the idea a lorelei might be able to transform herself. Not the tomes kept by the ink witches in Sankt Goarshausen or the Palatinate Coven Library. Not bloody C.R.O.W. and their grimoires.

It was another lie, another omission of fact, to regulate the desecrant and shoe-horn them into a specific place and function. Narrowing the walls and tightening the leash to keep the creature from acting out to the detriment of the witches tasked with keeping her in her place.

Keir's stomach twisted and soured at the parallels between his treatment and hers.

"I cannae do this, Toby." He whipped around to face the spalování. "Cannae cleave a desecrant, not when she's just like … just like …"

"*Ich verstehe,*" Toby gripped his arm. "Can you hold her if she gets close?"

"I dinnae—" Keir stopped himself, remembering how the Shades slipped away from Réalta time and time again. Could he grab hold of the lorelei's Shade? He had yet to try, and she could change her form just like the merman. What if the two were related? Doubt hollowed a pit in his gut. Doubt and the realization that he'd never cleaved a desecrant. Not truly. He had detained them, injured them, delivered them to other members of his team, but cleaving? Ripping their Shade free and bending it to his own will? He shook his head. "I dinnae ken if I can."

Toby frowned. "Before she sings again …"

"Tobe—"

"Any idea why being enthralled by her song feels like when you have hold of my Shade?"

Keir's jaw dropped. The Shades surged protectively, or perhaps defensively, behind his eyes. "Come again?"

Toby blinked, blue eyes going glassy. "The lorelei cannot cross onto dry land, nor can she tolerate the salt. She is not yet on the bridge, but the meteomantic is getting close. Once the overpass is flooded, she will try to cross and deliver her message. You have to stop us." With each word,

Toby's throat seemed to tighten. The humming from the turbines grew louder, and a vein throbbed on his forehead. He ran a hand over his hair, sweeping back the white blond and staring across the overpass. In the absence of flame and steam, the road and frozen seas were illuminated in pale moonlight, reflecting off the ice crawling across the overpass.

"What message?"

"For the witch," Toby intoned. "In the crescent sea." He blinked and dazedly stared at Keir. "Where is your friend?"

"In the water." Keir hooked a thumb over his shoulder, cocking his head at the dream-like quality of Toby's question. Then he glanced back with a frown. "At least, I hope so. What witch?"

"The song took neither of you." Toby wrung out the hem of his sweater, leaving it hanging loose and stretched out. "Why is that?"

"I've nae idea."

Toby cocked his head, studying the Dark Witch with a quiet, thoughtful expression. "He is not like her."

"He is not like anyone or anything I've ever met." He turned his face toward the Waddenzee, distracted by his worry for Réalta and the fear that he'd frozen beneath the ice. Could merfolk tolerate water that cold? He said he'd studied the polar star and the northern lights, which bred confidence, but it was little assurance when Keir couldn't *see* the merman with his own eyes.

"*Meine Göttin*, can you hear her?" Toby took a step. The humming of the turbines rose in pitch, and the overpass rumbled beneath their feet, water sloshing against walls of ice. "So *wunderschön*."

Keir jerked back around. "Tobe?"

He grunted, clutching his head with both hands. Flame burst, gut-tered, and burst again, crowning the spalování in blue. He bent at the waist, forcing words through clenched teeth. "Go, Keir. Get your friend."

"And leave you here?" Keir hissed.

"She is ... distracted, trying to manage myself and the meteomantic. Use that."

"Nae, I'm nae leaving you alone to—"

"Then strip his Shade and mine if you cannot get hers." Toby jerked his face to the Dark Witch, eyes blazing. The blood rushed from Keir's cheeks. For all the years and all the missions and the odious tasks they had handled together, the spalování had never once issued that command. "Can you do it?"

"I—"

"Can you do it and maintain control?"

"Toby—"

"*Ja, oder nein?*"

"*Nein!*" Keir shouted, slashing a hand through the air. Midnight stretched thin between them before bursting and drifting away like smoke. He'd stepped too far already and had barely been able to come back to himself before leaving Toby to drown in three inches of water like a mad Bavarian king. "I cannae, not without losing myself."

"Then go and seek out your friend. Use him as your anchor." Toby straightened, gliding through the water. Blue flame licked up his wrists. His voice rose above the humming in a haunting, dream-like tone. "She is calling for me. *Meine Göttin*, it is beautiful."

"Shite. Hang on, Tobe." Keir turned his back, nerves speeding him across an overpass lit by the moon, stars, and an eldritch flame. Each footfall cracked the newly formed ice and brought him nearer to the Waddenzee and Réalta.

A fist of wind howled off the Ijsselmeer, slamming into his back. It knocked him off balance, and the witch stumbled over the frozen ripple of a wave. He skidded and slipped on the ice, pinwheeling his arms and calling on the Shades to keep him upright. The frozen walls he had mistaken for berms fell away on either side to reveal the on-ramp for the causeway.

Keir threw his hands down, twisting his wrists and pulling Shades up to brace his thighs and wrap around his waist. He severed enough of himself to add weight and body to the smoke-like summonings. The Shades pulled taut, slowing his momentum but nowhere near enough to stop him entirely. He threw his hands forward, catching himself against a red-and-white striped barricade at the end of the road. The force of his collision rocked the barricade back onto two of its four legs, and together, they teetered at the edge of an overpass still under construction.

There was no guardrail or fenceline, and the road fell to nothing, revealing a straight drop to the hard-packed Waddenzee twenty feet below. A sheet of ice stretched out to the horizon, meeting the winter night as a harsh clashing of white and black.

Heartbeat slamming in his ears, Keir wasted one last clear thought to calculate how much it would hurt when he toppled off the bridge. In a rush of wind and cold, the Shades tightened around his waist, struggling against his weight and that of the barricade.

"Let go," they grunted in his ear, barely audible over the roar of blood and fright.

Keir willed his fingers to release the barricade, and the sudden loss of his weight was like the snapping of a rubber band. The barricade teetered and fell over the side of the overpass while he and the Shades flew backward. They tumbled onto the ice with twinned groans of pain, and only then did it register that the Shades could not talk.

SEVENTEEN

"For a not-human, you certainly are acting stupid." Réalta lay pinned on the ice and salt by the lanky witch. He tightened his arms around Keir's waist, face visible from the corner of his eye. The remains of the third eyelid blinked before it vanished, and black eyes stared up at the clear sky and stars overhead. The merman's muscles twitched and bunched in a full-body shiver, jolting Keir into action. He jumped to his feet, grabbing the merman by still-blue wrists and panicking at all the nakedness.

"You're naked."

"Magnificently stupid." The tendons on his neck pulsed as a smooth stretch of skin swallowed the last of the gills.

"You cannae be out here *naked*." Keir swept his hands down Réalta's arms, rubbing his palms up and down the limbs and wiping away a faint pink foam that had accumulated over scratches and puncture marks. "Goddess, what happened?"

"I was delayed."

"How did you *get here*," Keir nearly shrieked.

"Tire iron."

"That ice has to be at least a foot thick."

"There was a boat." The merman shrugged out of Keir's hands and cradled his cheeks. The tips of talons not yet swallowed by fingers prickled his jaw. "Docked in the harbor," Réalta explained as if that explained it. He jerked his head toward the man-made harbor on the Waddenzee side of the dijk.

"Was a boat," Keir repeated.

"I saw the flashes of light from below and used the anchor to break through the ice." Réalta shuddered, his normally stoic expression wavering with something akin to fear.

"What happened to the tire iron?" Keir asked. "And what do you mean 'there *was* a boat'?"

"It is still there," he admitted, "only, it is no longer at the dock. That is how I was injured; the squid dragged it down into the depths."

Keir blinked. Blinked again. "Sorry, did you say 'squid'?"

"A very large one."

"A *Kraken?*" Keir pressed a hand on top of his head. The swells in the salted ice made a hideous sense now, and the knowledge that Réalta had been swimming in the sea with a Horned God-damned Kraken made his stomach churn. "Ohhhh, that is far worse than *each-uisce*."

"Sneezing already." Réalta peered at him, concern drawing a line between his brows. "I told you not to be out here in the cold."

"What? Nae, Toby said her message was for a witch—what would the lorelei want with a Kraken?"

"Perhaps he was to deliver the message to the witch?"

Keir stepped out of Réalta's hands and dropped his gaze low. Lower. "And where did you get those shoes?"

"I took them from the boat."

"*Ó, a Bhandia, tabhair neart dom.*" He rubbed his temples and dropped low, tugging his laces and pulling off his boots.

"Keir—"

"Bloody baltic out here," he grumbled, wriggling out of his rip-stop pants and tossing them at the merman. They slapped against his muscular chest and fell to the ground. "Gonnae freeze your baws off. Cannae have a mer-sicle to worry about while I try to capture a lorelei."

"So you discard your pants?"

Keir rose to his full height, salt and ice crusting his socks as he strode to the merman. Stopping only when they were nose-to-nose.

"*Put. Them. On,*" he seethed, livid and worried and *frightened*. "Dinnae fancy asking you twice."

Réalta's nostrils flared, a keen light flashing in those dark eyes. Holding Keir's livid gaze, he ducked low. Intentionally brushing his chest against the witch's stomach, his thighs. Réalta grabbed the discarded pants without releasing Keir from that intense stare. Just as slowly, he straightened.

"My body is well-suited to the cold." His breath puffed warm and soft against Keir's cheek, voice a low, delicious rumble beneath the panicked humming that had sharpened to a tinnitus-like ringing. "But for you, I will wear these."

"Thank you," Keir exhaled, shaving off the barest amount of his Shade to brace himself against the cold. Because it was *heavy* cold, standing there in his boxer briefs as he was. He steadied Réalta while the merman stepped into the tactical pants, filling him in on all he'd learned and what Toby had told him.

Bright, caustic blue flared from the far end of the overpass as he spoke, and in the pocket of the pants Réalta now wore, Keir's E.R.I.E. began shrieking its alarm. He thrust his hand into the pocket, earning a startled grunt from the merman, and retrieved the device, lighting up the screen to read the scan.

"Meteomantic and spalování — Toby," he amended, holding the mobile between them. "There's nae sign of the desecrant signature next to them."

"Can you help your friend from here?"

"Nae." He tucked the phone in a pocket on his sleeve. "She wasnae on the bridge yet, but Toby said the meteomantic was close. Any minute she could —" Cold lapped at his shins, flooding into his unlaced boots. Keir looked down as another wave of near-freezing water hugged his legs. "Aaaaand that's our minute up." He blurted the slip-shod plan as it formed. "I need tae disarm Toby and the meteomantic. Get them out from under the lorelei's thrall and keep her from crossing the bridge to deliver her message."

"What do you need me to do?"

Keir could have kissed the merman for that question if the timing weren't so piss-poor. Not a hint of doubt nor shred of fear laced those words. Only support and unwavering trust that the witch knew what he was doing, what he needed to do. It was enough to make a man swoon, which he did. Quietly. Firing a silent prayer to the Triple Goddess, asking for the time to thank the merman properly. Later. Right now, he needed Réalta to—

"Anchor me." Keir swallowed. "If I cannae bring myself back after handling the lorelei and the other ... man, I'll need a-a reminder of—"

Réalta tugged Keir forward, catching his mouth with a kiss. Hard against the lips until the witch opened to him. He swept in, fierce and unyielding. Stealing the oxygen from the world until Keir's head spun, and his heart hammered wildly in his chest. He pulled away, grazing teeth along the witch's lower lip and chuckling at the moan it dragged free. "Would that work?"

"Oh, aye." Keir shivered. He leaned back from the merman and ran a hand down his face. "Am nae gonnae be distracted. Not in the slightest." He eyed Réalta and huffed a tiny laugh. "The promise in your lips might be enough to keep me grounded altogether."

"Then be a good boy and behave," he rumbled in reply. Parts of Keir that had no business being acknowledged at a time like this puckered at those words. One specific part of his anatomy became *very* obviously interested. Réalta noticed this and released his grip on Keir's arm, dropping his hand to squeeze his hip. "Go, I will be right behind you."

"Goddess, you say the sweetest things." Keir grinned and stepped back, shaking out his hands and stretching his neck. "If she gets past me ..."

"I will stop her."

Another pillar of flame shot up, raising a cloud of steam that obscured the far end of the overpass. As before, Toby's shadow stretched long against the white cloud, marking his location at the far end of the overpass. Giving his hands one last shake, Keir summoned the shadeblades and mustered the last of himself.

Are you there, Little Shadow?

Always, the Shade unspooled from behind his ribs, creeping up to peer over a shoulder. Behind him, Réalta let out a choked gasp at the appearance of a shadow curling around Keir's arm. *Oh, he's cute when he's surprised.*

Keir winked at the merman, tucking a smile into the corner of his mouth. "Even cuter when he sleeps."

Réalta blinked. Keir smiled and put his back to the merman. *Yell at me if I go too far, Little Shadow.*

Always.

The Shades flooded his vision, painting the world in charcoal and gray. Fine threads wove through the air, leading across the icy expanse to the form of a flame witch burning the world. The Dark Witch followed those threads and spread his lips in a wide, terribly sharp grin. "It's showtime."

One step, another, and another until the witch ran across the overpass. Water flooded his boots, slogging his stride, but on he ran. Twenty feet from his target, he threw out a handful of shadeblades, snagging Toby with each arrow-sharp shadow.

His cry of pain fell on emotionless ears. The Dark Witch easily ducked the wild flight of a blue fireball, dropping into a slide and snarling as shards of ice bit into his bare skin. Just as quickly, he was up and running headlong into the steam. His hand worked a sigil, and Shades streaked free, seeking their own among the billowing white. They silently shrieked through the air and collided against an unknown, a Shade not yet brought to heel. Ribbons of black wrapped around the meteomantic, tasting his fears and woes and sipping his joys, learning his Shade to create a waypoint in the nothing.

The Dark Witch grinned wider, finishing his sigil in the empty air and stepping into the dark—

—through the dark—

—and directly in front of the portly Witch of the Demesne.

The meteomantic was deep into his Way, burbling intent from swollen, purple lips as he worked sigils with frostbitten fingers at the end of an outstretched arm. He yelped at the sudden appearance of a Dark Witch — a thing of nightmares, a story told to little witchlings as a warning of the Forbidden and Foule—striding out of the nothing.

The black smoke of the Neitherworld tainted the pristine white steam. Serpentine stygian tongues lashed out, reaching for the Witch of the Demesne to drag him into the boundless expanse that was their home.

"*Alsjeblieft!*" The meteomantic quivered. Crystals formed at his fingertips, and an icicle emerged from his palm. He sobbed, arms jouncing as he fought against using his Way. His sweater strained against burly arms, and he pleaded with the over-tall terror looming before him. "*Laat me stoppen.*"

The Dark Witch hesitated, calling out to his legion, *Do any of you speak Dutch?*

A chorus of, *No!*, rang across the Neitherworld.

He rolled all-black eyes and widened his terrible grin, smoke curling from his lips as he bent closer to the witch. "Boo."

The meteomantic pissed himself.

"Pitiful." Clawing his hand, the Dark Witch slammed it over the center of the meteomantic's chest. Nails digging through cable knit to press against his sternum. "*Liomsa.*"

Cleaving the witch took less than a thought, and when the Dark Witch pulled his hand away, the paunchy Dutchman teetered forward and splashed face-first into the water.

The water, Little Shadow prompted.

The Dark Witch stared down at the body.

Don't forget about the water, dummy.

He prodded the body with the toe of his boot. When the thick witch did not move, the Dark Witch crouched and turned him over, staring blankly down into a sputtering face. A wet, rattling breath left his lips, and the Dark Witch dropped his head back. "Ach, aye. The breathing."

Goddess, you're the worst.

"That's why I have you," he replied. Assuring himself that the meteomantic's Shade was secure, the Dark Witch rose and scanned the steam cloud. It was warmer at this end of the overpass, damp and muggy like a Finnish sauna the nearer he was to the spalování with his ridiculous blue flame. Still, silly as it was, the Dark Witch was poorly dressed for the weather, and he half dreaded taking the spalování's Shade.

Again.

It would be bloody cold without it. Though he could not feel the cold this deep in his Way, his body was not impervious. And the job was the job, and it needed doing.

The Dark Witch shook out his arms, running his fingers through the sigils. He backed up a step, water sloshing at his knees as he turned to face the steam.

A taloned hand swept out of the cloud, and the lorelei came shrieking her song behind it. She caught him across the chest, wool parting beneath razor-sharp claws. Warmth blossomed over his heart, followed by the delayed sensation of distant pain.

The Dark Witch gasped, staggering back stunned before a decade of training took over. He plummeted headfirst into his Way, releasing the Shades to restrain the desecrant. The pain from her blow became a distant memory, and any fright he might have felt was successfully packed away for another day. There was only the desecrant. Only the job.

Shadeblades flew from his hand, battering against and through the lorelei, shredding the pieces of *her*. Her song rose to a fever pitch, no longer an irritating humming but the heinous discordant clamor of keys that had rattled his head so thoroughly only days before.

Still, the Dark Witch was relentless, a roiling storm intent on destroying the desecrant. He bound her in his Way, wrapping shadow around her wrists, neck, and waist, corrupting the beauty of the Shades into something wicked and cruel. He fueled them with his fear and terror, feeding the lorelei every minute of every day that the witch thought he would be found out, that he would be discovered and detained by the Fine and Faire witches of C.R.O.W. He imbued the Shades with shreds of his tortured self and drowned the lorelei in utter dismay. Urging her to surrender to the inevitable—that she was wicked. She was cruel, Forbidden and Foule, and she would be eradicated.

The desecrant howled her rage, clawing at the Shades and slicing open her own mottled, soggy green skin instead. Thick, oily blood oozed from the wounds, piranha sharp teeth gnashing as over-wide eyes like boules glimmered vividly in the blue light. What remained of her song was a gallows cry, but still, she fought, slipping an arm free, ducking beneath a ribbon of midnight, and lunging for the Dark Witch. Her talons opened bloodied seams along his thighs, shredded his sleeve, and tore a gash at the collar of his wooly-pully. The jutting bones in her legs dug into the Dark Witch's waist as her teeth latched onto his shoulder, chomping up the side of his neck, breaking the skin, and raising bruises.

He grabbed at her, hands slipping off of skin slick like algae and coming away coated in a viscous mucus that disallowed any solid grip. Curling his hand into a fist, he pommeled the side of her head instead. A quick succession of jabs stunned the lorelei enough that she let go, splashing down in the now knee-deep water streaming across the overpass. The Dark Witch snarled, thrusting his hands into the water to grab the desecrant—and felt nothing.

He rose and whirled, fanning water out in all directions. On the Ijsselmeer side of the bridge, the spalování worked his flame, melting the ice walls to flood the road. The meteomantic was still down, and Little Shadow quietly wondered if the witch was any good at floating. The Dark Witch ignored her, shedding a handful of Shades like a cloak. They bled into the water, diluting themselves into a thin miasma just beneath the surface, and—*there.*

Clawing his fingers, he took hold of the Shades and coalesced them into a jagged point of shadow aimed directly at the lorelei. A simple hex, a quick binding, and a severing of Shade from Soul and body. A task he had performed countless times to countless Shades, claiming them as his own and bringing them to heel before their rightful master. It would work; it had to work because if it didn't, he did not know what to do.

"*Mianach.*" He clenched his left hand into a fist and jerked his arm from the water. "*Liomsa.*" Ready to absorb the Shade of the lorelei and be done with this nasty business, except —

Nothing came. No newly severed Shade. No desecrant.

"*Liomsa!*" He snarled, plunging his arm into the water. The caustic blue flame died and winked out, the steam dissipated into the winter night, and the Dark Witch glared at the star-strewn waters. "*Liomsa.*"

His Shades reached and reached again, brushing against the desecrant and slipping away. An aggravated growl left him feeling scraped raw. How dare the Shades fail; how *dare* the desecrant not obey him. It was unfathomable. He was the Dark Witch. A thing of nightmares sent by C.R.O.W. How *dare* she refuse to submit herself before him?

"Keir?" A voice rumbled at his back, familiar and foreign. He angled his face to the side, spotting a muscular, moon-pale figure. Again, Little Shadow whispered. A name this time, the reminder of an anchor, a lodestar in the night. The Dark Witch heard this, saw the man—*no, not a man*—approaching, and disregarded him as Not a Threat.

"*Liomsa,*" he growled, both hands in the water now. Seeking and seeking the lorelei with every Shade that he was and willing to empty the Neitherworld to send out more. He would make of himself little more than a gateway for unholy terror to bleed into the world, all for the sake of succeeding where he always failed. He would cleave this bloody desecrant. He had to. It was what he *did*. It was all he was good at—stepping too far into his Way, working too much magick Forbidden and Foule, and if he couldn't do this one bloody thing, what use was he to C.R.O.W.? "*Liomsa.*"

"Keir, you need to stop."

A heavy hand came down on his shoulder. The Dark Witch snarled, jumping to his feet and darting away, only to drop to his knees and begin anew. The Shades were there; *she* was there, just out of reach. If he could grab hold of the lorelei, then he could sever the Shade. Cleave the bloody desecrant like C.R.O.W. wanted him to. He could go home and leave this dijk behind. Leave this job behind, and then maybe he could *live*. Use his degree to help the desecrants who did not deserve the fate C.R.O.W. had chosen for them. All he had to do was this one thing and he could be free.

"Let her go, Keir."

You should listen to him.

"I cannae," he sobbed. The Dark Witch *sobbed*, spooling more of himself from the skein and surpassing the rigid bounds of control he kept himself within. Just a little more of his Way, of himself. A little more, and he could reach her, could end her, could escape the perpetual hell that was his life. Just a little more, and then he was falling, falling too far into his Way, and soon there would be nothing left of the man and all too much of the Dark Witch.

Too Much.

"Oh, Keir," Rai shook her head, deep brown eyes wide and wary, *"it's too much."*

"It's too much," he rasped, splaying fingers wide in the water. Shades shot out in all directions, blotting out the reflection of the moon and stars.

The Dark Witch juddered to a halt mid-descent into the shady depths of his Way. He blinked at the boundless expanse of power untouched. The triskelion sigil on his chest burned, a final reminder of what he was, what C.R.O.W. had made of him, and he severed his Shades.

The sudden release jerked him back to the surface, reeling Keir into himself like a fish on a line. A wet cry rose from the far end of the bridge and a portly form lurched up from the water only to collapse back in a heap. Elsewhere, a Shade joined his roiling horde for the briefest instant and was released. "Goddess," Keir sobbed. "It's too much, and I cannae"—he gasped. Hiccuped—"I couldnae —"

Keir sank to the ground, curling over himself as frigid water swallowed him to the waist. Without Toby's fire, the temperature was dropping rapidly. His teeth started chattering, and his muscles twitched and danced as a full-body shiver set it, but his sorrows drowned the cold. The effect of falling too far, experiencing too much, and *failing*.

Réalta dragged him to his feet, walking Keir back towards the Waddenzee. Goddess, the water was over their knees now, and neither was a small man. The lorelei had gotten close to burning out Toby and making a human popsicle out of the meteomantic. Too close and still, Keir had failed.

"Did you free your friend?"

All he could do was nod and sob. Covering his face with his hands, his legs barely able to hold his weight. She was gone. The lorelei was gone, and what would C.R.O.W. say after all of this?

"The meteo—the other man?"

"Fine," Keir croaked. "They're fine. I got their Shades, gave them back."

"And you came back." Réalta turned the witch to face him. Elegant fingers brushed his hair back and away from his face and pressed against his jaw, forcing Keir to look at him. "You came back. There was no death today. This is good."

"I failed."

"This is *good*," The merman doubled down. "She has not crossed the bridge; you have not had to kill her. Is that not what you wanted?"

"She'll try again."

"Let her," Réalta stated. "Her message will not make it to the ocean. My folk will see to that."

"Réalta—"

"Keir." He tipped their foreheads together, black eyes to black eyes. "Soon, this water will freeze. Unless your Toby wishes to light his fire again, we must seek shelter."

"Toby," the witch repeated, dazed. "Toby." His best friend's name jarred a loose screw back into place. "Toby!"

"Keir?" The spalování's voice called from the other end of the bridge. Distant but alive. Angry, even. "Keir, *wo bist du*?"

"Here!" He hollered, turning out of Réalta's arms. "We're over here." He stepped away from the merman, an arm raised to hail his friend, and the lorelei rushed up from the water.

Talons outstretched and her face a vivid mask of fury, she latched onto the Dark Witch. Clawing and shrieking, her razor-sharp nails scored the side of his scalp. Keir staggered back, struggling to get his hands on the algae-slick desecrant. She was too fast, too furious in her near defeat.

Her teeth tore at his left shoulder, turning his begun intent into a ragged cry. Those talons struck again and again, forcing the witch back and back and back.

He barely registered the merman shouting and his attempts to grab hold of the desecrant. Barely noticed the change in the surface beneath his retreating feet from sloshing water to crackling, salt-capped ice to gravel. He was too busy fighting to keep the lorelei from gouging out an eye or wrenching a finger free from his casting hand. Unable to land a solid punch to buy himself a second to think and then —

Nothing.

Nothing at his back, nothing beneath him, behind him.

Nothing but frigid wind and the lorelei's ruined song in his ear.

Eighteen

"Keir!" Réalta's voice followed him over the edge, with a glimpse of over-wide dark eyes on a moon-pale face. His name and then a sickening *crack.*

Pain exploded across the back of his skull. Utter, blinding pain warbling down his neck and out from his shoulder, his hip. The wind *whooshed* from his lungs at the impact, and try as he might, Keir could not breathe. He was drowning again, only this time on top of the ice and not in the watery depths below.

Dark Witch?

Out of the corner of his eye, he made out the shape of the fallen barricade tipped on its side, one end higher than the other, and he understood. Despite his pain, he felt a curious warmth coating the back of his skull, puddling under his neck, and he understood.

The heavy weight of the barricade, a fall from that height, the newly formed ice.

Goddess, he understood.

Dark Witch, get up. Little Shadow sounded far away, her voice small and scared. *Please, get up.*

The lorelei gurgled beside him, moving over the ice with wet, fizzing sounds like baking soda doused with vinegar. Keir tried to turn his head, and the world flashed red, sending a lightning bolt down his right arm that tingled in his fingertips. Something was wrong, desperately wrong, and the lorelei was coming, and he couldn't get his hands to form sigils. Couldn't get enough air to hiss his intent.

Get up!

She moved again, dragging herself across the salt-covered ice with high-pitched keens. Keir raised a knee, gritting his teeth against the pain the effort earned. The lorelei lifted her head, that terrible visage now twisted in fear and anguish rather than rage. She saw him trying to move and panicked, throwing herself at the witch.

Elbows and knees slammed into his broken body. Keir bellowed, a jagged, throat-scouring cry cut off by a hideous *CRACK*.

It was the sound of his death stalking across the ice, shaking his bones as a loud boom that the witch felt more than heard.

The ice beneath him gave, dropping Keir an inch, two, and then he fell again, this time in horrific slow motion.

Frozen, black waters swallowed the witch and the desecrant, dragging them to their mutual doom. Keir was a heavy witch, made of dense muscle and bone, further weighed down by a lorelei. She began writhing the moment her body hit the saltwater. Algae-slick skin fizzed and foamed, hardening to a crust. She latched onto the witch as though he could swim them both to the surface, but her weight was an anchor, sending them deeper with every passing second.

Still, he fought, scaling his one good arm at the water and weakly cycling his legs. He fought against the pain, against the weight of the dying lorelei, reaching for a surface that pulled further and further away until the little bit of light that trickled through their hole in the ice was blotted out altogether.

At least this means the end of the lorelei, Little Shadow proposed. *Oh! And your Shade can come hang out with me all of the time, and not some of the time. So it's not a complete loss?*

Keir laughed. Or sobbed. There was no way to tell beyond the bubbles in front of his face. The water he swallowed was beyond cold, the shock prompting a second gasp, a third. His body seized beneath the weight of the lorelei, twitching and jerking like a marionette puppeted by a palsy victim. Still, they sank. Deeper and deeper into the Waddenzee where a Kraken awaited the message that would never come.

A current rushed past, buffeting Keir to the side. Then again, and the lorelei was pried off of him, the absence of her drowning weight a momentary reprieve. He was too tired to drag his arm in the water, too hurt to kick, too *useless* to do anything but drown.

Hands braced against his back, prickling fingers dug into his aching body, and then he was surging through the water. Up, up, up, too fast to keep his eyes open. He broke through the surface, all but tossed onto the ice before a hand cradled the back of his head, and he was rolled onto his back. The motion spun the world, blurring the black-and-white line between sea and sky into a nauseating Fraser spiral.

It hurt, it hurt so Horned God-damned bloody bad. His brain was pounding in a skull three times too small, but that was nothing, *nothing* compared to the pounding against his sternum. Jarring his body again and again in a rhythm he could almost place, the knowledge of the *what* slipping through his fingers and vanishing altogether. A warm, plush mouth pressed against his. Air filled his cheeks, struggling down his throat.

"Breathe, Keir."

Breathe, Dark Witch. You need to breathe.

The pounding resumed. Stopped. More air forced itself into his lungs, filling Keir with a desperation that brought him clawing back into himself.

A wheeze left his lips, rattling in his chest, and the pounding stopped. In his chest, not his head. His fingers and toes were numb, his joints felt swollen and close to bursting, and his head swam—dizzy from the drowning and the fall, throbbing from the head wound. It left him too disoriented to fully comprehend what was happening beyond the passing thought that the come down from a betel nut high was far more preferable than *this*.

"Keir," a hand cradled his face. "Look at me, Keir." He tried, Triple Goddess, he tried to look at the source of that voice, but his eyes wouldn't focus. They burned beneath his contacts, and his vision blurred at the impossible sight, and Goddess he *hurt*. "Keir, good boy, look at me."

"Cannae," his protest escaped as a wheeze, which made the pain in his head explode, and the world blurred to black. Unconsciousness dragged him under, warmer and softer than the water he'd been dying in. Fuzzy like a blanket in which Keir would happily remain wrapped.

A painful jounce of his skull jerked him screaming back into consciousness.

Be careful!

"Careful," a new voice hissed. "Get him out of the water." A hand slipped beneath his head, and Keir and the voice hissed together. "*Meine Göttin*, what happened?"

"He fell," that first voice again, warm and threaded with worry. Hands gripped his calves, needle-like pricks digging into the cramping muscle, and Keir was pushed away. His fingers flexed, reaching for the source of those hands. "She attacked from the water. It was too fast for me, on land, the gravity—"

"He fell from the overpass?"

He knew that voice almost as well as he knew his own. Toby. His friend and his keeper. Toby, with his fire and his desire to burn the evil out of the world.

A coddling warmth blossomed over the center of his chest as though he heard Keir's thoughts fizzle into being. He struggled to open his eyes, wincing at the caustic burn of the spalování's blue flame. As much as it hurt his eyes, it was a welcome heat.

"Get out of the water," Toby directed to the other voice. "My flame is enough to warm you both."

"I can tolerate the cold better in this form." The hands at his legs slipped free, and in the next moment, strong fingers laced through his own. The palm that settled against the back of his hand was warm and wet. An odd webbing braced his knuckles as talons prickled against his palm. Keir twitched and tried to sit up, groaning at the pain the attempt sent lancing through his body. A weight pressed down on his chest, and warm breath crashed against his ear. "Be still. Do not hurt yourself more."

Don't be stupid, Dark Witch.

And he obeyed. What choice did he have when the darkness consumed him once again?

"—went down with him, his wounds ..."

A finger trailed Keir's neck. He moaned, beyond pain and relieved at that soothing voice dragging him back to wakefulness. The weight that had pressed down on his sternum remained warm and heavy. A comfort amidst the pain. None of this made any sense. The pain, the drowning, the lorelei. How did he get out of the water? He couldn't swim; the lorelei was a dead weight, but here he was, freezing on the—his fingers twitched, flattening against rough gravel.

Gravel?

"She is nowhere in the depths; the salt must have destroyed her."

"That quickly?"

There was a long silence that stretched between Toby and the voice that dragged Keir in the direction of life like a pole star.

The weight readjusted, and Keir belatedly realized it was an arm draped over his chest. The fingers of a large hand were splayed over his heart, rubbing gently to stimulate his nerves and blood flow.

"How," he rasped. Toby stood a short distance away. He jerked around at the sound of Keir's voice, his face a hazy collection of features capped by bright blue orbs where his eyes should be.

"*Leise bitte*, Keir," he advised, striding purposefully over and dropping to meet the Dark Witch's cloudy-eyed stare. "We had to move you off of the ice. I know the gravel is uncomfortable, but this was the only place Réalta would not have to change." *Réalta*. The word was a balm and a guiding light, calling Keir's blurry gaze to the being beside him. He squinted, seeking out the strong features that had turned to watercolor swatches from saltwater in his contacts and pain blurring the world. "C.R.O.W. is on the way with a team of hippocromantics."

"C.R.OW.," he managed to force out of a choked throat. "Nae, they cannae—"

Goddess turning his head *hurt*. *Why* did it hurt so bad? He only wanted to see the face attached to the voice calling him back. To burn Réalta into the backs of his eyelids and remember the sweeps of his cheekbones instead of the blurry nothing that he saw instead.

"Be still," Réalta rumbled, his voice wide and worried.

You should listen to him. Little Shadow bloomed across his chest, her silken cold trailing around Keir's neck like a brace. *You hurt yourself real bad, Dark Witch.*

Réalta cradled the witch's cheek in his hand, angling his head back and setting it down gently. Pain from the movement had Keir's eyes watering, blurring his vision even more. "You fell a very long way and landed on the ice. The injury to your head is—" water sloshed as he bent forward, dark tendrils of hair falling as a curtain to obscure Toby from view.

It's really bad, Dark Witch. Like, really *bad.*

"You did so well, Kee-ear." Lips dusted his forehead and his nose. "So brave and so fragile. Be a good boy and remain still."

Keir fought to raise a hand, wanting to cup the cheek of a statue come to life, but his arms weren't working. His hand wouldn't move more than a few sad inches, and the herald of Réalta's voice was so impossibly beautiful that it couldn't be real. None of this could be real. It was the dream of a dying man. He was still trapped beneath the ice, grappling with the lorelei even in death.

A shrill klaxon broke through the labored silence, drilling its wail into Keir's skull. He groaned, heels kicking uselessly in the gravel. Réalta dragged his face away to look up at Toby.

"They are here," the spalování sighed, gently gripping Keir's shoulder. Distantly, he noted the trembling in Toby's fingers and the high tightness in his voice. Fear, he realized, worry for him.

Toby rose, stepping away from the pair. He raised his arm and shot a ball of blue flame into the air, a flare telling the hippocromantics their location. Keir whimpered, willing his mouth to work, and Toby glanced back at the sound, his voice shaking as he pleaded. "Hold on, Keir. Just a little bit longer."

"Nae—"

"Keir." Réalta swept a hand down his arm, threading their fingers together. "It is alright, they will help you. Be still."

"Nae, you cannae, they cannae" —Goddess, words wouldn't form— "Tobe, please." Thoughts wouldn't take root. There was only panic and fright. The sickening feeling that something terrible was about to happen and he needed to warn Réalta that ... that ... "Dinnae let them see."

"*Scheisse*," Toby blurted. He jogged over, hollering as he ran. "Réalta, you need to leave."

"What?!"

"You have to go, now, before they see you."

Réalta tore his hand away, pressing his fists into the gravel and straightening as much as he was able. From the corner of his shit vision, Keir noted the dark cast to his skin shimmering beneath Toby's flame. Blue light curved along the stretch of Réalta's backside half submerged in water and the deep, onyx-black fin where his legs would be. A large, powerful fluke kicked up as the merman argued with the spalování. "Are you as stupid as a human?"

Keir worked his mouth, trying to form the words, but the approaching siren was too loud, the argument between Réalta and Toby too fast. The cacophony drowning out the world in soothing, blissful black.

No. Nonono, stay awake.

"You want me to leave him?"

"Either that or change. *Jetzt.*" Toby hissed. Flashing lights strobed across the landscape, painting a jumble of stones in red and white. "They do not know what you are, and Keir does not want them to know."

"Réalta." Horned God, was that his voice? It was so quiet. Wispy. As intangible as a Shade. But the merman heard it. He ripped his glare away from Toby and dropped his elbows, working closer to Keir. "Please."

"No begging," the merman hovered over him, filling the world. "Not from you."

"Please," he wheezed. The world dimmed at the rise of sound as his battered, broken body sought to protect itself. "Go."

"No, no, Keir." He shook his head, wide, black eyes rounding.

"Dinnae let them leash you," the witch managed. Toby let out a sound stuck between aggravation and woe. "Please."

"No begging."

"Den Helder," the spalování snapped. "At Fort Erfprins. They will take him to the hippocromantic hospital there." Tires crunched over gravel, doors slamming as choppy, Dutch voices shouted over the klaxon. "Now, *go*." He whirled around, arms waving over his head as he shouted back to the witch doctors.

"I will find you," the merman promised. He dropped low to seal the oath against Keir's lips. "Look to the sea." He pressed a last, gentle whisper of a kiss against the witch's mouth. "But for your god's sake, stop going in the water."

"Good advice," Keir murmured, shoving all of his strength into raising his hand. It dropped against the base of Réalta's back, where marble-smooth skin fused into slick, enticing scales. "Cannae swim."

The merman huffed, and in the last waking moment before unconsciousness swept in, Keir saw him smile.

Nineteen

He rose and fell out of the dark. The journey to the hospital passed in a series of vignettes, clouded and fuzzy at the edges like a silent film scored by his screams and howls.

In one, fluorescent lights burned his eyes. The ambulance jostled his broken body, and he struggled against hands that groped his arms and pinned his legs. The light vanished, the Dark Witch succumbing to his trauma only to surge into consciousness as they set his bones. An explosion of pain had him seeing red, and he was under again, floating in a narcotized nothing until the gurney jostled on a curb and an achingly familiar voice called him back to life.

"Get me the bloody corpomantic, immediately. And call Cyrus!"

"A chronomantic is not what he needs," Toby argued, his stark features coming into focus. Lights whooshed overhead, and the gurney juddered through another set of doors, jolting every painful broken bone in his body. "Treat him, Lou, do not try to reverse the damage."

"This wouldn't have happened if you'd stepped in earlier, *Tobias*." Blue-green eyes gleamed in the harsh light, flitting over Keir before widening in horror. "The bleeding isn't stopping. Oh, Goddess, why isn't the bleeding stopping?"

End scene. Cut to black. Fade in, tight shot on a popcorn ceiling.

"There was a man, a—"

"A staid," Lou spat.

"A desecrant," Toby whispered. Silence. A hissed inhale from Lou before her cool hand settled on his arm.

"Bloody fool."

"C.R.O.W. cannot know," Toby pressed. "And you know how he gets with drugs in his system."

"Chatty." Lou's hand tightened on his arm. "Are you asking me to do what I think you are asking me to do?"

"You're the only witch who can do it without their interference."

Her grip on his arm eased. When his sister spoke next, Keir's addled mind thought he heard pleasure where there should have been pain. "He'll hate you for this if he ever finds out."

Toby sighed, and in a last conscious moment, Keir heard him mutter, "Then it is one more thing you can hold over me."

Wake up.

This time, the lights faded up slowly, revealing gray shapes developing like a tin type. The world remained fuzzy at the edges as an unfamiliar face leaned in close, shining a light in one eye, the other, before pressing Keir's eyelids closed with a hand.

Oh, please, please wake up.

"Can't you hurry?" Lou demanded from elsewhere in the room. "I've a plane to catch."

"Give me a minute, kiddo." An unfamiliar voice replied, the accent American. Southern. That much Keir could place. "This sort of thing takes time." Cool metal from a ring on his finger gently grazed Keir's eyelid. The weight of that hand kept him blind, but Keir wanted to see, wanted to know. How bad was it? What was wrong with him? Why couldn't he move his arms and legs, and *where* was Réalta?

"Where—"

"He's gone, Keir." Lou's slender hand slipped into his, her lilting voice singing like a lullaby in his ear. "But he'll be back. I promise."

Dread overtook him, panic at the fear that Réalta hadn't gotten away in time. He was supposed to go, supposed to swim far away from C.R. O.W. before they learned what he was. *Who* he was. She couldn't know because if Lou knew, then C.R.O.W. knew, and if C.R.O.W. knew, they'd ruin everything.

"Nae." He tried to sit up, to fight off the hand over his eyes and pull free of his sister's too-gentle grip, but his body wouldn't listen to the demands of his brain. The best he could manage was a twitch of his shoulders before a blazing pain engulfed his shoulder and right arm. Someone screamed, a ragged, agonizing cry that echoed in what must have been a tiled room.

"Whoa, easy there, big guy." The other witch was near, too near, but Keir couldn't open his eyes. He couldn't move. Oh *Goddess*, what had he done to himself? A rush of warmth coated his chin and his lips, whoever it was bellowing their pain was silenced.

"Toby will be back; he just needed to step out momentarily. Shush now," Lou soothed her hand over his head.

Not Toby, Keir wanted to sob. *Not Toby. I need to know he is safe. That he got away, that C.R.O.W. doesn't know.* But his mouth wouldn't work, he couldn't form the words, and when had the pressure at his eyes left? Why couldn't he open them? Why couldn't he see his sister as she lied to his face? Goddess, Horned God, and all the deities of all the religions, why couldn't he open his eyes?

"Put him under." Her hand slipped out of his, and any soothing tones that might have lurked in the shape of her words were drowned beneath clinically cool logic. "And leave the room."

"Now?" The other witch asked.

"Now," Lou stated. "You know it has to be now, else we'll run out of time."

"Yes, ma'am." Fingertips crowned Keir's skull, and in the most American-accented German he had ever heard, the witch spun his intent. There was a wet-blanket rush of magick over his limbs, pressing Keir's bones into the surface he lay on, dragging him down...down...down....

Wake up. Please wake up.

Dark Witch?

You're back! You're back, you're back! Now wake up. We need you to wake up.

Someone is here, and I don't know what to do. Dark Witch, pleasepleaseplease wake up.

Weak light struggled through cream-colored curtains, a winter sun working its damnedest to warm the earth. Keir squinted at the room, letting his vision adjust to the living world. It was a harsh awakening compared to the blessedly empty night he'd been wandering for Horned God knew how long.

His contacts had been removed and though crusted from sleep, his eyes no longer burned from the salt water. Closing one eye, he stared down the length of his body with the other, trying to bring the image in front of him into focus.

He lay in what he assumed to be a hospital bed if the series of tubes and tape attached to his person were anything to judge by.

And the Horned God-awful sheets.

Scratchy polyblend linens and a horrid, puke brown fleece blanket covered him from the waist down, tucking him firmly against a concrete slab of a mattress. He longed for silk. Twenty-two momme, grade 6A, black silk on a king-sized bed. Preferably in a room with heavy blackout curtains keeping out the light but allowing the sound and scent of the sea to waft through his cracked window.

A careful turn of his head showed Keir that his right arm was braced at a ninety-degree angle, wrapped in miles of gauze and plaster up to his shoulder. Dimly, in the back of his head—which felt like it had been pommeled with a hammer and what in the nine rings was *that* about? This was a hospital; did they not have *drugs*?—he remembered the feel of gravel digging into his back and legs. A comforting weight pressing him into the stones and a whispered promise he could not grasp.

A wisp of a memory. A half-formed Shade there and gone.

His focus settled on his feet, tenting the coarse sheets and blanket. He waggled the toes of one foot and the other, unsure *why* but needing to know he *could* and doing it nonetheless. A sigh in the room had him opening his other eye, squinting at the figure curled in a chair shoved into the corner.

The furniture was far too small for the long, sleeping body it hosted. One leg was bent at the knee and curled to a chest, while the other leg dangled awkwardly off the cushion and onto the floor. Long arms hugged the bent knee, fingers half curled into loose fists. The overall posture was ridiculous, especially when considering the seriousness of the person it belonged to.

"They couldnae get you a bed?" He sounded like a toad, and his throat felt like he'd swallowed the stones from a dry sauna.

The figure in the chair snorted awake, lifting their head at the sound of his voice. Bright, blue-green eyes widened to saucers, and Lou practically threw herself across the room. She wrapped long, strong arms around her brother's shoulders and sobbed. He hissed at a surprising flash of pain from his shoulder.

"Oh, Goddess, Keir." Lou pulled away, eyes darting from his face to his forehead, his neck, then back to his face. "You scared me so bloody much!"

She batted his thigh, shuddering with relief when he tried to return her embrace. The PICC line attached to his left arm made it difficult to hug his sister as tightly as he wished, so he grumbled his annoyance until she eased off.

Lou settled on the edge of his mattress, frowned, and jumped to her feet. A twist of her wrist summoned his glasses to hand, and she slid them onto his face, pressing buttons to lift the bed so Keir could sit up. She busied her hands by fluffing the pillows and adjusting them to support his back. The mother henning annoyed him, as it always had, but he was grateful for her smothering care when the effort of sitting upright had him breathing heavily.

Muscles in his torso fluttered from the strain of use after Goddess knew how long. He fisted a hand, punching the mattress as he drew a long inhale, hissing through his teeth.

Once recovered, Keir scratched a bearded cheek and frowned down at his feet, assessing the weak state of his body.

"It will get better," Lou's voice was softer than he was used to. She ran fingers through her white-blonde hair, pulling the thick, glossy mass back into a tail. "We'll get you a physical therapist and a personal trainer. We can fix this, but Keir ... you should know that you were unconscious by the time they had you stabilized. The hippocromantics thought it was best to induce a coma—"

"A *what?*" Keir jerked his head up, wincing at the white-hot burst of pain behind his eyes. "Ach, fuck." He fell against the pillows, bringing fingertips to his temples and freezing at the feel of gauze and medical tape. "Lou?"

She opened her mouth, forming the words, but unable to speak them. Grabbing Keir's wrist, she pulled his hand away and laced their fingers together. A sheen overtook her eyes, and when Lou blinked, tears fell free. The sight of them was enough to horrify the witch. He could count on one hand the number of times he had seen his sister cry, and both of those instances had involved him and near death.

"Multiple contusions and closed fractures on the base and crown of the skull," a new voice supplied. Keir blinked and twitched his attention to the doorway. Toby stood there, frowning with his arms crossed and a shoulder dropped against the frame. Dressed in denim, a worn Ben Folds Five t-shirt and flannel, the German witch looked like he'd been called away from his farm in the Carolinas. "Lacerations along the throat, torso, and thighs. Fluid in the lungs and brain, symptoms of hypoxia, hypothermia, and decompression sickness." The frown deepened. Toby's eyes fell to the cast on Keir's arm. His throat bobbed, and he continued. "Multiple transverse and comminuted fractures to the scapula and humerus."

"That's nae funny," Keir murmured, stunned by his diagnosis.

Lou scoffed. "This is hardly the time for jokes."

"Agreed." He raised a hand above the bandage, intending to sweep fingers through his hair. He jerked it away, horrified at the stubbled growth crowning his skull. Goddess, what had he done to himself? Weak, broken, and damn near *bald*.

He searched back, the last moments he remembered being hazy at best. Toby sending a flare into the sky, the loss of feeling in his arms and legs, the riotous pain whenever he moved his head, and a comfortable weight over his heart.

"Harlingen," he murmured. Lou smiled, encouraging. "We were in Harlingen, chasing the lorelei."

"And what else?"

"I ... I fell?" He looked to Toby for confirmation. The spalování nodded, his face grim. "Off of the overpass, fighting the lorelei."

"The hippocromantics warned it would take a moment to remember everything," Lou smiled, though her bright eyes remained hard and assessing. "You did so well, Keir."

Those words rocked him back against the pillows. His attention drifted to the window and the blue horizon beyond closed curtains. Toby strode past the foot of his bed without a word. Jaw firm, he jerked the curtains open. Weak winter light flooded the room as the channel leading out to the North Sea was revealed. Lazy waves rose as frothing strips of white, breaking up the monotony of the deep blue. Keir's heart thudded at the sight of the ocean, a sense of longing overtaking the panic he'd felt at all the damage done to his body.

"I had to leave for the job in New Orleans, but the hippocromantics assured me that the craniotomy was a success..." Lou was still talking, her fingers dusting over his shorn skull and dancing away as lightly as her words. "...mitigate the risk of stroke or seizure. I'm sorry I couldn't be here, but I flew back as soon the dust was settled around Lightner's disappearance—"

"New Orleans?" He blinked, struggling to keep up. Lou frowned at him, quirking her head like she'd expected him to say something else. But what else was there to say? New Orleans had been the next job on the list; one Keir would have happily taken, if only to get out of lovely but somber Edinburgh for a week and experience the light and color of Mardi Gras. Maybe disappear into a swamp afterward. "I missed New Orleans?"

Still facing the window, Toby glanced over his shoulder, hands crossed behind his back and feet shoulder's width apart. His casual ready stance, one the spalování only adopted when he thought he'd need to lurch into action at a moment's notice. He watched Keir with an impassive expression, warning him that whatever Lou said next would be worse than what she'd already given away.

"Last week. Keir." She set her hand on his knee and squeezed gently. Carefully. "Honestly, I thought you'd be more concerned over Lightner."

"What happened to Ezra?"

"We can discuss that later when you're rested."

"There was an attempt to access the Gate," Toby stated. "Through the Neitherworld."

Lou whipped her head around, ponytail scything through the air. She glared at Toby before turning a much softer expression on her brother. "Everything is going to be alright."

"How long was I out?" Pushing his left hand against the mattress, he kicked the blanket, needing to move, to get out of this room and use his legs. Needing to find ... something. Someone?

"Three weeks," Toby answered, staring out at the water.

"As I said, everything will be alright." Lou eased him back against the pillows. "I'm in the process of assuring the Tribunal that you're—"

"Why would you need to assure the Tribunal of anything?"

"They are ..." she caged her words behind white teeth, selecting them carefully and slipping each one out like contraband. "They are upset that you were unavailable to act as a defense."

"Unavailable to act as ... I was in a bloody coma!" He slapped a hand against the mattress, jostling the PICC line. A machine started pinging, and a nurse rushed in, fiddling with knobs and glaring at Keir's visitors. Toby threw up his hands in playful surrender, a sheepish grin on his face. Keir would have laughed at his friend's predictable deference toward nurses if he weren't so angry. Lou rose to her full height, arms crossed, watching the nurse work and nodding curtly when she scurried away. The diversion gave him the space to think, to feel, and what he felt was — nothing.

I'm trying to help you, a little voice chided. *Stop pushing.*

Beyond his window, the waves formed and furled, crashing over themselves only to be subsumed by the fathomless blue. The chaotic monotony of nature soothed Keir's nerves, allowing him to disassociate from the wretched things his sister kept saying. He'd done his job, had nearly died, and couldn't make sense of anything. What else did they want? He was C.R.O.W.'s pet Dark Witch. Caged and tamed and too afraid of testing the door to see if it was even locked.

Just, ugh, try to remember what you can, Little Shadow demanded, her tiny, sweet voice strained and weary. *And don't cut any more of yourself off. It's really hard trying to keep all of you together when the bits keep wandering to the stranger at the gate.*

The what? Keir startled. What Little Shadow proposed was impossible, no one could wander the Neitherworld, much less make it to the Gate, other than him and his Shades. *Who is it?*

Honestly, I thought you would know.

"Now that you are awake, I should speak with the hippocromantics about getting you discharged." Lou's weight dipped the mattress, a hand settling lightly on his knee. "It's time we got you home to Edinburgh. You'll stay with me and Donmar until you're fully healed."

"Nae." Keir adjusted his seat, pulling his knee away from the tender weight of his sister's concern. "Ye ken I dinnae fancy Corstorphine."

"Keir—"

"I want to go home. To my home." He felt the roil of Shade in his eyes as he glared at Lou, mollified when she frowned. "Portobello."

"I don't think you should be left unsupervised—"

"I'm nae a child, *Lou*," he snapped.

"Then stop acting like one, *Keir*." She snarled back, standing with her hands fisted at her thighs. "Stop treating all this like a game and pretend, for a moment, that you are a grown witch, an Enforcer, for Goddess' sake, and start taking this all seriously."

"You dinnae think I take this seriously?" He scoffed, shaking his head at the ceiling. A bit of his Way slipped free, and Little Shadow bloomed across his shoulders, curling a protective tail of midnight around his throat.

Ahh, this is nice. She wriggled, nestling deeper among his collarbones. *Oh, I missed you.*

Missed you, too, Keir thought to his familiar, comforted by her odd, weightless presence.

Lou narrowed her eyes at the Shade. "Put that away."

Little Shadow gave the impression of a huff and pouted. *Why is she being so mean to you?*

To us, you mean?

Whatever, Little Shadow replied with a tone that implied rolled eyes.

Her indignancy bolstered him, just as the day the Ways opened up to Keir and she found him wandering lost in the dark. He looked his sister in the eye. "This is my *life*, Lou. You bloody well know I take it seriously."

Lou hesitated. The briefest of pauses that the untrained eye would have dismissed altogether. But Keir knew his sister. He knew her unruffled calm was a carefully honed weapon. One she deployed time and time again against the brother who felt too much.

"Yes, truly, you must take it seriously as you decided to *seduce* a desecrant rather than put it down." Near the window, Toby tensed. Lou narrowed her eyes, sniffing. "I wasn't going to discuss this with you until we were *home*, but again, you've forced me to be the villain in your petty dramas." Raising her hands, Lou performed a limp-wristed golf clap dripping with sarcasm. "Well played, Keir, well bloody played. I hope the lay was worth the broken bones and concussion. Was she better than the *vodyanoi*, at least?"

"Seduce—" Keir clacked his teeth closed. His brow furrowed as his mind raced back over the lost weeks to the events in Harlingen, playing through what he remembered or thought he did. Images formed and faded, memories hovering just beyond his reach. Whether it was the drugs, the concussion, or the Horned God-damned *cranial surgery*, he couldn't form a proper history of his time in Harlingen. Only abstract scenes that, collectively, made no sense.

"—any idea how embarrassing it is to have to request a kit and a bloody corpomantic to ensure you're clean—"

Humming from the wind turbines and floating on his back beneath a clear blue sky. Was he in the water? Or on a dock?

Oh, keep going.

"—recovered with no pants on, seriously, Keir. The marks on your neck were damning enough, but did you have to—"

Goddess, his head hurt, but the memory was right *there*. So close he could almost see the dimly lit bar and hear the waves lapping as he ran along the jetty. And lurking in the shadowy depths of his pock-marked memory was a being with eyes as black as his. The feel of strong arms holding him in the water. Teeth at his neck as he was tossed in the waves, salt on his tongue, and ... bliss. The overwhelming memory of a bliss so acute it bordered on painful.

I liked him, the little Shade purred.

Him?

His gaze drifted to the windows, the sea. A dull throbbing began in his skull, the building pressure of an oncoming migraine. "I didnae ... there was a ..."

"Can you argue his results?" Toby interrupted, moving from the window to stand at Keir's shoulder. "The lorelei was handled just as C.R.O.W. asked. What do the means matter if the result is satisfactory?"

"I'm not having this argument with you again, Toby." Lou pressed her palm in the air. "It was your responsibility to keep him on task and out of harm's way. You're as culpable in this as Keir is. Goddess, the shipping lanes are only now clearing from that storm you had the Witch of the Demesne call."

"I still hold that Keir's means of detaining the lorelei were sound. She would have claimed the Witch of the Demesne and myself, regardless. Were it not for his quick thinking—"

"His intense desire to embarrass me by fucking every known desecrant listed in our e-grims."

"—the lorelei would have made her crossing to the sea." Toby finished. He glared at Lou, blue flame twisting in his eyes. "His tactics, questionable as they may be, are the only reason we are alive today. That has to hold merit, Luminescence. Enough so that you uphold your end of the bargain."

"Oh?" His sister arched a brow. "Making rulings on bargains now, are you?"

"As his keeper?" Toby leveled. "Never. But as his friend? Absolutely."

Lou pinched her lips and scanned Toby from head to toe. Shifting to face Keir, her expression eased, regret darkening her eyes. "Keir—"

"Lou, please." He gestured to his broken arm. "Have you seen me?" She frowned, shoulders dropping. "I cannae do this anymore. I'm not built for the job like you and Toby."

"Neither was Donny," she relented. That she used Donmar's nickname was telling. "The both of you feel too much, but he learned through necessity and experience, so can you."

"I cannae." The words were small, as tiny as Keir felt at that moment. Again, he pleaded his case with his sister, knowing she would never agree. She firmly believed he was safest by her side and beneath her thumb, where C.R.O.W. could see the length of his sturdy leash. Better to have a trapped and caged Dark Witch ready to deploy than to let him forget he'd ever been involved with Shades and cleavings and desecrants. "This job almost killed me, Lou. I dinnae want to fall into my Way as deeply as I did on that overpass, I—" his voice cracked. "What will it take for you to let me go?"

She stared down at her brother, broken and bruised, then collapsed onto the chair in the corner. A glance at Toby had her jaw hardening and back straightening.

"Probation."

"Pardon?"

Lou bent over her knees, wrists dangling and her face to the floor. "We can place you on judiciary probation, say it is until a full and exhaustive investigation has been conducted."

"That's nae what we—"

"It's the best I can do, Keir." She speared him with a gleaming, Light Witch gaze. "The whole affair with the lorelei is a bloody PR nightmare, and that is before we even begin to unpack what occurred in New Orleans while you were out of commission. There is no chance the Tribunal will agree to your separating from C.R.O.W., not right now. A Dark Witch is too much of a risk, but probation—I can buy you time to heal and work through whatever is in your head keeping you from understanding that I'm only trying to help you."

She reached low, scooped a bag from the floor, and rose. With little more than a glance at Toby, Lou dumped the contents onto Keir's lap. "I asked Rai to put something together since I know you're too stubborn to ask her yourself." Keir flinched at his ex-girlfriend's name, staring down at the collection of paraphernalia in his lap. Vials and jars, a bag of his preferred herb, his grinder, and a new vape pen. Lou cupped his right hand and squeezed gently, kissing the crown of his head. "I love you, wee yin. Ye ken?"

"Aye," Keir nodded, dazed from the conversation's turns. Probation was not what he wanted; he wanted *out*, but it was something. A reprieve. One he might be able to stretch. Absently, he trailed a finger along the glossy side of the vape pen, already adding up the intent behind the

collection of herbs in his lap. Clove and Solomon's Seal, barberry, and —
a sniff of the baggy confirmed — skullcap. Maybe probation wouldn't
be all bad if he could still lean on Rai's skills for help. "Love you too, big
yin."

"The hippocromantics won't bother you about that." She gestured
to the herbs and vanished her bag into the aether. "I'll go speak to them
about your discharge."

She swept from the room. After a handful of minutes in terse silence,
Toby leaned against the windowsill and stared at the witch in the bed.

"How much do you remember?"

Keir plucked a baggy from his lap, eyeing the finely ground clove and
thinking back, back, back. "Seducing a lorelei certainly sounds like me."

"Does it?" The spalování moved to the end of the bed. His jaw ticked
when Keir summoned a mortar and pestle. "I thought you were done
with that *scheisse.*"

"I almost died, Tobe; give a witch a break."

Toby frowned, watching Keir fumble through grinding the herbs
one-handed. "Is there anything else you remember?"

Think back, Dark Witch.

"Did I—" He stopped himself, knuckles blanching from his grip on
the pestle. White heat bubbled behind his eyes, and he winced, dropping
the pestle into the mortar to rub his temple. "I was in the water."

"You were."

"I ne'er go in the water."

He laid his hand in his lap, palm up to trace the lines with his eyes. The
ache in his skull subsided as he backed away from the memory of strong
hands at the base of his spine, the there-and-gone quirk of a smile, and a
deep, rumbling voice saying, "Please."

"There was someone else." He looked up at Toby, reading the intensity in his friend's gaze. "Another desecrant?"

Toby chewed his cheek, dancing his gaze over Keir's face. He finally sighed and tapped the Dark Witch on the foot. "C.R.O.W. will never know."

"Never know what?" He pleaded.

Instead of answering, the witch jerked his chin at the door. "She'll come around, Keir. Eventually."

"Hm."

"You should sit by the window." Toby shoved the chair across the room. "Get some sunlight and watch the waves. Maybe it will help you recall."

"Mm," he gave a non-committal nod, letting the spalování help him from the bed and get settled before leaving him alone with his thoughts and weed.

He watched the sea while waiting for the chamber to heat. The sun dropped low as he studied the waves, raising the pen to his lips every few minutes, willfully retreating into the haze of herb and letting it soothe thoughts he could not conquer on his own. Thoughts like memories that kept slipping beyond his reach. The timbre of a voice, the broken syllables of his name, and the delicate, precious feeling of being treasured.

Little Shadow hummed quietly, still draped across his shoulders and watching the sun as it kissed the horizon.

Do you remember? She finally asked.

"'member what?" A cloud of sweet smoke billowed from his lips.

The Shade quivered and dripped off his shoulders to puddle in his lap. She watched him as he inhaled, the peaceful, reassuring chill of her presence keeping his feet firmly bolted to the ground while his head soared a mile above the earth. *Do you remember what happened?*

Do you?

I wasn't there for most of it, Little Shadow bristled. *You said it wasn't appropriate.*

He huffed and set the pen on the windowsill, lifting his glasses to rub beneath an eye with a knuckle. "I cannae grasp it, Little Shadow."

Keep trying.

A glint of sunlight off of something in the harbor dropped his gaze low. He jumped from the chair, vape pen clacking against the glass as he pressed his hand against the window to keep his balance. Little Shadow crawled onto the sill, stretching tall like a curious stoat popping out of its burrow. Below, Toby walked along the pier with a somber expression, disappearing out of view as he re-entered the hospital. The water in the tiny harbor rose and fell in lazy waves, empty save for a dingy tied to the end of a dock and—there!

Ohh, Little Shadow sighed at seeing a broad, black fluke breaking through the surface, only to vanish beneath the waves. A seal or a whale. Whatever it was, Keir wished he were as free to leave the continent and C.R.O.W. behind. Free to travel the world or the waters without end. Perhaps he could disappear into the Neitherworld and wander the boundless expanse, seeking out a polar star within the nothing to hold his course.

Or maybe he could just—Keir raised the vape pen to his lips, inhaling deeply and holding his breath for as long as he could before exhaling and rocking back on his heels—forget.

Little Shadow angled her shadowy not-face to the side. *Do you even want to remember?*

How a Shade could sound so judgmental was beyond him, but he loved her for it.

"Ye ken, Little Shadow," he mused to the ceiling, the tiles spinning as the world slid out of focus. He swept a hand at the curtains, pulling them closed and teetering to the hospital bed. "I'm nae so certain I wish to."

How come?

Black eyes and broad shoulders. Skin like a starlit sky. Hands at his hips, a plush mouth trailing his jawline before traveling low. It was so close. Just there, obscured by the haze of drugs and injury. Close enough that if he just reached out and grabbed it—his vision flashed white. Searing pain lanced along the dome of his skull and shot into the backs of his eyes. He curled onto his left side, cradling the vape pen in his hand as Little Shadow puddled in the crook of his knees.

"It hurts."

TWO OF CUPS

EPILOGUE

Two weeks. Two bloody weeks, she'd been calling and reaching nothing but his voicemail. Two weeks of evasive texts and missed appointments. Two weeks of asking Donmar and Rai to check on him, only to be met with their staunch refusal.

"The two of you need to work it out," Donmar had replied, kissing her temple and tucking Lou closer into his big body. "I cannot always step in when Keir shuts you out. He usually has a good reason to do so."

"I hardly think I am the appropriate person to ask." Rai had swirled the wine in her glass; dark eyes lowered to watch the legs fall. "It is one thing to continue shipping him herb, but Lou, you know where your brother and I stand."

And they were right. Goddess, even Lou knew that, but this was a delicate emotional matter which was *not* her forte. She needed someone he trusted and cared about to help her get through to him. To help him understand that *she* was the only reason C.R.O.W. let him live. Why was that so hard for Keir to comprehend?

Still, two bloody weeks of her brother playing coy and disappearing into the shadows if she dared to grace his presence was a bit excessive, especially as she hadn't bothered him regarding C.R.O.W. and Enforcer tasks for close to two bloody years.

Ducking through his bedroom window, she glared at the fire escape and the tell-tale thudding from the roof.

"Good." Stepping out of her heels, Lou tossed them through the window and stripped down to her camisole. Folding her sweater, she placed it on the charcoal gray Le Creuset Dutch oven that served as her brother's cauldron. "Broad bloody daylight today, and you've got yourself on the roof." Gripping the bottommost rung, she braced a foot on the railing, stretched her arms, and hauled herself onto the ladder. Over forty, she might be, but never let it be said Lou was anything less than the pinnacle of physical perfection. Fluid and limber, she scaled the fire escape, congratulating herself on choosing stretchy ponte trousers for today's outfit. This climb would never have been as graceful had she chosen to wear a skirt. "No chance of you slipping off into the shadows."

The thudding grew louder as she climbed, joined by the rattling of chains supporting his punching bag. In short order, she popped her head over the low wall ringing the rooftop, smiling viciously at what she saw.

The last two years had been hard on her brother. After that ridiculous job in the Netherlands landed him in the hospital, he'd sunk low. Low enough that Donmar agreed to let her interfere, and looking at him now, it was a good thing she had.

The weed they couldn't do anything about, and honestly, Lou had little desire to take that away from Keir. He certainly needed to pursue therapy, but at least she had been able to help him recover from the physical injuries. Looking at him now, swinging a wicked right cross and following it with a hook that rattled the bag on its chains, one would have never known he'd been comatose in a hospital bed with a shattered right arm.

His wasted form was now lean and well-muscled, broader in the shoulders from all the boxing. Though pale as a ghost, his cheeks were flushed from the exertion of his workout. His build and appearance were that of a man who cared to a worryingly vain degree, even though he desperately needed a haircut.

Lou had done that. She had dragged her brother as far out of his depression as she could. Throwing him at a boxing gym, calling Toby and convincing him to "surprise" Keir for a six-week job in Edinburgh, and, oh yes, could he crash at his flat? She had dropped off cookbooks and his weed. Had "happened" upon small venue concerts for the bands she knew he liked and purposefully steered every conversation away from C.R.O.W. and Enforcers and the Netherlands until one *glorious* day over tea and pastry, he had looked at her and smiled. Eyes clear and jade green, not a shadow to be found. He had smiled at his sister and said, "Thank you, big yin."

So then, what in the nine rings was his problem *now*?

"I know it's only a punching bag, but keep your hands up," she called out, trying to keep her tone light. Friendly.

The only tell that Keir heard her was a slight hunching of his shoulders before he unleashed holy hell. A series of quick-tempo jabs that had the bag seizing on its chains from the force of each punch. He finished with a cross that sent it swinging wildly. Chin tucked, Keir stepped back and dropped his arms, shoulders rising and falling with each rapid, heavy breath. He took a moment to center himself before turning around to face her.

"Aye?" Keir's usual greeting was more of a bark than a welcome. He eyed Lou as he strode past, tugging at the velcro strap of a glove and pulling his hand free. The glove was tossed onto one of the wicker couches she knew he liked to lay on while stoned out of his mind, and the other followed. Keir, however, remained standing. Feet held in a hard-trained defensive stance, his face impassive and — *Horned God-dammit* — smoke licking over his eyes.

"Oh, stop with the defensive act." Lou swung a leg up over the wall and the other, raising her chin and striding to the loveseat. Sitting, she crossed her legs and closed her eyes long enough to step into her Way and drag her Soul into focus. Just enough to speak with emotion and treat with the tedium of empathy. "I only came to see how you're doing."

"Wellness check, is it?" He picked at the ends of a hand wrap, unwinding the nylon and draping it over his shoulder. "Here I thought we were beyond these little visits."

"You're my brother, Keir." She fidgeted in the chair, wicker ribs digging into her back. On a whim, she gripped the armrests and pulled herself to her feet, long legs carrying her to the punch bag. Keir kept his boxing gear in a crate tucked beneath an eave, and Lou knew from experience that spare gloves and wraps counted among the contents of said bin. Rummaging around, she pulled free a worn pair of purple gloves. "Wellness checks are part of being your sister. Especially when you avoid me for weeks on end." She held up the gloves, eyes gleaming, and grinned. "Can't believe you still have these."

"You came here to box?" He raised an eyebrow. To Lou's delight, he stopped unwinding the wrap on his left hand, hesitating before reversing the action and re-wrapping his wrist and fingers. The ghost of a smirk dimpled his cheek for half a second, and in that, Lou knew she had him.

"I came here to speak with you." She hooked her thumb through the loop at the end of a hand wrap and tightly wound it around her wrist. "As I've been trying to do for weeks now."

Keir pulled the tie from his hair, working his fingers through the coppery mass and pulling it back into a tight bun. Wrapping his right hand, he tugged on a glove and secured it, easily pulling the velcro tight around his wrist. The left caused him to fumble. Biting the end of the flap, he addressed Lou through his teeth. "Dinnae want to talk about whatever it is you're hounding me about."

"I think," she tugged the flap of her gloves tight, "you'll be interested in this."

Jabbing the empty air, Lou worked through a warm-up combination. One she'd learned early on while escorting Keir to the gym and sticking around long enough to see that same healthy flush pinken his cheeks. He'd been shy at first. Uncomfortable in his body, which was jarring to them both. Standing timidly, settling on his heels, and hesitant to swing his right arm with what she knew could deliver a cold-cocking, knockout punch.

Keir snorted, repeating her combination and adding a series of jabs and a final cross into the mix. Lou copied him with a smile.

"It's a job." She finished the cross and added an uppercut. Her brother rubbed a glove under his nose. If Lou were not mistaken, it was a gesture of begrudging respect.

"Dinnae want a job."

"A job that—"

"Dinnae care," he growled, repeating her sequence perfectly. "Thought that was clear by now."

"You do realize you're only on probation." Lou again added to the combination, a quick double-jab. This time, she landed each strike against the punching bag. Her knuckles barked at the impact, but it was worth it. She needed to speak Keir's language to get through to him. She needed to find a way to relate, and maybe in reminding him of all the work she put into his well-being, he would remember that she wasn't his enemy.

She was his sister. His only family.

His *protector*.

"So have the Tribunal issue a subpoena." His fists flew, each jab, cross, and hook pommeling the bag with a precision that only hours of training could produce. "Call me in through the regular channels. Dinnae scale my flat and approach me as a friend."

"I'm not your friend." Jab, cross, hook, cross, jab, jab, hook, uppercut, jab, cross. "I am your sister, and I have a job to offer you."

Keir punched the bag once, twice, thrice. Faster and faster. Foregoing the combination and seeking only to destroy. When he'd spent his frustration, Keir wheeled around to face his sister, eyes blazing, cheeks flushed. *Alive.* "What."

"Florida."

He blinked, shoulders dropping. "What?"

"Florida. A Witch of the Demesne and a curious surge of necro-magick. You would act as an Aural Insurance Adjuster, determining what threat the witch poses, if any."

"Necro-magick." He rubbed his chin with the curve of a glove, eyeing Lou and pacing like a caged predator in a zoo. Of course, he latched onto the idea of Forbidden and Foule activity and not the witch in question.

Good, Lou thought. *Better he gains his focus now than get distracted on the job.*

"Why send me?"

"You were requested." She tugged a glove off and tossed it aside. "By the Morgenhexe."

That dropped his arms, clearing the smoke from his eyes once and for all. His Adam's apple bobbed, and he worked his jaw, turning her words over in that clever mind. "Morgen. Former member of the Tribunal, Morgen Tage, requested me?"

"The matter concerns her foster daughter. Considering Morgen's knowledge of your Way and the sensitive nature of the job, she requested a witch who would treat the matter with the utmost discretion. One with experience in dealing with the Forbidden and Foule."

"Speak plainly."

"The Tribunal is re-opening the case involving Ezra Lightner's disappearance. Morgen's foster daughter is Ezra Lightner's former apprentice."

Keir rocked back, his cheeks paling. "The one who—"

"Was initially suspected of Foule play," Lou confirmed. "One and the same. She earned herself the title of Witch of the Demesne in a small city south of Jacksonville."

Keir chewed that for a moment. Lou knew he was weighing the emotional cost of the matter. The suspect's closeness to Ezra Lightner. His former relationship with the witch. And she saw the moment he was hooked, willingly swallowing the bait so preciously laid before him.

"The surge was when?" He finally asked, gloves discarded and hand wraps draped over a shoulder. The vape pen appeared in his hand, his thumb on the button to warm the chamber, which Lou assumed he kept packed and ready.

"Two weeks ago, after almost a year of silence from the demesne."

"And this is the same apprentice who participated in the ritual that lost us Ezra?"

"It is indeed." Lou stepped close to her brother, meeting him eye-to-eye.

Keir brought the pen to his lips, inhaling as he scratched the center of his chest. His fingers absently trailed the topmost whorl of the triskelion Soul Sigil, Lou's sigil. A binding she'd placed on him years ago to help control the Shade.

"Ken what I think?" His eyes sharpened with suspicion, the green brightening to vivid chartreuse.

Any other witch would have wavered beneath that keen, assessing stare, but Lou recognized the set of his shoulders and the close way he watched her. How he had to keep his hands busy to clear his head enough to think, all the while clouding his mind with Rai's blend to keep himself safe from the feelings those thoughts would stir.

Her brother was a clever witch with the degrees and the letters after his name to prove it. When he wasn't hiding behind a cloud of pot-smoke and intent-laden herbs, he could be downright terrifying in how capably he used his nature and his Way to manipulate the scene.

Those were the skills he needed for this job. Lou had recognized that the moment Morgen submitted her request. Any daughter of the Morgenhexe, foster or otherwise, was bound to be a keen opponent, as skilled in hand-to-hex as she would be in building walls to hide her truth. Walls that only a Dark Witch could scale.

"I think you came here knowing that my nature and my past relationship with Ezra Lightner would make it nigh impossible to turn this job down."

"And if I did?"

Keir narrowed his eyes, vape pen pressed against his lips. He pulled it away, pushing his mouth to the side and turning his head to not exhale directly in Lou's face. Already, the brightness in his eyes had muddled, the harsh green softening to a cloudy jade. But with the retreat behind his safety blanket came a loosening of his limbs. So she pressed her hand.

"Lightner's apprentice is an un-registered vestic."

"A seer?"

"Mm-hmm." Lou brushed non-existent lint from her thigh. "She runs a curio shop in the city center and still lives in the house she shared with Lightner."

"A vestic runs a demesne?" Keir pulled his hair free from its ludicrous man bun, running a hand through the copper strands. "That seems unlikely."

"That's because she isn't a vestic." Lou painted a pleasant smile on her face.

"What is she?"

"Determining that is part of the job." She plucked the knee of her ponte trousers and smoothed the fabric at her thigh. "I'm willing to go to fifty percent. If you accept, of course."

Keir hesitated, mouth opening, then closing. Lips pulling into a tight line.

Then he stepped forward, the toes of his shoes brushing her bare feet. Lou smiled warmly this time and rose to cage the core of the Soul Sigil with the tips of her fingers.

"I'll do this, Lou." He lowered his voice, speaking with a terrifying steadiness she rarely heard from her brother. Each word was imbued with the power of promise and threat. "And when the job is done, I want out."

"Out."

"For good. No more jobs, no more probation. You undo the Soul Sigil and let me lead my life."

Despite her nature and Way, Lou felt a prickling at the base of her neck. He would do this, of that there was no doubt. After the lorelei and her machinations with the Tribunal to keep him on the payroll, even Keir knew he had no choice but to take this job. But when it was done?

A problem for later. Once I've had time to find a workaround.

"Understood." Lou leaned into her Way, warmth blossoming at the back of her head as though she'd dipped back into a thermal spring. She pressed harder against her brother's chest and whispered the release to grant him the use of his Way.

"Oscailte."

Open.

He inhaled sharply, pupils dilating and stretching beyond their bounds before he clenched a fist, shivered, and reined his Way under control.

"Horned God, it's been a while." Teetering back, Keir half-stumbled to the wicker couch. He plopped his lank down, dropping his head against the backrest. The pen was immediately at his mouth, and a skein of black silk blossomed and wrapped around his arm. A tiny smile flittered across her brother's face, and the Shade on his arm wriggled in reply. "Anything else I should know?"

The question surprised Lou. Mentally, she reprimanded herself. Of course, he'd read between the lines and make assumptions about what she wasn't saying. The job required a witch with knowledge of the Forbidden and Foule. It was a delicate task that C.R.O.W. wanted to keep quiet due to the high profile of the witch's parentage and upbringing. Her relationships. *Of course*, her emotionally intelligent brother would sense she was keeping something from him, something vital, even if he were well on his way to being stoned out of his mind.

Before she could spin together an answer, Keir's smoke-thick voice rambled on. "Am I getting a new name? Staying in a hotel? I'd rather have a cottage, truly. With a kitchen and walkable to the downtown. Near the waterfront."

"Of course." Lou cleared her throat and resumed her perch on the loveseat. "And a rental car, though I expect you to walk when you've been smoking."

"Naturally," he chuckled.

"The job is fairly straightforward. Observe the target, assess her Way, and report back to C.R.O.W."

"M'gonnae go to the beach," he announced, sounding half asleep.

"So long as you don't go fucking a mermaid, I don't see why that would be a problem."

Keir shook his head, smiling lopsidedly at Lou. "Dinnae be daft." He settled against the cushion, eyes drifting closed. "There's nae such thing as mermaids."

Holy Horned God, what happens in Florida? Find out in

Read the first three chapters now.

RITUAL INCOME

A WITCH OF THE DEMESNE NOVEL

B.L. BROWN

COCO INTENSE PRESS

LAKE PONTCHARTRAIN
NEW ORLEANS, LA

He turns his back. He always turns his back.

Every single time she relives this moment, he turns his back with the surety and unassailable faith in his own ability that only narcissism can provide. And that is his fatal mistake every damn time. That unswerving trust in himself and the natural extension of that trust to her.

Ezra glances back, the teal crackle of magic bright and painful in his eyes. "No matter what you See, Milla, believe in me."

"I will."

"That's my Millapet." He takes a step. Another and another, and for a heartbeat, she thinks he might manage it this time. He might succeed in pulling the world apart. And then her vision fractures into three, the pain in her head debilitating. The tether between them frays; it rips out of her grip and shreds her to her soul.

"Ezra!" Her feet slide in the silt, and she grabs the tether with both hands, bearing her weight down on her heels.

"Hold tight, Milla, believe in me!"

Snap. Snapsnap.

"Ezra, come back!" Strands snap and coil away, the tether slips and tears her palms, lashing her forearms and spraying blood across her face and her clothes. Her vision continues fracturing; nine, twenty-seven, eighty-one. A bone in her arm shatters, and she closes her eyes against the scream. "I can't hold on. I don't-I don't know—"

Snap.

"Ezra, please!" The tether burns against her palms, and the tension fails, whipping against her wrists and the back of her hands. His scream echoes hers, a pain cut deep to the center of their very being. "Come back!"

And then he is gone. The only sound is her ragged breathing and the staggered cessation of chanting as she struggles to piece together what is left. Of her, of him.

No. That wasn't right.

There was nothing left of him.

ONE

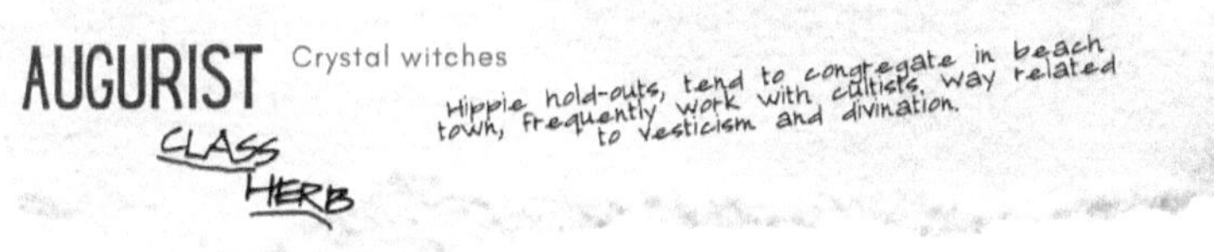

If it weren't for the customers, Milla's job would be ideal.

There were days when all she did was sit at the front counter, sipping her drink and waiting for something to happen when she wished nothing would. Glorious days when the only person she spoke to was her room-mate and co-worker, Diego, and all their sales were made online.

"Hey, hon!"

And then there were days like today when Milla had to remain calm in the face of Southern passive aggression.

"Me, again." Her sole customer approached the counter, flapping the garment in her hand. Milla paused mid-sip, identifying the vintage nineteenth-century asymmetrical bathing costume being treated as a handkerchief as The Pinkerton.

She frowned into her bubble water. The Pinkerton was an antique bathing costume she had painstakingly restored under Diego's watchful eye. It had been the first magick she'd attempted in months. Her blood, sweat, and the echoes of her curse words lived on in each thread of the asymmetrical banding and delicate frill on the collar.

The woman was still talking, probably complaining about the ventriloquists' dummies being creepy or the Tiffany lamp in the corner flickering whenever she walked by. Tourists had no end of complaints when it came to Milla's store and its eclectic collection.

She took another small sip, let the sharp tang roll over her tongue, and swallowed her annoyance. "What."

Okay, so maybe she wasn't so good at swallowing her annoyance.

"Excuse me?" The woman's eyebrows arched, which was a feat. Milla honestly did not think eyebrows drawn with Crayola could arch with such disdain.

"You're excused?" She extended a hand, palm up, gesturing at the Pinkerton. "Did you want to buy that?"

"Well, sort of." The woman's eyes dropped to her hand, indignation wrestling with and losing to sick curiosity. Her hands had that effect on people. It had been over a year, and even Milla wasn't entirely used to the webs of spidery white tissue marring her palm.

The woman sneered, shoving the Pinkerton into Milla's waiting hand. Her fingers brushed Milla's palm, and the unnatural chill had her darting away, the sneer widening to alarm.

Even before the incident that earned her those scars, people said she was too cold, her skin clammy when it should be warm from the Florida sun—chilled when it should be flushed from heat or exertion.

No one had liked touching Milla until Ezra.

Ezra who ran hot and wore bags of ice tucked into the waist of his running shorts. Ezra who slept in the buff and sweat through the night, even with the a/c running itself to exhaustion.

Ezra who was Gone.

"Sort of?" Milla raised her eyebrows.

"I was wondering if you had this in a larger size?"

She held up the garment, using it as a shield to hide the incredulous look on her face. "A larger size."

"You know how it is when you've had kids." The woman patted a hip in a manner that might have been cute had Milla not noticed a torn seam on the bathing costume.

"Did you—this is a 19th-century bathing costume, originally sold by Pinkerton's on the Boardwalk in Atlantic City." The woman smiled, nodding. "Atlantic City, New Jersey." Another nod. "In 1886."

"Uh-huh." She smiled broadly, still not understanding.

Oh, Horned God.

"This is an antique." Milla prodded the torn seam and tried counting backward from ten. She made it to seven, which, truth be told, was an achievement. "One-of-a-kind. I had to outbid a collector in New Haven for this."

"Incredible." The woman nodded, clearly not picking up what Milla was putting down. "So, do you have it in a bigger size? Maybe in the back?" Eyelashes fluttered, her lips pressed together in a pink, glossy pout. "I won a cruise through my company. I'm a Diamond Qualifying Executive for Icy Me, and this little bathing suit"—Milla's eye twitched—"is just perfect." She paused, lips pursed like a sturgeon, and Milla could have sworn she was holding for questions.

She had just the one, but Diego would be pissed if Milla asked this woman, this customer, if she was fucking serious.

So she cleared her throat and reached for her sparkling water. "Nope."

"Aren't you even going to check?"

"What part of 'one-of-a-kind' is confusing you?"

"I ..." The woman's smile finally faltered. Milla relished the war of emotions playing out on perfectly contoured cheeks. The eyes lost it first, then the right corner of her mouth, followed by the left, disappointment altering the scenery of a lovingly painted face until the final transformation from cheerful Southern Gal to Bitch Queen was complete. It was utterly mesmerizing. "I would like to speak to your manager."

Had Milla not been the owner and operator of Southern Gothic Antiquities and Curios, she might have quaked in her boots.

Might have.

But the point remained: it was the *Pinkerton*. She couldn't sell it to just anyone.

"I'm afraid I'm the only one here."

"I see." The woman whipped her phone from the oversized beach tote on her shoulder, thumb swiping at the screen. She was no doubt crafting a rude post of her experience for Yap! Reviews, which was fine. Milla didn't need in-person sales to survive; the store was mostly a way to fill her days and keep her mind from wandering.

Believe in me, Milla.

Not that it was working very well.

A shutter snapped, and Milla blinked, jaw hanging open at the sheer *gall*. "Did you just take my picture?"

"You don't have any signs saying I can't."

"I...wha...you..." Milla fumbled, her usually sharp tongue struck dumb. "I think you should leave. *Ma'am*." The woman's nostrils flared at the layers of insult Milla added to the honorific. "Maybe Shopaholic has something more in line with what you're looking for." She gestured to the front door. "They usually carry plus sizes."

"Did you just *body shame* me?" The woman flushed, though it was hard to tell beneath the caked-on makeup. Her neck turned an alarming shade of red, as did her ears, but her face remained the same painstakingly contoured shades of peach and pink shimmer.

"I—shit," Milla stammered. "No, it's just, that's an antique. People in the 1800s were, um, smaller."

The woman slammed her palms down on the glass. "I've decided I don't want that moth-eaten fabric you call an antique," she snarled, which would have been intimidating were it not for the beach tote choosing that exact moment to slide down her arm. She jogged her shoulder to readjust the bag. "You've made a big mistake. Huge. I'm going to tell everyone I know about the appalling customer service at …" She squinted at the business cards beside the register and snorted. "Southern Gothic? Guess I shouldn't expect someone who designed their entire personality off of Wednesday Addams to be creative."

"Whatever," Milla rolled her eyes, "Karen."

"Kayleigh." She sniffed, then screwed her mouth into a purse of disgust. "This entire establishment reeks like the gin in your coke."

"It's juniper-scented bubble water," Milla huffed.

"Whatever." Kayleigh jabbed her phone screen with a finger. "What kind of trash store only sells clothing in one size."

"An antique store." Milla swept her arm at the curio cabinet behind her, pointing out the porcelain figurines, heirloom jewelry, and the broken but beautiful Berthoud marine clock. "Full of antiques, which this bathing suit—I mean *costume*—is."

"Do yourself a favor, sweetpea, and sell something people actually want to buy," Kayleigh hissed. "Not like it'll do any good by the time I'm done with you." She whirled in a swirl of floral polyester and shoved the door open, muttering insults under her breath. "You body shaming piece of …"

Milla fumed, palms itching, as Kayleigh stormed across the road and disappeared down Toques Place.

"That went well." Diego's mocking voice hummed from the hallway to the rear office, bathroom, and sewing room.

She drummed her fingers on the glass display case, chewing on her lip. "She wanted to buy the Pinkerton."

"Diosa forbid we sell anything." Diego sidled in front of the display, slipping a hand beneath the bathing costume and whisking it from the counter with a flourish. "You are obscenely attached to this shift."

He was shorter for a man but tall for an Iberian, or so he claimed. Thick, shoulder-length black hair was pulled into a bun at the nape of his neck, and the shadow of a beard clung to his jaw, adding warmth to an already deep olive complexion. From the wireless headphones looped around his neck, Milla caught the synth-loop refrain of Chaka Khan's "I Feel For You."

"Already in 1985?" Milla asked. For the past few months, after he'd figured out his smartphone, streaming services, and Bluetooth, Diego had been painstakingly reviewing music of the twenty-first century, in order.

Diego made a face, squinting behind his thick-framed glasses. "Chaka's later catalog is so frivolous. I much preferred her collaboration with Rufus." He held the bathing costume at arm's length, examining the torn seam with a critical tailor's eye. "Not much can compare to Cher's Best Works of the 1970s."

"Obviously," Milla agreed. "Nothing beats 'Dark Lady'."

"How you can say that when 'Rescue Me' is on the same album, I do not know." Diego turned his attention to the Pinkerton, shaking out the garment and muttering an allure. "*Muéstrame.*"

The fabric swelled and curved in the intended places, tapering around a modest waist and flaring over sweet hips as though it clung to the body of a turn-of-the-century model. As a Stitch Witch, Diego had a Way with fabrics, especially those from previous centuries, and he delighted in these impromptu displays of his magick.

He tilted his head, pressed a finger to the torn seam, and muttered a second quiet intent. A faint crackle of magick rose the hair along Milla's arms, and the stitching at the hip wove itself back together. Diego smiled, releasing his Way, and the bathing costume sagged in the way of all woolen things.

"She wanted it in a bigger size." Milla leaned against the curio cabinet. The figurines, jewelry busts, and vases rattled, and Diego lurched to steady the hutch. "Oh, calm down, I'm not that heavy." The broken clock thumped off of its display, and Milla flinched.

"Not at all what I was suggesting." Diego gripped the glass vial he wore around his neck, unable to completely wash away the sick look on his face. "You should have called for me, pequeña bruja, rather than frighten away a customer."

"Right, because I'm so scary." Milla rolled her eyes. "I can handle an angry customer."

"Like you handled that one?"

"It's not my fault that Karen tried to squeeze herself into an antique bathing suit."

"Kayleigh," Diego corrected.

"Whatever. We don't even have a dressing room; where did she even try it on? *And* she tore a seam."

"Which I have fixed."

"Well, aren't you special," Milla grumbled. "Not all of us have the luxury of old age and Stitch Witchery to fall back on."

"Old age?" Diego narrowed his eyes and flicked his fingers at her with a hiss. "Do not start insulting me because *you* were rude to a customer."

"I—" Milla started. And stopped, immediately regretting her words. She covered her face with her hands. "Shit, I'm sorry. That was ... that was unacceptable."

"I will not say it is alright." Diego held her eye, forcing a weak smile. "But I understand you are frustrated, Milla."

He did. The Horned God and the Triple Goddess knew he did.

"Doesn't excuse it." Milla peered at him over her fingertips. "I'm sorry."

Diego's smile warmed. He stepped around the glass display, grabbing her cold, clammy hands and tracing his thumbs over the ruin of her palms. Not for the first time, she wondered if a Stitch Witch could see the seams beneath the scars.

"What sort of tío would I be if I did not forgive you?" Milla managed a tiny smile. He let go and fixed her bangs before tucking a dark lock of hair behind one ear. "Si, I forgive you," he smiled, eyes crinkling. "Also, there is a rat stuck in the trap."

Milla set the rat free in the alley and clung to the store's corners while Diego worked the register. Another attempt was made at getting the Berthoud to work, which ended with Milla storming out the rear door, hollering with the ship's clock in hand, "To the dumpster with you!"

Diego wrestled her for the clock, cursing a stream of Spanish as he stalked inside, and finally, it was sunset—closing time.

"Big plans tonight?" Diego called from his sewing room.

"Feed the raw-head, cup of tea, and my regularly scheduled ugly cry." She turned the lock on the front door, flipped the sign, and headed down the hall.

"Ah, yes. The Tuesday Special. Is this an R.E.M. 'Everybody Hurts' or Taylor Swift 'White Horse' kind of night? So I am prepared."

"I was leaning more towards something by Heart or Adele." Milla tugged open Diego's mini-fridge to grab a can of sparkling water and a hunk of raw meat wrapped in paper. "Or My Chemical Romance."

"Oh, please let it be an Adele night." Diego grinned with a sewing needle clenched in his teeth. A beaded collar stretched across his work table beside a handful of black and white pearls piled on a velvet cloth. Placed with some reverence beside them was an antique cameo—the centerpiece of the genuine Whaler's Wife mourning collar from the early twentieth century. He pulled the needle from his teeth, threading it with ease and wiggling his fingers over the pearls. "She always brings out the good wine."

"Because I do this for you." Milla pulled the tab off her can and flicked it at him. Diego winked, brown eyes twinkling.

"Naturally." He plucked a pristine black pearl from the pile and threaded it through with the needle.

Diego had spotted the collar on one of the many occult boards he trolled. Milla didn't know how he selected the gold from the veritable sea of pyrite that was online browsing, but he always knew which pieces to bid on, their essence speaking to him through the computer.

Or something.

She stopped questioning his skill after the third purchase in a row, a nineteenth-century top hat worn by an usher at the final performance of *Our American Cousin* at Ford's Theater, had proved legit. The black silk stovepipe arrived, and at a glance, Milla knew the hat carried a scrap of emotional memory—a Shade of terror—imbued in the very fabric of its being. After restoration, the antique hat was sold to a collector in Belgium for five times the purchasing price.

"I am only going to be here a few more hours," Diego said. "Not long enough for you to get into any trouble."

"Noted; I'll hold off on my tea until you get home."

She left the shop to his care, hurrying onto Spanish Street and keeping a wide berth around the mortals ambling the cobblestones or crowding under wisteria arches and narrow Spanish balconies.

Agatha waved her down from her usual spot on the corner of Spanish Street and Treasury. The old augurist was a holdover from the influx of hippies in the sixties and seventies and a St. Augustine institution. Her cart boasted an assortment of crystal necklaces, earrings, charms, and purple geodes sparkling under the orange-yellow glow of gaslight and salt lamps.

Things in St. Augustine changed, but Agatha did not.

The witch and her augury cart had sat on the corner of Spanish and Treasury for half a century, ready to ensnare inebriated tourists stumbling into the daylight after having gorged themselves on alcoholic slushies. It was one of the first places Milla's foster mother had brought her when she was a girl and nearly twenty years later, she still wore the lavender-hued geode shard the old augurist had gifted her.

Milla returned the wave, lifting her necklace to show Agatha the smudged and cloudy amethyst shard dangling next to a woven dream-catcher.

"Your aura is looking a bit thin, dear!" Agatha cried out.

"I'll be sure to drink more tea," Milla replied, veering onto Treasury Street. The crowd bled from sunburned tourists to tanned, laughing Flagler students. Skirting the Governor's House, she crossed Plaza de la Constitucion and pointed towards the Bridge of Lions, a two-lane drawbridge stretching across the Matanzas River.

A pair of Medici Lions protected the St. Augustine side, their teeth bared in what Milla thought resembled pained laughter. As if the city were a bad joke they were forced to protect. She often felt the same and, over the years, had developed a kinship with the lions. Named Firm and Faithful, Milla could never remember which was properly which, so she'd designated the right-hand lion as Faithful and ran a tingling palm over his paw whenever she passed by.

Tuesday night was Feed the Raw-head Night, a task Milla neither relished nor forewent. A task that, unfortunately, fell to her as the Witch of the Demesne.

Raw-heads were nasty pieces of work brought over to the Americas by Cornish sailors. How one had ended up in her Spanish Floridian demesne remained a mystery but nevertheless, here it was.

Humanoid in design, the raw-head in question was all knobby knees and elbows, a gaunt belly, and skin stretched tight over a frame too lean. Flaps of flayed skin dangled around its neck like a macabre daisy, and the wretched thing had the habit of taunting mortals and witches alike through fleshless lips.

"Bad words, bad deeds," the raw-head hissed when Milla stepped onto the bridge. The rasp of jagged nails against metal followed her every step. She only went far enough to place herself over water and in danger. It was the only way the raw-head would come close, Milla being a thing Forbidden and Foule as she was.

"Nice to see you, too." She picked at the tape keeping the paper closed around the raw meat. The horrid flap-slap of the raw-head's flayed skin scuttled closer, and the fine hairs along the back of her neck rose.

"Unpunished." A blood-blistered eye reeled at Milla through a metal grate.

"Not for long, pal." She curled her lip, pinching the—*Oh, Goddess, ew*—chuck roast between two fingers. Thrusting her arm through a gap in the pale-green iron bars, Milla dangled the meat over the water. The raw-head edged closer, and when she felt the heat of its breath on her wrist, she released the steak and jerked her hand back through the guard rail.

"You invite grief," the raw-head grumbled, its version of a curse ... or a threat. Milla hadn't quite figured that one out. The raw-head might have meant it as a compliment.

The meat ka-ploshed in the Matanzas River, followed by the heavier ker-splash of the raw-head chasing its dinner. Milla allowed herself one full-body shudder before power-walking off the bridge.

The house she shared with Diego was a one-hundred-dred-and-change-year-old Victorian across the street from Flagler College. Painted a pale yellow Milla likened to room temperature butter, the dangling trim, now more of a mossy light green with gray dust edging, was due for some attention, as was the sagging front porch. At some point in its more than a century of existence, the house had been split into a duplex. Milla had rented the left half of the property since her freshman year at Flagler, while the owner, an elderly woman from New England, leased the other half as a vacation property.

Electric candles flickered warmly in the windows of her half, a welcoming light for the wandering and the lost. She paused at the front door, bracing herself before stepping inside an empty house haunted by a ghost that wasn't there. Even now, she caught Ezra's scent in the heavy, humid air: bourbon and praline, the herbal bite of his shampoo, and the subtle sweetness of his lotion.

She dropped her forehead against the fogged glass pane in the door, closing her eyes and counting to ten before thrusting her key into the lock. The door swung open at the gentlest pressure.

The door of the duplex she shared with Diego and Ezra's not-ghost ... a not-ghost that was in no way capable of unlocking a door, which meant—

"Horned Goddammit, I left the door open again." She thunked her head against the frame twice before stepping inside, helping the door close with a heel kick.

Milla headed down the hall, stopping in the kitchen to grab a tub of hummus, bell pepper slices, and a beer. She stepped out of her checkered slip-ons in the hallway and charged into a dining room that had long ago been converted into her bedroom, complete with built-in cupboards and drawers in the closet that had once served as a butler's pantry.

A wingback upholstered chair sat by the bay window opposite her bed turned to overlook the small yard she shared with the other half of the duplex. A low bookcase formed a window seat, and in a brief spurt of get-it-done-ness, Milla had added shelves along the walls framing the window.

Her grimoire sat on one of these shelves, opened to an unassuming page on the benefits of hemlock and drawbacks of hawthorn in regards to the limbic system and aural display, and waiting patiently in her chair, with the poise of a witch who expected to be noticed as soon as she entered a room, was the Morgenhexe.

TWO

"Hello, Ludmilla." The Morgenhexe's lips twisted upwards in a sadistically feline manner. She rose from the chair with straight-backed grace and crossed the room in three gliding steps, whisking the can of beer from Milla's hand. "How kind of you to remember my preference for a crisp lager."

"Blessed be," Milla squeaked, setting her hummus and veggies on the edge of the bed to proffer a bow to her *jezibaba*—her first mentor and foster mother.

"Blessed be," Morgen cracked open the can and took a tentative sip. A Black Forest witch, Morgen was as tall and imposing as the trees blanketing the hills of her birthplace. She had a look of austerity about her, with the cunning kindness that forms around the eyes from a life well lived. A master conjurer and illusionist, the Morgenhexe was a former Aural Insurance Investigator—an Enforcer—for the Coven Aural Review Board, conversationally known as C.A.R.B. They were the witches called in when magick Forbidden and Foule reared its ugly head, hunting down the those who dared practice the illegal craft.

In this room with Milla, however, she was a mentor first, a mother second, and an Enforcer never.

Morgen brought light to hand, illuminating the room as she studied the label on the can. The art depicted a cartoon image of Ponce de Leon guzzling a can of beer bearing the same image. "Ferment of Youth, *bezaubernd*." Smiling at the recursive headache that was the label, she took another sip and smacked her lips. "It is good to see you, Ludmilla."

"What brings you all the way up from the Keys?"

"Can a mother not visit her daughter?"

"When the mother is you, there tends to be a reason." Milla sat on the bed, drawing her feet up and crossing them at the ankles. "I take it my dues are due?"

"Tch," she waved a hand, "I took care of those last month. And the month before that, before that, and before that ..."

"I get it." Milla pulled the tub of hummus closer and pried off the lid, ignoring the dour glare from her foster mother. She opened the bag of bell peppers and plucked out a slice. "Doesn't necessitate a visit." She swept the bell pepper through the hummus and popped it into her mouth. "So, to what do I owe the honor?"

"To good standing."

Milla choked on her bell pepper.

To be a witch in good standing, one was expected to renew their Practical License every five years with an appearance before C.A.R.B., which was managed by the Coven for the Regulation and Oversight of Witches, or C.R.O.W., for the word adverse. An aural reading was performed, the witch demonstrated the Fine and Faire application of their Way and, ideally, walked out of the coven headquarters as a witch in good standing, able to fly under the radar for another decade.

Morgen sipped the beer, eyed Milla, and examined the room and tchotchkes on the bookshelf. Her eyes skimmed over an origami tiger, settling on a chunk of graffiti-ed cement taken from the ruins of a wall.

"Is it wise to have this on display?"

"Like anyone even comes in here." Milla tried to keep the annoyance from her voice. Her face, on the other hand, was a lost cause. "Can't you speak on my behalf to C.A.R.B.?" She jabbed another slice of bell pepper into the hummus and shoved it into her mouth. "As you can see, I'm doing marvelously. Couldn't be better. It was nice to see you, now please return my Jericho Stone to the bookshelf and leave me and my hummus in peace."

Morgen replaced the stone and moved her hands, face impassive. The beer can vanished from the left while her right scoured the air, conjuring a fist-sized pale yellow sun out of nothing. With less than a glance her way, the Morgenhexe lobbed the glowing sphere at Milla. She dove from the bed, flinging the container of hummus at her *jezibaba*. The tub twisted and rolled in on itself a foot away from the witch, disappearing altogether.

"Hey!" Milla clambered to her feet. "That was my dinner."

In response, Morgen conjured a second orb, flicking her wrist to send it flying. This time, however, Milla's hands were free. She braced her feet and cupped her palm, digging at the air as she swept her arm like a lacrosse stick. The orb tingled against her scars, and Milla tossed it to her right hand, redirecting the energy with a grunt and sending it flying back at the Morgenhexe.

Morgen bent to the side, and the orb curved around her. She held out the back of her hand, and the gaseous yellow ball alighted on her wrist as a tweeting yellow canary like the witch was a damn Disney princess. Nary a hair was out of place; even her clothing was unruffled.

Not. Fair.

Milla panted, glaring at her mentor. The exertion of absorbing, re-shaping, and redirecting Morgen's magick was tiring on a good day, and Milla was out of shape. She hadn't sparred with her foster mother for years and had barely touched magick since Ezra.

At least, not the combative sort. Her magick these days was quiet and contemplative. Stitches and lace. Simple mechanics and sachets of hawthorn, hellebore, hemlock, and clove. Not surprise brawls in her bedroom with a master illusionist.

"Milla," Morgen tutted, "you used to spar with me for hours."

"Yeah, when I was seventeen and hormonally enraged that My Chemical Romance had broken up. Then you apprenticed me to a twenty-one-year-old Mind Witch. You think we spent our time sparring?" Milla spat the last word, trying to keep her thoughts from what she and Ezra *had* spent much of their time doing.

Morgen cocked her head. With a flick of her fingers, the beer can wobbled to rest at Milla's feet. She eyed the summoned lager and gazed up to meet her foster mother's.

"Was there a point to that gross display of magick?"

"Of course." Morgen flapped a hand between them, gesturing to the beer. "My apologies for startling you." Chair legs screeched over the hardwood as she turned the wingback to face the bed. Milla sat without being told. It was her room, her house, and Horned God-dammit she was a grown-ass witch of twenty-six. She didn't need permission from Cate Blanchett's magickal doppelganger to sit on the edge of her bed; thank you very much. "I am worried about you, Ludmilla. C.R.O.W. is worried about you." Morgen began. Milla drank.

C.R.O.W.

Of course, it was C.R.O.W.

Their sole aim was to keep every witch under their jurisdiction in line and to eradicate those who dared to push against the narrow confines of their covenants.

"Why would C.R.O.W. be worried about me?"

"You are the unregistered Witch of a Demesne, you have clearly not been using your magick and, judging from your grimoire, have been experimenting with"—Morgen glanced over at the book. A curl of her finger turned the page to an entry on the benefits of lilies—"warding and banishment?"

"At least you know you're welcome in my home," Milla muttered into her beer.

An exquisite eyebrow raised. "Or you performed the incantation wrong."

Milla snorted.

"You stopped returning my calls, you have stopped using the magick I taught you while pursuing that which Ezra desired you to perfect, and the worn pages of your grimoire lead me to believe you wish to disappear." Morgen pursed her lips, waiting.

But what was there to say? That her body was slowly heading down the same path as her dead heart?

Two years. She had survived without Ezra for two years, keeping her head low, her magick muffled, and avoiding the notice of C.R.O.W. What more did they want from her?

"Is that it, Ludmilla? Should I have left you in that filthy apartment in New Orleans?"

"No," she whispered.

"Ludmilla." Morgen had moved across the room and stared down at her, fingers laced at her front. "You were meant to recover here, not claim the title of Witch of the Demesne."

"It was an accident."

"I am beginning to think your return to St. Augustine was a mistake." She curled a lock of Milla's hair around a finger, the gesture one of maternal care borne from years as a foster mother. "There are too many ghosts wandering these streets. One too many shadows in your mind. It was my wish that you return with me to Key West, where I could keep an eye on you."

"*What?*" Milla's heart clenched at the veiled threat. It took a moment for the implication of her words to settle, and Milla lurched to her feet when they did. "Wait, what do you mean *was*."

"C.R.O.W., however, has different ideas."

Milla snorted. "Because they've known what's best for me in the past."

"After seeing what you have made of yourself, Ludmilla, I am inclined to agree with them." Dread curdled in Milla's stomach. She pressed her lips together and clenched her fists, willing the tingle in her palms to cease. "As of now, you are being promoted to *polednice*"—Milla blinked. A *polednice* was a Mid-day Witch, the intermediary membership level with C.R.O.W.— "and will be assigned a *čarodějnice* of your own."

"An *apprentice*? How can I have an apprentice? *I'm* still a *čarodějnice*." Milla rattled the Czech title off her tongue, the word as familiar as her own name.

Little Witch, entry-level.

Nothing and no one to be concerned with as far as C.R.O.W. and their Enforcers were concerned.

"Considering your status as Witch of the Demense, C.R.O.W. feels it necessary to promote—"

"This is insane. I'm barely managing the demesne; how am I expected to manage a witchling? Look at me. I'm a mess!"

Morgen acquiesced, dragging her deep blue eyes from Milla's ankle-socked feet to her pale legs with their assortment of random bruises from working in the store, running into cabinets, and climbing under displays. A corner of the Morgenhexe's mouth twitched at Milla's high-waisted black shorts, fallen suspenders, and her cropped band t-shirt. Self-conscious under that critical eye, Milla ran her fingers through tangled hair. Thick, black, falling just past her shoulders. She exhaled, fluttering blunt bangs, and forced herself to meet Morgen's eye.

"True, you do not look the part of a *polednice*," her foster mother began, "but perhaps a youthful bent in leadership is what C.R.O.W. needs."

"You can't be serious. Morgen, please." Milla's voice cracked, and the sound finally pulled something like emotion from the Morgenhexe. "Don't make me do this."

The elder witch flinched, her cold exterior crumbling. She embraced Milla, smoothing her hair as the younger witch leaned against her.

It was odd, being held. Letting herself be held. Milla relaxed into the embrace, wrapping her arms around Morgen and holding tight. Touch was such a simple thing, and while her friends often gave quick hugs or high-fives to Milla, no one had truly held her since Ezra had ... Gone.

"Shh, shh, *Millamäuschen*," Morgen whispered. "It will be alright. Goddess knows you have had enough experience with magick, both Faire and Foule, to set another young witchling successfully on the right path." Milla sniffled against the velvet of Morgen's gown. The older woman gripped her shoulders and pushed Milla away to look her in the eye.

"It is already done; all that remains is to prepare yourself and convince C.R.O.W."

"Convince C.R.O.W.?"

"I am only a summons away, Ludmilla. You understand?"

She managed a nod, and Morgen shared a soft smile, the kind that brooked no argument but managed to convey sympathy all the same. "We cannot have you fading away, *Millamäuschen*. Give it a try for this old witch, hm?"

Milla nodded, and Morgen let go, striding to the bay window and staring out at the moon-drenched yard, the out-of-season lilies, and the pale green burst of petals on the witch hazel tree. Her mouth pinched as a bushel of crumpled hay tottered out of the shadows and tossed an empty plastic bottle on the patio table. "A *polevik*?"

"He showed up a year ago." Milla shrugged.

"Hm." Disapproval drew a tiny line between Morgen's eyebrows. "Your *čarodějnice* was previously assigned to a technomantic who trained with me on Big Torch Key."

"Why is she moving to Florida?"

"A disturbance Forbidden and Foule in her home demesne." Morgen rapped her knuckles on the window, startling the *polevik*. What resembled an arm of hay rose, stalks bending into the imitation of a middle finger before the Slavic field sprite toddled back into the shadows. "Or so I am told. The official story should hit our grimoires in a day or so, though the rumor in Český-Krumlov is that C.A.R.B. has dispatched an elite team of Enforcers to handle the matter."

Milla's skin prickled at the mention of Enforcers, and she wondered if Morgen wished she were among them. "So something happens elsewhere, necessitating the presence of Enforcers, and you thought *I* was the best choice to take over as a mentor?"

Morgen waved a dismissive hand. "The girl has relatives in Vilano Beach, and as St. Augustine is your demesne, her education in the Ways falls to you. Congratulations on your promotion, Ludmilla." Morgen lay a hand against the glass. Ice spiraled out from her fingertips, crawling across the pane. It was a simple piece of illusory magick Morgen had performed time and time again, always to prove a point. Present enough pieces of reality, ice gathering on a window pane, a well-placed shiver, a puff of cloudy air as one spoke, and a person could and would believe whatever they were shown. An old lesson but one Milla took to heart.

Believe that you can do this, Milla. Or, barring that, fool yourself until you do.

Right on schedule, Milla shivered from the imagined cold. "Understood."

The Morgenhexe smiled.

"There is one more thing." She spun and folded her arms, slender fingers resting near the crook of each elbow. "C.R.O.W. remains to be convinced of your qualifications as *čarodějnice* and Witch of the Demesne. They are sending an Aural Insurance Adjuster down to St. Augustine. You will be expected to meet with him—"

"I'm sorry, what?"

"—and allow him access to the demesne." Morgen hooked her finger under one of Milla's suspenders and placed it back on her shoulder. "Will that be a problem?"

"Is an A.I.A. necessary?" She gripped her beer in both hands to hide how they shook. "My demesne was reviewed by an aural adjuster when I took over stewardship. I thought they only did that on, like, a ten-year cycle."

"Indeed. Regardless, it is a condition of your promotion—"

"Which I didn't ask for."

"—and for your having a *čarodějnice*."

"Which, again, I did not ask for."

"Consider, then, the mystery behind the witch involved in the disappearance of Master Ezra Lightner winning stewardship of a demesne. And not only that but stealing it from a witch that had successfully held the territory for nearly four decades." Milla suddenly found her ankle socks very fascinating. "The ritual you and Ezra performed required massive magick, *Millamäuschen*. It cost a witch in good standing his life. That is not an act easily forgotten." Milla bit her lips to keep from correcting Morgen on all the details she had gotten wrong. "C.R.O.W. is willing to ascribe your participation to youthful ignorance; as such, they require assurance that you are sound enough in mind and magick to tend the demesne."

"Or else?" Because there was always an "or else" where C.R.O.W. was involved.

"Or else you will have to account for your actions." Morgen pinched between her eyes. "And no one lies to C.R.O.W., Ludmilla. Not even me."

"But I haven't done anything," Milla said too quickly. Morgen raised an eyebrow. "I've been leading a low-C.A.R.B. lifestyle."

"That is, at least to me, painfully obvious." The elder witch ran a finger along the top of Milla's grimoire. The book made a sound like a too-long ignored dog on the receiving end of a solid ear-scratch. "It is C.R.O.W. you must convince, Ludmilla, so I suggest you put yourself together."

THREE

Morgen departed after her dire warning, leaving Milla with an un-comfortable amount of self-realization to attend to and little desire for her tea. Morning light dripped through the window too soon, and the demesne beckoned. She struggled into her running clothes and staggered from the bedroom, making it all of two steps before tripping over her discarded shoes in the hallway.

"Agh, fuck." She caught herself on the kitchen counter, avoiding faceplanting on the linoleum.

"O, por Diosa!" Diego whirled around with an egg pan in his hand. He ripped an earbud out and glared at Milla with an expression devoid of pity. The same expression he'd worn the last time she tripped on the stairs. He had given her that look, tended to her bloody nose, and packed up all of Ezra's things the next morning, moving into the upstairs bedroom and banishing Milla to the ground floor.

"Morning, Diego." Milla hoisted herself to her feet. His nostrils flared, eyes narrowing, and Gloria Estefan hit a high note underscored by samba horns in his headphones.

"How much did you drink last night?"

"Like half a beer, I tripped over my shoes." She rubbed her knee, jerking her chin at the offending footwear.

"No tea?" Diego blinked at the shoes in the middle of the hall. Milla wasn't sure which hurt worse: seeing that tired, angry look or the utter surprise that she was sober and had indeed tripped over a pair of shoes.

"Morgen dropped by for a surprise visit." She quickly filled him in on the news, emphasizing that she, and therefore *he*, would be under the observation of an aural insurance adjuster. "Tea didn't seem like a good idea after that."

"Oh." Diego's eyes went wide behind his glasses. "What are you going to do?"

"What can I do?" She pouted. "They've already made their decision, and Morgen backed it."

"Why would she do that? She knows what you—"

"I know," Milla cut him off. "I've kept us hidden this long; we just have to be extra careful for a few weeks, is all."

"Well," Diego exhaled, clearly unhappy. "Outside of *that*, you left the door open again."

"No, I didn't." Milla grabbed a fresh coffee filter from the stack. Gone were the days of Ezra's French press and pour-over with hand-ground beans. Making coffee had been a ritual for him, one that he delighted in perfecting, like the good witch he was. Before Ezra, Milla had been satisfied with cans of double espresso energy drinks, stating, "They have ginseng and Vitamin B, and you can hardly taste the coffee at all." He'd ruined that within a week of her apprenticeship, and it was like they said:

once you go hand-ground fair trade Colombian, you never go back. "I specifically remember kicking it closed after Morgen left."

"It was wide open when I got home," Diego retorted. "Bruja, you have to remember to lock up."

"I lock the door at the store."

"Yes, my mistake. One locked door makes up for you leaving our home open to criminals."

"We live in St. Augustine."

"Si," he countered, "and they let anyone open a store these days."

Milla pressed the button on the burr grinder and glared at Diego. He leveled a smile her way, popping the earbud back in and returning his egg to the stove.

Coffee prepped, she headed down the hall, hollering at Diego, "Off for a run!" before closing the door hard enough to rattle the glass in its frame.

The sun had climbed midway up the palm trees, and the first snatches of commuter traffic along Cordova set a pleasant soundtrack for her run.

She set her pace to the drone of cars and random bursts of music: snippets of Mellencamp and The Boss, the newest auto-tuned pop hit, and the deep bass and wobble of Dirty South hip hop. To chatter floating through open windows and from sidewalk cafes until circling the park turned the music into children's laughter. The songs of her demesne fueled the witch, who fed power back into the city with each footfall and brush of tingling fingers against trees, gates, and lampposts.

The loop around Maria Sanchez Lake was always where Milla felt her best. Legs limber, breathing steady, she opened up her stride. The gentle lapping of the reservoir and call of the birds focused her mind and pushed her through to home, finishing her charge of the demesne with a clear head and peaceful heart. Her Way settled for the time being.

Diego was already gone when she finished her run, though he had left a note on the kitchen counter reminding her to lock the door. The urge to roll her eyes rose, but next to the note was a mug of coffee topped with the appropriate amount of milk and a swirl of Redi-Whip.

"You are forgiven," she told the note, tapping a cupboard door closed as she left the kitchen.

She showered quickly, not wanting to be alone with the not-ghost of Ezra. It was infrequent, but whenever she was tired, sad, or lonely—like right now—Milla swore she could see him out of the corner of her eye, reading in a chair or opening a cupboard. The echo of his footsteps would creak on the stairs, or the ghost of his fingers would brush her spine.

But Ezra was Gone.

Not dead, Gone.

People who died left behind bodies that could be found and mourned or an echo to be traced. A Shade or a fragment of Soul. An aural stain where they had last stood.

Ezra had left nothing.

Nothing but Milla.

She dressed, took care to lock the front door, refreshed a few of the sigils protecting the house, and began her walk into the Colonial Quarter. The day was cooler, reaching the low seventies around noon and lingering on into the perpetual stasis of Floridian twilight, so she had chosen her outfit accordingly: cuffed black shorts, an a-line halter in bold black and white stripes, a floppy black sun hat, and clunky ankle boots.

In black, of course.

She was a witch, after all.

Diego was already hunched over his sewing table when she entered through Southern Gothic's rear. Milla rapped her knuckles on the frame in greeting as she passed by, and he raised two fingers in a wave.

She opened the store, flicking on lights, unlocking the door, and powering up the tablet that served as their register, and was on her second can of sparkling water when the bells over the door tinkled merrily. Glancing up from her phone, she smiled as Julie Kettler waved hello.

"I thought you worked today."

"Mm-mm," Julie shook her head, red curls bobbing. She dropped her purse on the counter and shrugged off an Army Green bomber jacket, revealing a loose-fit v-neck and worn jeans. "Took the day off to meet a friend from out of town."

"Nice," Milla tucked her phone away and propped an elbow on the counter. "Taking her to Fountain of Youth?"

"Coffee first," Julie said, "then after that, maybe. I'm not sure what she wants to get up to." She eyed the earrings, necklaces, and rings in the display case. "She evacuated or something from Hattiesburg, got in town a couple of days ago."

"Evacuated?" Milla straightened. "What's going on in Mississippi?"

"Haven't you watched the news today?" Julie frowned when Milla shook her head. "There's been an outbreak of something in the Delta; a bunch of people were hospitalized, and someone died. I think. Ooh, can I try that one on?" She pointed to a large square-cut emerald in a white gold cathedral setting with black diamonds running along the band. "It's the Art Deco, right?"

"Nah." Milla crouched to unlock the display. "The Art Deco is the one with the triangles. This is the Victorian. Do they think it's going to be serious, like COVID?"

"No idea." Julie drummed her fingers on the glass. "I just hope I don't get furloughed again."

"Ahead of an outbreak?" She set the ring in front of Julie, who excitedly clapped her hands. Her wandering in to try on a ridiculous amount of the ridiculous items in Southern Gothic had become a ritual. Secretly, Milla loved it. Outwardly, she had a carefully curated persona of gloom to defend. Julie knew her well enough to tell when Milla was having fun, and seeing the nurse strutting around in a can-can skirt and beaded headdress tugged over her red hair was always a delight.

"You remember what it was like when everything calmed down, too many nurses, not enough patients. I'm still trying to pay off my credit card debt from that side hustle I started to make ends meet."

"I told you it was a bad idea," Milla said. The bells over the door tinkled, halting Julie's reply. Both women looked over—Julie with a delighted squeak and clap of her hands and with Milla a wide-mouthed look of surprise. "When did you leave?"

"Half an hour ago." Diego grinned at her, balancing two stacked cups of coffee in one hand and holding a bag of Old City Biscuits in the other. "You were doom-scrolling Blather; I did not wish to interrupt." He raised the bag. "Left my phone in the back, but I got your favorite: sundried tomato, spinach, red onion, and a fried egg. Light aioli."

"Oh, my Goddessssssss," Milla danced out from behind the register, grabbing the topmost coffee and reaching for the bag. "Bless you."

He swept his arm back, taking the bag out of reach. "Did you really not know I had left?"

"Nope." She popped her lips on the *p*. He chuckled and shook his head, dropping the bag on the counter. Milla pulled it closer, peering within. "Been quiet, haven't had a single customer."

"Um, hello?" Julie waved.

"Are you going to buy anything?"

Julie gave the store a speculative scan. "No?"

"Not a single customer." Milla doubled down.

"I am not surprised." Diego grabbed the bag from Milla's greedy hands. "The line at Shopaholic is out the door, though from what I saw of the window display, I do not understand why."

Milla snorted, smirking. "What hideousness are they shilling now?"

"Birds of Paradise floral spandex *everything*." He gave an exaggerated eye roll and headed for the rear of the store. "Some new brand I have never heard of."

"Ooh?" Julie arched back from the counter, peering out the window. "What's the label?"

"Excuse me, you are my customer." Milla fake pouted, and Julie laughed.

"Thought you hadn't had a single customer today."

"Semantics."

"I'm just saying," Julie put her hands up in surrender, "Southern Gothic is very ... niche."

"And that's a problem, why?"

The nurse paled, stammering as she backpedaled. "It-it's not. Everything in the Quarter right now is neon leggings and pastel scarves. It's what sells, that's all. Colorful Florida florals, not the ... the specialty shops like you and the crystal cart."

"And the torture museum."

"That is not a shop, Milla," Diego called from down the hall.

"Could be, if that's your thing," she hollered back.

Julie poked the glass in front of the diamond and sapphire band. "Well, if you want to spice up what you sell, let me know. I still have boxes of inventory."

"I don't see why we should change what we sell to please a crowd," Milla replied, ducking low to grab the Art Deco ring. She set it in front of Julie, who squeaked and clapped her hands. "We don't need the foot traffic; Diego makes most of our sales online."

"Lucky you, then." The nurse slid both rings on her finger. "But as someone who spends twelve hours a day in scrubs and a sports bra, cheerful tights are kinda nice now and then."

"Okay, so buy them at Shopaholic," Milla unwrapped her biscuit and took a large bite, speaking around her food, "and let me sell my antiques in peace."

"Only saying, if you wanted to broaden your market at all, you could—"

"What did you do?" Diego stormed out of his sewing room and slammed his phone on the display case. Julie jumped back, covering a startled yelp with her hand. "Lo siento, Julie. Sorry. For that. And for this." He turned the full brunt of his righteous Iberian anger on Milla. "What did you say to that woman?"

"What woman?"

"The one from yesterday, to whom you refused to sell the bathing suit."

"Who," Milla corrected.

"The *customer*," he seethed.

"No, you used 'whom,' not—never mind. Are you talking about the Pinkerton bathing *costume*? I didn't refuse to sell it to her; it didn't fit. I told her to go to Shopaholic to find something in her size."

"Yikes," Julie whispered.

"We are a shop, Milla. We sell things." Diego pressed a punctuative finger against the display case. "It is a time-honored transactional sequence of events. Customer enters, customer selects an item, shopkeeper keeps their opinions to themselves and takes their money. Shopkeeper does *not* send customer to another store!"

Julie glanced between the pair. "What happened?"

"Some Karen got mad at me," Milla explained.

"*Kayleigh*." Diego hollered.

"Kayleigh?" Julie asked.

"Whatever." Milla waved a dismissive hand.

"Whatever?" Diego jerked his head back, eyes blinking rapidly. He picked up his phone and shoved it in her face. "Look. Scroll. Read. Absorb." Milla startled back, hesitantly taking the phone. The screen was open to their Yap! page, which had been flooded with new reviews. "Fix."

The first review was harsh but not out of line. "Weird shop, weird owner, go in with low expectations."

"Fair enough," she muttered.

From there, however, they got progressively worse.

"Shitty clothes and broken furniture," "buncha dead flies," "reeks of mildew," "questionable stains on the carpet."

She looked at Diego. "We don't even have carpet in here."

"You have the Persian rug," Julie offered.

"Hyderabadi," Milla and Diego corrected. "Keep reading," he continued.

Milla scrolled until her eyes landed on a novel-length review, each sentence worse and more fabricated than the last.

My girls and I stopped in here on a port call during a recent cruise. While promising at the outset with an eclectic and funky owner—

"Not so bad." Milla attempted to smile and kept reading.

— Southern Gothic quickly disappointed. Not only did the owner refuse to help us find items in our size, but the store is absolutely disgusting. Cockroaches everywhere, I saw a dead rat in the bathroom, the whole place

reeks of gin and, I hate to be so rude, but, a morgue. It smells like dead bodies in there. Maybe it's all the old crap, maybe it's the risk of operating an antique store in the Colonial Quarter but Jesus Christ, have some pride. Take a shower and sober up when you get to work.

Milla looked at Diego, stunned. His glower told her to keep reading.

The next review was worse, calling her illiterate and saying they would never trust the store to give out the correct change. Accusations of turning away customers of a certain racial make-up, refusal to allow returns on vintage Keds ("I have never in my life sold a pair of Keds."), out of date and out of touch ("We sell antiques! It says so on the sign!"), more accusations of a drunk salesgirl, an especially creative review that compared the store to a unicorn in that they could not believe it existed, and finally, a review from Kayleigh Masterson.

"At least she's kind of honest," Milla muttered, reading her account of their argument.

"Who is?" Julie peered at the screen, squinting to read the poster's name.

"The Karen."

"Kayleigh," Diego corrected.

"Whatever," Milla snapped.

Julie cleared her throat. "What does it say?"

"It's only half the story," Milla protested. "And that bathing costume is one of a kind. We literally don't have it in any other size."

"Again, Milla, not your problem." Diego snatched his phone out of her hand. "You take money from the customer. The customer leaves with an ill-fitting garment, we keep our ratings up and then sell more ill-fitting garments to the next batch of idiots that wander in." He paused and glanced at the two rings on Julie's finger. "Those look lovely on you, by the way."

"Thank you?"

Milla covered her face with her hands and groaned. She had messed up. Again. Another mistake added to her very long list of mistakes.

"I hate to leave when you are obviously having a ... thing," Julie shot Milla a sympathetic look, sliding the rings off her finger, "but I need to head out to meet my friend. Want me to bring you back anything?"

She shook her head, face still covered in her hands. The bells tinkled as her friend left, and Milla slid her hands down, covering her mouth with her fingers. "Diego, I am so sorry."

"No, you are not."

"Yes, I am. I had no idea that woman was serious."

Diego's warm, brown eyes were hard behind his glasses, his laughing mouth a thin, angry line. "My tailoring is quite literally all I have. You saw to that when you, you —," he curled his fingers into claws, tearing at the air between them and appealing to the ceiling. "Tonto del culo ... fix this. Call Yap!, apologize to this Kayleigh woman, I do not care what you do, but fix it."

"It's not that big a deal," she protested. "They don't even know Bimini Bespoke is attached to my store."

"Oh?" He raised an eyebrow and stole his phone back. Within a second, he had the profile for his tailor services, Bimini Bespoke, pulled up.

Someone needs to call ICE on Southern Gothic. The owner is clearly smuggling aliens into our country.

"What the fuck—" Milla stole the phone back, scrolling, her eyes catching snippets.

Send him back to where he came from...immigrant stealing our jobs... sorta faggot owns a sewing shop...can someone say 'slave labor'?

Diego snatched his phone, gripping it hard and pointing at Milla. She could not help but notice the tears limning his eyes and the tremble of his finger. "Fix it."

Urban fantasy romance and magick Forbidden and Foule

Milla is a witch who deserves a *break*.

After saving the women of St. Augustine from a soul-sucking Loa, she and Darkly head south in search of some peace of mind and a chance to navigate their budding relationship.

But once again, C.R.O.W. has other plans for the formerly wicked witch.

When a spate of mysterious rituals backed by a power suspiciously similar to hers wreaks havoc across the southeast, Milla must team up with a coven of Enforcers, the witches she despises, to clear her name and stand once again for the Forbidden and Foule.

AVAILABLE NOW

Author's Note

Thank you, patient reader, for swimming along on this journey. And what a journey it has been.

Shady Depths was born from a joke, a dare, and a writing exercise.

The joke involved a friend/critique partner/fellow author sending pages from her novel, and my many questions regarding mer-anatomy and the physics of zero-gravity ... congress.

The dare was her throwing up her hands and saying, "Fine! You write it, then."

The writing exercise involved a certain brooding not-Scotsman and wondering just who he was before ~waves hands at *Ritual Income*, Ludmilla Probuditna, and St. Augustine ~ all of *that*.

What made him tick? What were his goals? His fears? What made him giggle and what clenched his heart?

The answers to those questions lie within the pages of *Shady Depths*.

If you enjoyed this aquatic romp, please let the crowd over at Goodreads and Amazon know!

I can't wait to share the rest of this wonderfully witchy world, and the rest of the team can't wait to meet you.

For news on upcoming releases, other published works, or maybe an odd recipe or two, consider wandering over to www.brittawritesthings .com

Thanks, Y'all!

Here it is, the page every author dreams of writing. There are so many people to thank for their patience, insight, and repeated readings of passages, and, in the case of the World's Best Hype Woman (TM), multiple readings of an entire manuscript.

Oliver - your talents as a DM lent themselves mightily to building out the World of C.R.O.W. Thank you for brainstorming ideas, fixing plots, arguing about the pros and cons of mind control (none, unless you are a dick; and surprisingly a lot), digging through your vast knowledge of corporate lingo and financial terms for the sake of a good (bad?) pun, and for not saying "no" when I told you I wanted to vanish to New Orleans for "research". The Sazeracs were delicious.

Molly - for the joke, the dare, and trusting me with one of your merfolk. Your insight, critical eye, and sick ability to spot a plothole a million miles away are invaluable. Whenever I can do the same for you and Polaris, just say the word. The dreamer that is Réalta is your beautiful creation, and I hope I did him justice. He certainly enjoyed himself.

Ana - The World's Best Hype Woman. You will be thanked in everything I write. Sorry my characters trash on *jamon* so much. Thank you for your proofreading, beta reading, and cheerleading. I'm a lucky person to have you in my corner.

Lianne – time and time again you have deciphered my word salad and turned it into the dreamiest, loveliest art beyond anything I could imagine. You have brought these characters to life in such a magical way, and I am forever grateful for your talent.

Kel – you're the best thing TikTok ever put on my fyp. I wouldn't want to travel this indie author journey with anyone else. Thank you for answering my initial, crazypants DM, and every unhinged message I have sent you since.

The Ladies of Fort Smut - I could not ask for better company on this writing, retreating, and charcuterie-eating life. Love you all, now where are we going next?

You - you lovely, lovely human being who read this book. I feel like we must frequent the same corner of Goodreads, KU, and scroll a similar fyp on TikTok. I feel like we could almost be friends. I hope you stick around for more ♥

About the Author

About the Author

Britta is the worst. She doesn't even publish under her real name and responds to things like, "Mom", "B", and "Brown".

As B. L. Brown, she publishes urban fantasy and paranormal romance. Her debut novella, *Shady Depths*, was released in April 2023, and her short fiction can be found in *Tails, Trysts, and Tentacles: One Monstrous Summer, Fireside: Modern Legends and Lore*, and *The Future of Us, A Moms Who Write Anthology*.

As Britta, she is a human-wrangling, word-wielding, musical theatre and beer-loving runner with a passion for fairy tales and folklore. She can be found under a pile of digital literature or begging her academic friends for their JSTOR logins.

Otherwise, she is in no particular order: lost in the woods, scanning the shelves at the bottle shop, flicking through a classic cookbook, or chasing a kiddo around the neighbor's yard.

You can follow her on Amazon, Goodreads, Twitter, Instagram, and TikTok. For less obnoxious updates, join her infrequent newsletter at www.brittawritesthings.com